Zugzwang

Zugzwang

RONAN BENNETT

BLOOMSBURY

First published 2007

Copyright © 2007 by Ronan Bennett

The moral right of the author has been asserted

No part of this book may be used or reproduced in any manner
whatsoever without written permission from the Publisher except in
the case of brief quotations embodied in critical articles or reviews.

Bloomsbury Publishing Plc, 36 Soho Square, London W1D 3QY

A CIP catalogue record for this book is available from the British Library

Hardback ISBN 978 0 7475 8711 8
10 9 8 7 6 5 4 3 2 1

Export paperback ISBN 978 0 7475 8731 6
10 9 8 7 6 5 4 3 2 1

Typeset by Hewer Text UK Ltd, Edinburgh
Printed by Clays Ltd, St Ives plc

Bloomsbury Publishing, London, New York and Berlin

The paper this book is printed on is certified by the © 1996 Forest Stewardship
Council A.C. (FSC). It is ancient-forest friendly. The printer holds
FSC chain of custody SGS-COC-2061

FSC
Mixed Sources
Product group from well-managed
forests and other controlled sources
Cert no. SGS-COC-2061
www.fsc.org
© 1996 Forest Stewardship Council

To Molly

Zugzwang

Derived from the German, *Zug* (move) + *Zwang* (compulsion, obligation). In chess it is used to describe a position in which a player is reduced to a state of utter helplessness. He is obliged to move, but every move only makes his position even worse.

St Petersburg, March 1914

One

O n a raw March morning, on the Moika Embankment
near Politseisky Bridge, two men accosted the respected
liberal newspaper editor O. V. Gulko. Witnesses later told the
police that the taller of the two appeared to berate Gulko in an
agitated manner and that Gulko, evidently perceiving himself
to be under physical threat, became anxious and attempted to
extricate himself from this unwanted attention. The same
young man then produced a knife and his companion a
revolver. A shot was fired.

Gulko did not fall dramatically but, according to the same
witnesses' accounts, slowly folded into a sitting position, as
one who suddenly feels faint might ease himself to the
ground in order to give his senses time to revive – except
that in this case a large hole had been torn in Gulko's
abdomen and blood was spotting the frozen snow on which
he sat.

The assailant with the revolver ran off, perhaps under the
impression that his work was done but more likely because he
had lost his nerve. If so, his companion was made of sterner, or
at least more unpitying stuff. He was dressed in workman's
boots, long leather coat and astrakhan hat – a fashion popular
among certain of the city's students who liked to affect a
revolutionary air. By now passers-by were beginning to recover from their initial immobilising shock, but before they
could go to the aid of the stricken man his attacker made

several hysterical thrusts. He then fled, making good his escape by reason of his youth and athleticism, the crowds on the Nevsky, and the trepid nature of common humanity in such circumstances.

The affectation of the murderers' dress led to speculation that Gulko had been assassinated by one of the Socialist Revolutionary Party's so-called fighting squads. But if so, why? The fighting squads were certainly active and unpredictable, but it would have taken a logic warped a degree too far for even these fanatical spirits to mark Gulko, who was no friend of the autocracy, as an enemy to be smitten like the Amalekite. Suspicion also fell on that other force of unpredictability and fanaticism, the Black Hundreds, but though Gulko was a Jew he was, like myself, barely so. Others whispered that he had been killed by German agents or a jealous husband. But in truth no one had the least idea of the murderers' identity or motives, and so, uncertainty being to the rumour mill what the scent of food is to an empty stomach, all of St Petersburg talked of little else – at least until the next spectacle upon which people could lavish their consideration should come along.

This duly arrived in the shape of the sensational St Petersburg chess tournament, a glittering occasion held in the ballroom of P.A. Saburov's magnificent house on Liteiny Prospect. The competition's distinguished benefactors, whose munificence provided the generous appearance fees and still more generous prizes, included the tsar himself, who subscribed one thousand roubles to the prize fund. Thousands paid to attend and watch their heroes. As a keen amateur player, I would have gone in any case to watch the games, time permitting. But there was another reason for my interest. I had recently begun to treat the great Avrom Chilowicz Rozental, that sad, shy man. Then thirty-two years old and at the height of his powers, Rozental was the clear favourite. He had defeated Lasker in 1909, Capablanca in 1911. The year 1912 was his alone: his spectacular run of triumphs at San Sebastian, Bad Pistyan, Breslau and Warsaw made him one of the most talked-about celebrities of the age. His introversion only added to his air of mystery. Across Europe, princes invited him to their palaces, gentlemen to their clubs, and fashionable hostesses to their dinner parties. At that time there was in his play – I know this will sound preposterous to those who do not love the game, but I stand by my comparison – something of the decisive, organic simplicity of a Mozart clarinet concerto, or the classical lines of Quarenghi, or the streamlined flight of the *Zwergschwan* as it passes over Lake Ladoga on its summer migration to the south.

And yet, tragically, Rozental's genius was flawed by acute psychological instability. At our very first meeting, arranged by a mutual friend, the renowned Polish violinist R.M. Kopelzon, Rozental apologised for his mere presence in my office, declaring himself to be utterly unbearable to his fellow human beings.

Kopelzon had begged me to help Rozental achieve sufficient psychological equilibrium to enable him to participate in the competition. I hesitated, for it was evident my new patient was on the verge of a complete mental breakdown and I doubted anything could be achieved in so short a time (our first meeting fell on 3 March; the tournament was scheduled to start on 21 April). I advised Rozental to withdraw but this he refused to contemplate. There was simply too much at stake. Chess was his life. Were he to win, were he even to finish second behind the reigning World Champion Dr Lasker, he would certainly have claimed the right to play a match for the crown. The outcome, given their respective powers at that time, would not be in doubt: Lasker was a worthy and great champion but he was past his prime, whereas Rozental

5

had not yet fully come into his. Born in the remote settlement of Choroszcz in Poland, the youngest of twelve children from an impoverished family, speaking only Yiddish and Hebrew until he was almost twenty, Rozental seemed destined to become the third World Chess Champion, feted everywhere from Berlin to New York, Tokyo to Buenos Aires. The St Petersburg tournament of 1914 was the most important competition of his life, and I could not refuse to do for him what I could.

Nothing is ever ordinary or routine to the psychoanalyst. Each patient has a personal history – which is just that: *personal*, highly particular – and his needs are individual and specific. Nevertheless, when Rozental came to me I assumed I would be dealing with the kind of repressed trauma that is the everyday fare of my profession. When our sessions began I had no idea that the two events in which Petersburgers had so much of their febrile imagination invested – Gulko's murder and the series of ingenious slayings that took place daily in the ballroom of Saburov's house – were directly connected in the person before me. The chess world can be bitter and unattractively petty, but it is rarely the stage for intrigue, if one discounts the gamesmanship of rivals and the interminable bickering over the conditions under which World Championship matches should be held. But as my analysis of Rozental progressed, I came to understand that there was much more at issue than the mere winning of a tournament, however prestigious.

Not that the competitors who came to St Petersburg to play chess were aware of this. Professionals habituated to long journeys by train and steamer taking them from country to country and city to city to ply their trade, they had, wherever they found themselves, little occasion to stray outside the itinerant chess player's triangle of hotel, tournament hall and restaurant. Since at St Petersburg these were of the most luxurious standard, they could be forgiven for thinking the city's founder was exaggerating only a little when he claimed it to be the promised land. St Petersburg *is* magnificent and monumental. But it is also horribly squalid, and where magnificence and squalor co-exist there will always be envy, rage, cruelty, paranoia and violence. Just as a superficial glance at a chessboard on which a game is in progress will reveal little of the fierce struggle implicit in the arrangement of the pieces, so the tourist delighting in the treasures of the Hermitage, the glories of the Summer Gardens or the exotic wares on display at the Gostinny Dvor will likely be oblivious to the vicious currents coursing through the very streets he meanders in such innocent admiration. Of the eleven players who took part in the great tournament of 1914, only Rozental came fully to understand that cruelty and violent death were not just part of St Petersburg life in the way they are routinely in any great capital but were the very essence of a city stalked by revolution.

Rozental came for no other reason than to play chess, but through no fault of his own he became embroiled in conspiracy, betrayal and, ultimately, murder. I should properly say *murders*, for Gulko's was not the last. I did what I could to help but it was not enough. Rozental's guileless nature made him susceptible to the machinations of his more unscrupulous friends, and the concerter of Gulko's death turned out to be as powerful as a Tartar warlord, and just as ruthless. He cared nothing for the innocents who strayed into his path, and he crushed them with the same icy calculation with which chess masters exchange the pawns cramping their game.

Rozental did not perish in the street like Gulko; his end was neither dramatic nor violent, but it was just as poignant. At St Petersburg, history passed the great Avrom Chilowicz by and life subsequently broke him in pieces. He was to finish his days as he had begun them, in poverty and grief – and all because of half a dozen barely inferior arrangements of a handful of carved boxwood and ebony pieces on a chequered board of sixty-four squares.

Two

G ulko was murdered on the morning of 14 March. Five days later my secretary came into my office. She was about to go home for the evening and we had already bid each other goodnight. I was waiting for one of my regular patients, who was due at seven, and was using the time to catch up on my notes of an appointment with Rozental earlier that day.

Minna murmured an apology for the interruption; I could see at once that something was wrong.

'There is someone to see you, Doctor,' she said. 'A policeman.'

Minna uttered the word with disdain; she was not at all well off but she was a terrible snob.

In the small outer office where Minna worked I found a slightly built man of about thirty-five. He held his hat before him and his dark hair fell in an unkempt fringe over his eyes.

'Dr Spethmann?' he said. His voice was thin and slightly nasal.

'Yes,' I answered him, politely but also somewhat warily.

'I am Inspector Lychev. I wonder if I might speak with you privately.'

I was curious. The work of the psychoanalyst is not unlike that of the detective: both involve bringing to the surface what is being withheld or hidden, with the obvious difference that the former deals in unconscious inhibition, the latter in very deliberate evasion and concealment.

'Of course,' I said. I turned to my secretary. 'I shall see you in the morning, Minna.'

Minna hesitated for a moment, appearing reluctant to leave me alone in Lychev's company, before skirting around him in an attempt to put as much distance between them as was possible in the cramped confines. She pulled to the outer door very gently after her; to Minna, noise or disturbance, however slight, was anathema.

'Please,' I said to Lychev, showing him into my office.

I went behind my desk. He sat opposite in the old armchair at the head of the couch. He took in his surroundings quickly and expertly, very much the trained observer. I saw his gaze linger over the gilt-framed photographs of Catherine and Elena on the wall to my left, then flick to the books on my shelves and the Inca and Moche artefacts arranged at intervals between them. Everything was being weighed and assessed for clues about their owner.

'How may I help you, Inspector?' I asked.

'You can start by telling me how you came to make the acquaintance of Alexander Yastrebov.'

It was irritation with his brusqueness that caused me to delay my reply. He seemed to think the hesitation suspicious.

'Does the question discomfit you?' he asked.

'Not at all,' I said. 'But I'm afraid I cannot help you. I do not know any . . . Yastrebov, did you say?'

'According to the papers we found in his possession, Yastrebov was a student at the Technical Institute,' he said.

The information did not assist me in the slightest.

'You're certain you don't know him?'

'Certain, yes.'

'How do you explain this?' Lychev said, reaching slowly into his overcoat. Withdrawing his hand from an inside pocket, he produced a plain, unused envelope, which he opened. I expected a photograph of Yastrebov. Instead he took out a *carte de visite*. The ink was smeared from what seemed to be water damage but the wording was still legible.

'Do you recognise it?'

'Of course,' I said. 'It is my card.'

'Can you explain why Yastrebov should have been in possession of your card?'

'I give my card to my patients,' I replied with a shrug, 'but also to colleagues and acquaintances, to people I meet at scientific conferences, or at receptions and dinners. They sometimes pass them on to others. I'm sure I don't know half of those who end up with my card.'

'Could you have given the card directly to Yastrebov?'

'If I did, it was without my knowing who he was. Who is he anyway? Does he say I know him?'

Lychev looked at me carefully in frank assessment of my honesty; he made no pretence otherwise.

'Yastrebov is dead,' he said; then added, with no more drama or emotion than if he were recalling the weather last Tuesday, 'He was murdered.'

I waited for him to continue with more details of Yastrebov's demise. Instead he got to his feet and looked around the room.

'Your office is very pleasant,' he said.

I hardly knew what to say. What did he want with me? He moved to the chess table I keep to the side of the window nearest my desk and picked up the white king. He tested its weight, which he seemed to find acceptable.

'A nice set,' he said, peering at the base on which was inscribed in tiny blood-red lettering *Jaques London*. 'English?'

'Yes,' I said.

'The Staunton is a good design. More simple and pure than our Russian ones.' Putting down the king, he next examined the proud-chested and bearded knights. 'Very nice,' he mused. 'You obviously play?'

'When I can, which is not often,' I answered. 'Nor, indeed, very well.'

'Who do you think will win the tournament?' he asked.

11

In view of what he had come to discuss, I found this turn in the conversation faintly ridiculous, but I answered anyway, 'Capablanca has a good chance.'

'I'm surprised,' he said, in a tone that seemed to imply there was something doubtful about what I had just said. 'Rozental is the clear favourite. For the last two or three years he has been all but unbeatable.'

I sensed there was something behind the question. Did he know Rozental was my patient? In Russia the police know many things.

'Rozental, too, has a very good chance,' I offered.

Spethmann–Kopelzon

Kopelzon has just played 34 . . . Kh5, attacking the white rook.

Exchanging on g5 gives White nothing.

What should Spethmann play to keep alive his chances of a win?

Spethmann–Kopelzon
St Petersburg, 1913–1914
Moves so far
1.e4 c5 2.Nc3 Nc6 3.g3 g6 4.Bg2 Bg7 5.d3 d6 6.Nge2 e5 7.h4 h5 8.Nd5 Nce7 9.Nec3 Nxd5 10.Nxd5 Be6 11.c4 Bxd5 12.cxd5 Bh6 13.b4 Bxc1 14.Rxc1 b6 15.Bh3 Nh6 16.Qd2 Kf8 17.0–0 Kg7 18.f4 exf4 19.Rxf4 Re8 20.Qb2+ Re5 21.bxc5 bxc5 22.Rxc5 g5 23.hxg5 Qxg5 24.Rc2 Kh7 25.Rg2 Rg8 26.Qf2 Qe7 27.Rf6 Kg7 28.Rf4 Kh7 29.Bf5+ Nxf5 30.Rxf5 Rxf5 31.Qxf5+ Kh6 32.Qf4+ Rg5 33.g4 hxg4 34.Rxg4 Kh5

12

Lychev replaced the king exactly in the centre of the square. 'What is this position?' he asked.

I explained it was a correspondence game I was playing with my friend Kopelzon. At the mention of Reuven Moiseyevich's name, Lychev's eyes narrowed. A policeman with an appreciation of fine music? Or a policeman with a professional interest in one of my oldest friends?

He appeared deeply absorbed in the position. 'Whose move is it?'

'Mine. I'm White.'

'What was Black's last move?'

'34 . . . Kh5,' I said.

'Exchanging on g5 gives you nothing,' he said pensively, turning down the corners of his mouth. 'What are you going to play?'

In all the years we had been playing chess together I had never beaten Kopelzon, but in this game I had come out of the opening with a slight advantage. My rather surprised opponent then decided to give up a pawn in return for an attack. Defending accurately, I had not only weathered the storm but held on to my extra pawn. However, by the time we reached the present position I had run out of ideas and my hopes of a first win over Kopelzon were evaporating; I was on the point of offering a draw.

'I don't know,' I said.

Although I felt it almost to be a breach of etiquette – absurd, given the circumstances – curiosity was getting the better of me. I said, 'How was Yastrebov murdered?'

Lychev turned his pale eyes on me. 'He was bludgeoned to death. His killers put the body in a carriage, then pushed it into the canal near Leinner's Restaurant.'

'I've read something about this,' I said.

I went to a stack of old newspapers in the outer office and quickly found what I was looking for, in *Russkie Vedomosti*, as it happened, Gulko's paper. The story appeared in the same edition as the report of Gulko's murder, though it featured much less prominently. It related the recovery of the body of a young man after a motorcar accident on the Moika Embankment. According to the newspaper account, the unfortunate victim had lost control of his car on an icy stretch of road near Leinner's and skidded into the canal.

'There's nothing here about it being murder,' I said.

'The murderers attempted to conceal their crime by passing it off as an accident. Evidently they succeeded in fooling the press.' He indicated the newspaper and said, 'Did you know Gulko?'

'No,' I said.

'You never met him?'

'No,' I said again. 'Why? Is there some connection between the two murders?'

'It's a possibility,' he said, his voice like a shrug.

'Why was Yastrebov murdered?'

'Like Gulko's murder, it's still unclear,' he replied in the same unemphatic way. I noted with relief that he was moving towards the door.

'I really have no idea how he got hold of my card,' I said. 'I'm sorry I couldn't be of more help.'

'I will see you tomorrow afternoon at police headquarters,' he announced matter-of-factly. 'Be there at five.'

'What for?' I objected. 'I've already told you – I know nothing about this Yastrebov.'

'Perhaps we will discover that you know more than you think you know. Surely you, as a psychoanalyst, will understand that.'

'It's impossible. I have appointments tomorrow.'

'Would you prefer to come with me now?' I did not answer. Lychev looked at me squarely. 'Five o'clock tomorrow, then.'

I was still in something of a trance when he indicated the

photographs on the wall. 'Who is this woman?' he asked, tapping the larger of the two.

'My wife Elena,' I said.

'Shouldn't that be "my late wife"?'

'Yes,' I said when I had absorbed the crassness of his provocation, 'my late wife Elena.'

'And this would be your daughter Catherine?' he said, tapping the second photograph.

The thought of this odious and slyly menacing man being aware of Catherine's existence induced in me a sensation of sinking.

'Yes,' I said quietly, as though hoping he would not hear my admission.

'Bring your daughter with you tomorrow.'

I do not think I uttered a single word for a minute or more but stared uncomprehendingly at my unwelcome visitor, and he back at me. Even when the shock subsided I did not ask why he wanted to see Catherine, or what he thought Catherine had to do with Gulko or Yastrebov or this business of the accident or murder, or whatever it was.

Lychev glanced back at the chessboard. 'You are not losing,' he said. 'At least not yet.'

I turned to follow his gaze. When I turned back he was sweeping his lank fringe out of his eyes. He carefully patted his hair and put on his hat.

'I will see you tomorrow, Dr Spethmann,' he said, and with that he was gone from the office.

Three

W ith my patients I am the good father: attentive, kind, calm, fair, strict, unreproachful and present. It would dismay them to discover that the man to whom they impute almost preternatural wisdom and serenity is, in reality, no more immune than they to anxiety or excitement, or other more turbulent and dangerous emotions. But this is the truth of me.

My most intriguing patient at that time – and here I include Rozental – was Anna Petrovna Ziatdinov. I was first introduced to her in the spring of 1913, at a levee for the German ambassador. Thirty-seven years old, she was one of St Petersburg's most famous beauties.

I had gone only at Kopelzon's urging.

'You must get out more, Otto,' he had said in his brisk, no-nonsense way. 'I know you are still mourning but it's been a year. No one will think ill of you – and besides, there's a woman I'm on the point of seducing and I want your opinion of her.'

'I should stay in with Catherine. She'll be lonely without me.'

'Catherine has battalions of young friends. Whole armies. Get your coat!'

The embassy building was colossal and monolithic, carved, it almost appeared, out of a single block of Finland granite. Everything was about scale, power and domination: the

16

massive architraves, the gigantic walls and, on the roof, the bronze giants holding the bridles of two huge horses, their manes long and flowing, their nostrils flared. War was on the horizon and tensions ran high.

'How can you bear to be in such a place?' I whispered to Kopelzon as we accepted our first drinks.

'Because only here can I speak to my true love,' he said airily, casting his eye about the room. 'There she is. Come. If her husband sees her alone with me, the game will be up.' He took me by the elbow and steered me in her direction. 'Isn't she the most beautiful woman you've ever seen?'

Anna Petrovna was of average height, with a fair complexion, full lips and large, honey-coloured eyes, the whites of which were very bright. Her black hair was lustrous but the hairline was low, making for a rather paradoxical beauty, an effect accentuated by an upper middle tooth that seemed to come from the gum slightly at an angle, the single rogue in what was otherwise a perfectly symmetrical arrangement. I was taken with the imperfection of hairline and tooth; they suggested another, faintly piratical side to her, as though behind the decorousness there was something secret and knowing. Or perhaps it was simply that I was generally relieved to find flaws in others, being so conscious of my own.

She seemed pleased enough to see Kopelzon but, to my eye, was more bemused than flattered by his attentions. He brought the same dedication to his seductions as he did to his recitals; his playing, however, was infinitely more subtle. After a time, Anna Petrovna excused herself.

'What do you think of her?' Kopelzon asked. 'Worth the risk, no?'

'The husband, you mean?'

'God no!' Kopelzon exclaimed with a dismissive wave. 'Boris Ziatdinov is a nasty piece of work but he's just a little lawyer with a violent temper. The risk is the father.'

'Who is the father?'

'The Mountain,' Kopelzon said in a low voice.

His look was serious, and with good reason. Peter Arseneyevich Zinnurov was one of St Petersburg's richest industrialists and was suspected of secretly funding the Black Hundreds; certainly, he had no difficulty defending their violent attacks on Jews and Jewish property. He would not be amused were he to discover that his only daughter was the object of a Jewish violin player's sexual attentions.

'Alas,' Kopelzon sighed, 'it does not look as though Anna Petrovna will be coming to my bed, not tonight anyway, and as I, unlike you, consider a night alone to be a night wasted . . .'

He had already turned his gaze on a full-bodied woman of about forty. I clapped my roguish friend on the back and wished him luck.

I was on my way out when I heard a voice say, 'Are you leaving so soon, Dr Spethmann?'

It was Anna. She introduced me to her companions, who were perfectly nice and friendly. They were rather categorical admirers of Blok.

'You're getting restless, Dr Spethmann,' Anna said after a while. She had by degrees turned her back on her friends so that we were in effect detached from them and their speculations on lyrical poetry.

'I'm sorry,' I said. 'I should go home to my daughter.'

'I hope she's not unwell?'

'Not at all, thank you, but she's young and she recently lost her mother.'

'I am so sorry,' Anna said, touching my arm. 'How terrible for you both. How old is your daughter?'

'She will be eighteen in August. She does not like me to be away from her and I promised I would be back by nine.'

'Then you must go home at once,' she said.

Before this, I had thought her talk witty and well informed

but I also felt it had something of the salon about it, something rehearsed, reviewed and honed for the next performance. Her solicitousness now, however, seemed to come from a nearer reality.

'It has been a pleasure to meet you, Dr Spethmann,' she said, putting out her hand. 'I've heard so much about you.'

'From Kopelzon?'

Anna smiled. 'Your friend really is quite unremitting. Tell me, do his sieges ever succeed?'

'They never fail, so far as I know.'

An amused look came into her eye. I held her hand in mine. We can usually find a way to get the information we want, and this is what I wanted to know: that Anna would not sleep with Kopelzon. I was not aware of it, at least not fully, as I stood in front of her and only later admitted to myself that I had proposed Kopelzon as the source of her information about me only so as to get her to talk about their affair, if that's what it was. In the year since Elena died I had felt nothing, unless exhaustion can in this context be described as a feeling. Only Catherine's contradictory need for me kept me going: she both wanted me and claimed to be suffocated by me. She would throw herself into my arms and tell me she loved me; and she would scream that I was the cruellest father since Abraham, the worst husband since Adam. I intend no melo-drama, nor do I mean that even in the emptiest reaches of the night I ever had any intention of seeking out death. But had death come looking for me, I am not sure I would have put up a fight or attempted to flee.

Now I was looking at a woman and I was thinking that I would like to know her better. I felt confused, and also ashamed, as I bade her goodnight.

I next saw Anna five or six months later when I bumped into her at the Mariinsky Theatre during the interval of a performance of *Don Quixote* with Vaganova. I was with Catherine who, that night, was carefree and talkative. That night I was the best father since Abraham.

'Hello, Dr Spethmann,' Anna said, coming up to us. She appeared rather tired and had noticeably lost weight. 'How nice to see you again.'

I was secretly delighted that Anna should meet Catherine now, when she not only looked so heartbreakingly beautiful but was also in such a charming mood. But once the formalities were done, Catherine lapsed into a sullen silence and, for the duration of our small talk, cleaved to me with the force of a guard taking hold of a prisoner. I saw Anna's gaze slide over Catherine's stiff fingers digging into my arm. Her expression gave nothing away but I knew she understood what was going on. She said she hoped we would meet again soon and graciously excused herself.

'Who was that awful woman?' Catherine said when she'd gone.

'Did you think she was awful?' I asked gently.

'Certainly. Who is she?'

'Anna Ziatdinov. Her husband' – I made sure to mention her husband – 'is the lawyer Ziatdinov.'

'How do you know her?'

'I don't really know her at all.'

'Don't you? She was exceptionally intimate for a stranger.'

'I hardly think so,' I said lightly.

'That's how you used to get out of it with mother,' she spat at me with sudden vehemence, 'by pretending you had no idea what she was talking about.'

'Shall we go back to our seats?'

But Catherine would not be diverted. 'You broke her heart the way you flirted with other women in front of her.' Those nearest us stopped talking and took a sudden interest in their shoes. 'You're shameless. You disgust me.'

'Catherine, please –'

She turned on her heels. I followed her down the red-carpeted stairs, through the ticket hall and out to the deserted square, where I found her standing stock still, her back to the theatre, staring at nothing in particular. I came up behind her. It was early September but melting flakes of wet snow were feathering her white-blonde hair. Be attentive, I told myself. Be calm and unreproachful. A daughter's anguish demands no less of a father.

She turned to me and said, 'Promise me you will never see that woman again.'

I did not hesitate. 'I promise,' I said.

'Swear! Swear on your life.'

'I swear I will never see her again.'

We returned to get our coats, then walked to my motorcar and drove home.

The following morning a liveried messenger brought a note from Anna Petrovna asking if I would accept her as a patient.

Four

Ten minutes after Inspector Lychev departed, Anna stepped into my office. She settled on the couch. I sat, as the practice was, at the head of my patient.

To look at Anna one would never have imagined that she was other than contented and personally and socially confident. Her story as she had revealed it during our first interviews was that during her late teens she had experienced periodic and partial numbness in her right hand. The lack of sensation would last for anything between an hour and a week. The solemn and expensive society doctors her father summoned were unable to find any physical cause, but noted that the numbness tended to come on a day or two before Anna was visited by nightmares of such terror that she feared to sleep. They concluded that her illness was hysterical but, the condition being then little understood, were unable to prescribe effective treatments.

Anna herself could think of no particular incident that might have provoked the numbness or her nightmares, nor could she think of any reason why, in her early twenties, they should just as suddenly have ceased. For more than ten years she had been free of them and, as her health recovered, had indeed forgotten all about them. Both the nightmares and the deadness of feeling in her right hand had, however, recently returned. She was sick with anxiety and fatigue.

We know that dreams provide the master key to illness of

22

this kind, though the patient will often resist being brought to its discovery. Anna and I discussed her nightmares, which seemed to contain both literal and symbolic elements, at great length. However, she claimed to remember little beyond the fact that they usually involved a large, rambling house, beautiful but fallen into ruin. She also recalled a compelling sensation of thirst. We discussed the possibility that the house was her own body and that its ruinous condition represented the natural anxiety we feel about the body's integrity, health and attractiveness as we get older. She did not dismiss my interpretation but I could see she was not convinced. Exploring further, she recounted that on feeling so thirsty she began to explore the house in search of water. However, the more she went from room to room, the more convinced she became that someone lurked. She approached the doors with mounting terror until she found herself quivering violently, terrified of what she would find on the other side. In her dreams she did not always open the door but when she did it was not to encounter a ghoul but to find food – smoked fish, bread, caviar, fruits and vodka – set out on a table. At this point she would wake up screaming.

Such was Anna's dread of what I needed her to confront – and such was her resistance to hypnosis and free association – that we made less progress than I had hoped. After consultation with colleagues, I decided to put aside her dreams and return to her life history. Psychoanalysis is like panning for gold, and in an earlier session I thought I had detected a nugget. It concerned a dimly remembered journey Anna had undertaken as a child to visit her grandmother in Kazan. She had mentioned the journey in passing only, and when later I pressed her for details she started to become anxious. I began to suspect that something significant might have occurred during the journey.

Unsettled by Lychev's visit, I was not sure I would be able to

23

bring sufficient concentration to our session. But Anna looked so exhausted that I felt it would be inexcusable to postpone it.

She flinched when I brought up the journey. 'Why do you want to know about that? It was nothing, just a trip I took when I was a child.'

'The fundamental rule of psychoanalysis is to ignore nothing, no matter how apparently trivial.'

'It was years before I started having the nightmares.'

'Tell me what you can remember.'

'I'm not sure I remember anything much, really.'

'How old were you?'

'I was thirteen and two months.'

'You remember your age very precisely. Did something memorable occur?'

She hesitated for a moment only. 'I menstruated for the first time.'

'How did you react to this?'

'I was curious.'

'What were you curious about?'

'Becoming a woman.'

'Did you travel alone to Kazan?'

'No, with my father.'

'Where was your mother?'

'She didn't come. I don't know why. It was just the two of us.'

'How did you feel about being alone with him?'

She paused to reflect. 'At home Father was always so busy,' she began slowly. 'Sometimes I didn't see him for days on end. Now I had him all to myself and I was excited. I remember at Nicholas Station when we were boarding the train people were looking at us admiringly. Almost as if we were . . .' She stopped, then added quickly, 'He was in his prime and very handsome.'

'Almost as if you were . . .?' I prompted her. 'Finish the sentence.'

24

'It's foolishness,' she protested. 'I don't know why I said that.'

'You haven't yet said anything.'

'As if we were husband and wife rather than father and daughter.' She gave an embarrassed little laugh, reprimanding herself for the absurdity. 'They didn't really think that, of course. I was thirteen and he would have been . . . forty-four. But the fact that the possibility crossed their minds, or so I imagined, was flattering to me. That and my secret – that I had begun to menstruate – made me feel very grown-up.'

'What else do you remember about the journey?'

'Nothing, except that it was long – first to Moscow, then on to Kazan.'

I would not accept that she remembered nothing, and when I pressed her it turned out she was in fact able to recall some details about other passengers – a glamorous woman in a blue coat who smiled at her and an elderly cavalry officer who tried to patronise her father – but there was nothing of particular help to me. However, I sensed a reluctance on her part to arrive, as it were, at her destination.

'Tell me about Kazan and your grandmother's house.'

She looked at me warily, as though suspecting a trap. 'It's not the house of my nightmares, if that's what you're thinking.'

'Why do you say that?'

'The house in my nightmares is very large and rambling. There was nothing at all frightening about my grandmother's house. It was modest and homely. I remember a small vegetable garden at the back, and a little kitchen with an oil stove and a small table.'

'Where did you sleep?'

'In a bedroom upstairs.'

'Alone?'

'No. I was to share the room with my father.'

25

'You say you *were* to share the room? Did you in fact share it?'

She looked puzzled. 'I suppose we must have. I don't think there was room for him anywhere else.'

I made a note and moved on. 'How did you get to the house from the station?'

'A carriage probably, but I really can't remember.'

'What did you do when you arrived?'

She frowned and was silent for some long moments. 'We were there for a week but my mind is absolutely blank.'

'Try to remember. Anything. What did your grandmother cook for you?'

'Now I think about it, I don't think we did stay a week,' she said slowly. 'We were supposed to. I remember my mother kissing me at the station and saying she didn't know how she'd live a week without me.' Her voice trailed off as she fished her memory. 'I'm sure . . . we were supposed . . . to stay a week, but . . .'

'Go on,' I said.

'I really don't remember anything at all,' she said, a hint of desperation creeping into her voice. When I tried to prompt her she cut me off with a plea: 'Please. Really, this is a waste of time. Nothing happened.'

Her vehemence only deepened my conviction that here was gold, and yet at the same time I was hesitant about bearing her from simple history-taking into the unpredictable realm of the unconscious. I did not want to run the risk of provoking a crisis, but I was her doctor and had a responsibility to get to the bottom of her illness, something that could only be achieved by prising her from this fixed, defended state.

'Was anyone else in the house?'

'Please!' she said.

She put her hands to her face, placing her thumbs on her cheekbones and spreading the fingers upwards in a curtain

26

over her eyes. She was silent for several minutes. 'I don't want to talk about this any more.'

No amount of persuasion on my part would change her mind.

At the end of the session I made her some tea. She asked about Catherine.

'She's well, thank you. At least as far as I can tell. Since she began her studies at the university I see very little of her.'

'She's a very remarkable girl. I only wish she didn't dislike me so.'

'She doesn't dislike you in the least.'

Anna smiled knowingly. She said, 'Have you ever thought of remarrying?'

'No,' I answered at once, the question taking me by surprise.

'Because of Catherine?'

'Not just Catherine,' I said.

'Then why?'

'I seldom go out,' I said, 'and with little opportunity to meet anyone . . .' I smiled helplessly and shrugged.

'That sounds to me like an excuse,' she said.

'Perhaps,' I conceded.

'Are you afraid?'

'Afraid?'

'Of meeting someone? Of falling in love again?'

I do not know why but the question upset me. I got up and went to the window.

'Otto, I am so terribly sorry,' she said. 'What a stupid thing to say.'

I stared down at the street below, dark now and almost deserted. She came up behind me and touched my elbow.

'Will you forgive me?' she said quietly.

I turned round to face her. She was so close we were almost touching. We stared at each other in silence for some

27

moments. Had I been Kopelzon, I would have kissed her. Instead, I moved past her to the safety of the chess table, and the kiss that wasn't was left in the air between us.

'You seem preoccupied,' she said after a moment.

'I'm sorry.'

'Can't you tell me why?'

I should never have told her: it was unprofessional and almost certainly unethical. She listened, at first incredulous, then indignant.

'What right has this Lychev to demand your attendance at police headquarters? You've done nothing wrong. It's an outrage.'

'I'm not afraid of going,' I said. 'But I am afraid for Catherine.'

'You must get someone to intercede on your behalf. A person of influence. Someone who will put Lychev in his place. And you must do it before you go to police headquarters tomorrow. Once the police process starts, it will be impossible to stop.'

'I don't know anyone with that kind of influence,' I said.

She fell silent for a moment, as though debating something with herself. She asked if she might use the telephone in the outer office.

A minute or two later she returned. 'I've just spoken to my father,' she said.

The Mountain. My heart skipped a beat.

'I explained the situation,' she went on. 'He would like to see you tonight to talk it over.'

'I should never have told you.'

'Don't be silly, Otto. It's the least I can do. Go and see my father. If anyone can help you, he can.'

I knew from what she had told me in our earliest sessions that the close bond between Zinnurov and his daughter had not endured, but she had never revealed the reasons for their estrangement.

28

'He will expect you at midnight at the Imperial Yacht Club,' she said.

Grateful and embarrassed, I helped her on with her coat. I let my hands rest lightly on her shoulders. She was perfectly still. Without thinking, I moved my right thumb a fraction to touch a curl of her thick black hair where it fell on her pale neck. She turned her head a fraction; I could not tell whether it was to encourage me or warn me off.

I took my hands from her shoulders.

We walked together from the office to the wide marble landing where I summoned the elevator. She got into the car and the uniformed attendant pulled the gate to.

From behind the crisscross of bars she said, 'Telephone me when you've seen my father.'

I stood listening to the electric whine and the clicks and jolts of the descending car, then turned back to my office. I had just reached the door when I heard someone on the stairs. Slow, heavy footsteps echoed.

'Who's there?' I called out.

The only reply was the continued scuff of unhurried steps. Two figures appeared at the top of the stairs. One, a tall young man, grinned unpleasantly. His companion had a dour look and was holding a revolver.

He said, 'Hello, Jew.'

Five

T wo weeks before Gulko's murder, Kopelzon had invited me to a private recital he was giving at the house of the shipping magnate S. I. Raetsky. Afterwards we dined together at A l'Ours. Usually after a recital Kopelzon would be expansive and excited, quite full of himself, but that night he was preoccupied and agitated.

'You are either dissatisfied with your playing or you are having trouble with a woman,' I said, trying to animate him.

'Is it true you are treating Anna Petrovna?'

'Yes,' I said, somewhat guardedly.

'Are you sleeping with her?'

'No,' I said, pretending to be more taken aback than I really was.

'Have you fallen in love with her?'

'Is this why you are so morose tonight? Because you failed to seduce her?'

'Who says I failed?' He summoned a grin, though it took some effort. 'All right,' he said, 'I failed. For once.'

'Why don't you let me treat you?' I said.

'Treat me?' he exclaimed with some aggression. There were times when I thought Kopelzon might despise me. 'What for?'

'Your very alarming priapism.'

The hostility in his expression faded. 'Your own lack of

interest in these matters is of much greater concern,' he said with a smile.

We had finished the meal and the wine. He ordered champagne and brandy.

'I have a new patient for you – Avrom Rozental,' he said. 'I'm serious – he's quite mad.'

'I hadn't realised you knew Rozental.'

'We're actually quite friendly,' he said, though rather vaguely. 'Anyway, he's going to need your help if he's to play in the tournament.'

'Does he want my help?'

'I've talked to him about you.' Again, there was a vagueness, a hint of evasiveness. 'When will you see him? Tomorrow?'

'What are his symptoms? Why do you say he's mad?'

'You'll see for yourself. By the way, Rozental has no money to speak of. I can pay something towards the cost of his treatment –'

'There may be no treatment,' I interrupted him. 'But if there is, you owe me dinner, nothing else.'

Kopelzon took my hand and squeezed it. 'Thank you, Otto,' he said. 'You don't know how important this is.'

The following day Minna showed Kopelzon and the famous Avrom Chilowicz Rozental into my office. I had never before seen Rozental in the flesh, though like thousands of others I had followed in the newspapers his triumphal sweep across Europe. His game against Rotlewi at Lodz in 1907 was his masterpiece; I had studied it as closely as I had the case histories of Anna O., Dora and Little Hans. On examination, everything was revealed to be perfectly logical. Yet such were the dizzying depths of imagination it seemed the work of a conjuror.

Kopelzon and I exchanged some commonplaces and

attentions. Indicating the chessboard, he asked if I had a
move ready for him. I apologised yet again and begged his
indulgence.

'Are you saying you want a draw?' he said.

'Would you mind if I took another day or two to think
about it?'

'By all means,' he said expansively, glancing at Rozental.
'But I think you'll find it's a draw.'

Kopelzon's performance was intended for Rozental's benefit, a way to put the great master at his ease. Rozental's
taciturn gaze wandered over to the Jaques pieces and rested
there. His features remained impassive. I felt embarrassed by
his scrutiny of our feeble efforts.

'Would you like some tea?' I asked.

He appeared not to hear me. I repeated the question.

'*Nu*,' he answered.

He muttered an apology at once, both for the refusal and
the Yiddish. His Russian was the Russian of the ghetto, fluent
enough but guttural and nasal.

'How long have you been in St Petersburg?' I asked.

Rozental glanced nervously at Kopelzon.

'Two weeks, Avrom Chilowicz,' Kopelzon said, addressing
him as though he were an infant in his care. Turning to me, he
explained, 'Avrom is staying at the Astoria.'

Just then Rozental's head twitched in a way that reminded
me of a small animal alerted to the presence of a predator. He
began to scratch furiously at his scalp. Kopelzon and I
watched in silence.

After some moments I turned to Kopelzon. 'Thank you,
Reuven. Minna will show you out.'

'Shouldn't I stay?' he said, evidently surprised by the
request.

'What goes on between analyst and patient is an entirely
private matter.'

'Of course. But we are all friends here. Avrom is my friend. I'm the only friend he has in St Petersburg. It was I who suggested he see you. I have to stay.'

'It's impossible, Reuven. Please.'

'You don't understand – I have to stay.'

'The answer remains the same,' I said.

Rozental, preoccupied with whatever it was that irritated his scalp, did not hear any of this, as far as I could tell. I managed to get Kopelzon to the outer office. He was plainly displeased with me.

'If you want me to treat Avrom Chilowicz,' I told him, 'you will have to consent to my doing so in private.'

Kopelzon made a dramatic, despairing gesture. 'Couldn't you just this once make an exception?'

'Why do you want to be present?'

'To save you time. Avrom rambles. God how he rambles.'

'A psychoanalyst cannot ignore anything his patient might say, you know that.'

'Trust me, you'd do well to pay no attention.'

'If I were to tell you to use only three of your violin's strings, what would you say to me?'

Kopelzon ran his hand over his brow like a man brought to immense suffering by the inability of others to appreciate the full weight of his concerns.

'The timing is terrible,' he muttered. 'There's so little time. Do you think you can cure him?'

'It depends on whether he will work with me,' I said. 'On whether he is prepared to reflect on his inner world and tolerate psychic pain. And not least it depends on whether his illness is treatable by psychoanalysis.'

'The tournament starts on 21 April. He has to be ready to play.'

'It's a chess tournament, Reuven,' I said. 'There'll be others.'

'No – there won't!' he snapped back. 'This is Rozental's chance to prove himself the rightful challenger for the World Championship. He must play.'

Kopelzon was an exacting and impatient man. Most people found him impossible. I was used to his rigour but even I found his vehemence on this occasion unnecessary and distasteful.

'Rozental is not just a chess player – he's a Pole,' he continued; and, with an unmistakable accusatory emphasis, he added, 'And a Jew. Or hadn't you noticed?'

There are successful men from humble backgrounds who adjust so effortlessly to the trappings of their new lives you would never guess their true origins. And there are those who know only the tailor and the baker, the rabbi and the inn-keeper, the tents of the Torah and fields of weeping; removed from this world they do not know what to do or say, or even think. I suppose I had expected a magician with secret and spectacular powers far remote from the resort of men. Instead I found Avrom Chilowicz Rozental, a poor Jew from the shtetl. Yes, I had noticed.

'I cannot treat him if you insist on being present,' I said.

He glared at me, but when he saw I would not be moved he capitulated and said, 'You will at least keep me informed of his progress?'

'In general terms, yes,' I said. It was clear this was no more to his liking than my refusal to let him in on the session. I said, 'I will telephone another doctor now – Bekhterev himself if you like – but I can assure you whoever it is will take exactly the same position.'

I went back to my patient to begin the first of our many sessions. Rozental did not ramble, at least not to begin with.

The tall intruder took off his hat and dropped into the chair behind my desk. He placed a yellow, bone-handled knife on the surface before him.

'You are alone here?' he said. 'I was hoping to meet Minna. I've heard she's quite beautiful.' He turned to his accomplice: 'Check the bathroom.'

The young man with the revolver moved behind me. I heard the bathroom door open and the light switched on.

'It's empty, Kavi!'

I made eye contact with the man in the chair. Kavi, apparently. He was a bear of a man, with a broad face and powerful shoulders. A Cossack, by his look and speech.

'It might be my name,' he said, reading my thoughts, 'and it might not.'

He nodded to his accomplice, a signal to get on with whatever work they had come to perform. I heard drawers being pulled open, papers riffled and the slap of discarded files hitting the floor.

'What do you want here?' I said.

He was staring at the chessboard on which my game with Kopelzon was set out.

'Are you a revolutionary, Otto? A Socialist Revolutionary? A Bolshevik perhaps? Or a member of the Jewish Bund?'

'No,' I protested. 'I certainly am none of those things.'

'Then you are for the autocracy?'

'I have no political allegiance of any kind.'

'None? How is that possible?'

'My work is very demanding. I simply do not have time to preoccupy myself with political affairs.'

'Our work, too, is demanding. Isn't that right, Tolya?'

'Never a truer word spoken!' came the laughing reply.

Kavi looked straight at me. 'He might be Tolya and he might not. We cannot be certain. However, Otto, you can take my word for it that our work is indeed challenging and often difficult.'

'From what I have seen,' I said, 'I feel no need to dispute your assurance.'

Kavi laughed. 'You see, Tolya?' he shouted to his friend. 'Didn't I tell you the Jew looked like he had balls?'

Tolya, still going through the files, chuckled. 'You're a good judge of character, Kavi. I'll give you that.'

Kavi continued, 'Are you pro-German or pro-French?'

'You're ransacking my office and you want to discuss international affairs?' I said.

'We're about to go to war, Otto!' he exclaimed with bogus outrage. 'Don't you care who we're going to be fighting? Think of our soldiers! Who are they supposed to shoot? Germans, Frenchmen, Austrians, Englishmen – who?'

'If all you want to do is talk about war,' I said, 'we could have met for coffee at Filippov's.'

He smiled and said, 'I just wanted you to know that no matter how demanding our work we find time for politics.'

'I don't know how you do it,' I said. 'I congratulate you.'

'Got it!' Tolya shouted from the outer office.

I turned to glimpse him holding aloft a file. I could not see which one.

'Very well, you go now,' Kavi said. 'I'll see you later.'

'Do you want me to cut the telephone line?' Tolya asked.

'No need,' Kavi replied.

What this portended I did not know. Why was Kavi unconcerned about the telephone? Because he intended to kill me?

He waited until Tolya had left. He said, 'You're a Jew, yes?'

In what sense was I a Jew? I was circumcised. I was Bar-Mitzvah. But I spoke no Hebrew and my father had forbidden Yiddish at home. I did not attend synagogue. Rozental I had first glimpsed as a gentile would.

'Why do you hate Russia?' he said.

'I don't.'

'You don't fool me for a second, Otto. Admit it: you hate our civilisation. You hate our religion and our values. You want to dominate the world and destroy us.'

'That is ridiculous,' I objected.

'So you're the exception – a Jew who is a good Russian?'

My mouth was dry. I was thinking of Gulko and the fate he met on Politseisky Bridge. I said, 'Are you going to kill me?'

'Otto, Otto,' he replied, with exaggerated hurt. 'Why would you think such a thing?'

I could have pointed to the knife on the desk. I could have repeated the details of Gulko's murder. I could have asked him if he'd heard the cry *Bei zhidov!* or the name Mendel Beilis.

His expression changed, amusement giving way to contempt and spite. He took the knife and stood up, towering over me. I smelled the leather of his coat. I smelled the city street on his workman's boots, oil and horse dung and cigarettes and dirty snow. He raised the knife.

I closed my eyes and began to rock slowly back and forth, the way Rozental and the baker and the tailor and the innkeeper would as they contemplated their God. I summoned Catherine before me. I saw her face as I glimpsed it once when she came running through the snowy woods to me, arms outstretched, calling 'Papa! Papa!' I was never her favourite. She adored her mother. It had been one of the few occasions when she showed me uninhibited and unconscious affection. She was seven years old. We were in Finland, the three of us, on a skiing holiday. Such joy in her fine-featured little face, such excitement. I thought it the look of a child who felt utterly loved and safe.

I heard the outer door close softly.

I opened my eyes. Kavi was gone. His knife was gone.

For ten minutes or more I could not move, I could not trust my legs to support me or my eyes to guide me.

I have never been systematic in my note-taking. During analysis I sometimes scribbled the odd word here and there but generally I preferred not to record the session for fear of inhibiting my thought processes and interrupting my responsiveness to the patient. It was my practice to make a full record in the intervals between sessions or at the end of the day. I also made notes on scraps of paper at home, on the tram and in Filippov's and Café Central. These I gave to Minna who, like all good secretaries, had an instinctive understanding of her employer's intentions. Her filing system worked perfectly insomuch as she was able to retrieve whatever I needed at a moment's notice. But it was also highly idiosyncratic; no one else would understand its organising principle, which is why it took me so long to work out which file they had taken.

What I could not work out was why. What possible interest could Gulko's assassins have in Avrom Chilowicz Rozental?

Six

T he doorman smiled ingratiatingly as he let me out of the building. I did not recognise him. A new man, I supposed. He offered to run to the stand to get me a taxi. I had planned to take the tram to the Admiralty and walk to Morskaya Street but, having spent almost two hours sorting out the files, I did not want to be late for my meeting with Anna's father.

'Where shall I tell the driver his honour is going?' he asked.

The question was normal enough and in normal circumstances I would have answered without a moment's hesitation.

'You're new here?' I said.

'Yes, your honour.'

He was tall and rather thin. 'What is your name?'

'Semevsky, sir. I'll get his honour's taxi. Where did his honour say he was going?'

'Never mind,' I said, walking away.

It had been clear and cold earlier in the day but snow had been falling since lunchtime. Gas lights flickered through the flurries. As I was about to cross the street, I glanced over my shoulder. Semevsky was still outside the building, watching me. Without looking where I was going, I stepped into the road. A small, dark-blue motor carriage braked sharply, slithering on the street and almost colliding with a droshky.

I crossed the Nevsky and went to the taxi stand outside the Gostinny Dvor. A driver was waiting for a fare.

In the back of the taxi I thought about the coincidence of Lychev's visit and the arrival of Kavi and Tolya. But if they were connected, how? My first instinct had been to summon the police. But until I knew what Lychev wanted I was not certain I could trust the authorities.

The driver was in a mood to talk. There had been violent collisions that afternoon in the Vyborg quarter between striking factory workers and police, he informed me. 'All got up by German agents,' he went on confidently. 'It's part of the Kaiser's plan. He's trying to ruin our industries and turn the people against the tsar. Then, when he's got us on our knees, that's when he'll invade. The Jews are all in on it, too.'

'Really?' I said.

'Didn't his honour hear the news this afternoon? The police raided apartments all over the city and arrested more than thirty Jews. They found bombs, guns, everything. They were planning to massacre us. Thank God someone is keeping an eye on them.'

I wondered if Lychev's visit was in some way connected to the arrests.

We were passing the Stroganov Palace when I casually turned to look out the back window. My eyes fell on a small motor carriage behind us. Besides the driver I could just make out a passenger in the front. We turned into Morskaya Street. The little car did the same. Was I being followed?

The taxi driver pulled up at the Imperial Yacht Club. 'Fifty kopecks,' he said.

I kept my eyes fixed on the car behind us. As it overtook us, I saw that it was blue. The same car that had almost hit the droshky near the Gostinny Dvor? I caught a fleeting glimpse of the driver and his companion, but their faces were obscured by their hats. They did not so much as glance in my direction. Perhaps I was being foolish. I was paying the driver when there was a dull boom in the distance. Roosting birds rose up in a sudden squall into the dark sky above. The driver and I looked at each other.

'Sounds like the police didn't get all the bombers,' he said.

I straightened my tie, went to the door and rang the bell. A servant in a dark-green uniform with red piping looked me over.

'I have an appointment with his honour Peter Arseneyevich Zinnurov. I am Dr Otto Spethmann,' I said.

Inside, two more similarly attired servants relieved me of my hat and coat and led me up a wide, sweeping staircase. At the top was a plushly carpeted landing. I continued with my escort until we reached the farthest door, which led into a private room. Inside were leather armchairs and a pair of butterfly-backed, cream-coloured sofas in the Italian rustic style. Two potted plants stood on either side of a glass-fronted, mahogany bookcase, and on the French Empire guéridon lay a carefully folded copy of the *Petersburg Zeitung*.

One of the servants bade me sit and said that Zinnurov would join me shortly. He offered me a cigar and asked if I would take some refreshment. I asked for coffee.

The room was terribly overheated. I went to the heavy, dark-green velvet drapes and pulled them aside. There was a good view of the golden caravel of the Admiralty, and Winter Palace Square. The church bells sounded midnight and when the cannon fired it took me a moment to realise it was the routine discharge from the Peter and Paul Fortress and not another explosion.

I sat down to read the *Petersburg Zeitung*, a pro-German newspaper I rarely saw. A front-page editorial lauded the tsar's brother Grand Duke Michael Alexandrovich for his recent speech praising the restraint of the Kaiser and the German people in the face of continued French and English provocations. Germany harboured no animosity towards Russia, the editorial continued, and warned that if the pro-French cabal in St Petersburg got its way, it would lead the tsar and Russia to ruin.

For all Anna's resistance, it was obvious that something traumatic had occurred during her trip with her father to Kazan all those years ago. There was an odious possibility that Zinnurov had made improper advances towards his infatuated thirteen-year-old daughter. For this reason alone, leaving aside his notorious public reputation, my feelings at the prospect of meeting the Mountain were wary and incomplete.

The man who bounded into the sweltering room and thrust out his hand was tall, trim and straight-backed despite being, by my calculation, almost seventy. His hair was probably thinner than it had been when he was a youth but it was still plentiful, not yet entirely grey, and, for all his hairdresser's expertise, a little unruly. He spoke loudly; he was used to being heard and appreciated. I imagined he usually over-whelmed his listeners. And why not? He was the Mountain, after all, self-made entrepreneur and confidant of princes. Only the week before the newspapers had reported at length a speech in which he denounced Russia's enemies as 'a league of evil': they included liberals, factory workers, students, artists, social democrats, anarchists, terrorists and 'a certain race that need not be named because every decent Russian knows who they are'. Was I in his estimation, even if ambiguously in my own, of that certain race?

A waiter entered with a decanter of red wine and two crystal goblets on a silver tray. The wine was French, Zinnurov informed me with an ironic shrug (the Imperial Yacht Club was famously the resort of the German noblemen known as the Baltic Barons and their friends).

'The French are impossible, don't you agree?' Zinnurov said with a smile that was only half playful. 'The alliance with France is immoral. We should have nothing to do with the

French – they are cynical and frivolous.' He put his nose into the glass and sniffed deeply, then said with a helpless smile, 'The same, alas, cannot be said of their wine.'

We toasted each other. The wine was big, earthy and forceful; Zinnurov liked his essence mirrored back to himself.

'I understand from my daughter that you are having some difficulty with the police?' he said without further formality.

'Earlier this evening and completely out of the blue,' I began, 'a police inspector by the name of Lychev visited me in my office. He said he was investigating the murders of the newspaper editor Gulko and a young man called Yastrebov.'

Zinnurov's eyes narrowed, his interest piqued.

'I should state unequivocally,' I said, 'that I know nothing of these crimes and that nothing of this nature has ever happened to me before.'

He nodded solemnly. 'Did you know Gulko?'

'I knew neither victim, though Yastrebov was apparently found in possession of my *carte de visite.*'

'You did not give it to him?'

'I did not.'

'Business cards are often passed on from person to person.'

'I said as much to Lychev. However, he insisted on my attendance tomorrow at police headquarters along with my daughter.'

'Did he say your daughter is suspected in some way?'

'No. Catherine is only eighteen. She is a respectable young woman and it is simply inconceivable that she would know anything about these murders.'

'You're quite sure about that? With one's children,' he said in a rueful, worldly tone, 'one never quite knows what they get up to.'

'I know my daughter would never get up to murder.'

He smiled, point taken. 'Is there anything else?'

I had already decided not to tell him about the intrusion of

Kavi and Tolya and their theft of Rozental's file. It would give the impression that my affairs must be more complicated than I was letting on and therefore more suspicious.

'No,' I said, 'except to emphasise again that I am completely unable to help the police in this matter.'

'If you are innocent you have nothing to fear,' he said.

'Of course this is true,' I replied. 'But it is equally true that mistakes are sometimes made. Suspicion can and does on occasion fall on those who are blameless.'

Zinnurov sipped his drink and lapsed into silence, as if following up some vague line of thought. I could smell the wine's dense bouquet in the air between us.

'What would you have me do?' he asked.

'If there was someone in authority to whom you could explain this error, I would be very grateful.'

Zinnurov clasped his hands together and leaned back in his chair. 'My daughter says you are an honourable man, Speth-mann, and I have no reason to doubt her estimation of you. But my difficulty is that I do not know you. You understand my position? I cannot go to, say, Maklakov, who is the minister of the interior, on behalf of someone for whom I am unable personally to vouch. You could be, for all I know, a Bolshevik or' – Did I detect a sly look here? – 'a Bundist. I am sorry, Spethmann,' he said with a helpless gesture, 'I never like to disappoint my daughter, but on this occasion I am afraid I simply cannot assist you.'

I got to my feet. 'Thank you for finding the time to see me,' I said formally. I did not feel disappointment, rather distaste – for the man in front of me but also for myself. What had I been thinking in coming here? To this man?

His smile was equally formal, a slight, quick tightening of the corners of his mouth. We walked to the door.

'How do you know my daughter?' he asked conversationally.

'I am her doctor.'

He threw his head back and squinted long-sightedly at me.

'I thought Dautov was her doctor.'

'I am a neurologist,' I said, 'and a psychoanalyst.'

'I see,' he said uncertainly. His features took on a thoughtful cast. 'Look,' he said, 'I may have been hasty.' He indicated the sofa. 'Please . . .'

Pride and principle dictated I refuse his invitation; my fears for Catherine directed otherwise. I settled in my seat again while he refilled my glass.

'Spethmann?' he mused aloud. 'I do not know the name. How long have you lived in St Petersburg?'

'I was born here.'

'Really?'

The Mountain's own origins were obscure. It was rumoured his grandfather had been a serf and his father a conscript in the war in the Crimea. What was certain was that all that he possessed, which was a very great deal, he had created for himself. His spectacular rise in the world was the work of an especially powerful personality. Everyone knew how, in the chaotic days following the Revolution of 1905, he made a speech in the first Duma declaring that those who sought to bring down tsarism might just as well try to demolish Mount Narodnaya with wooden spoons and subsequently earned himself his nickname – the Mountain.

'A psychoanalyst, you say? Is something wrong with Anna? Is there some doubt as to her . . . sanity?'

'Not at all,' I hastened to assure him. 'Anna is perfectly sane.'

'It's the nightmares, isn't it,' Zinnurov said, a shrew look coming over him. When I did not answer, he said, 'Has the numbness also returned?'

'I am not at liberty to discuss my patients' condition,' I said.

'Even with a father?'

45

'I'm afraid not.'

'I hope you understand that Anna is, sadly, a confused and unstable young woman.'

I said nothing. He stared past me to his own reverie. 'She was such a beautiful child,' he said, making his voice nostalgic. 'Everyone loved her. When a child is happy, completely untroubled by anything in the world, or indeed anything in herself, she is surrounded by a glow. You're a father, Spethmann. You know what I mean. A real, physical glow that adults can actually see with their eyes. If you could have seen her face then, Spethmann. When you were with Anna you felt as though you were being touched by magic.'

He paused to draw in a deep breath. 'Her mother died,' he said. 'That was it – the beginning of her troubles.'

'I understood the nightmares began before her mother's death?' I ventured.

'Is that what she says?'

'It is the impression I have received,' I said.

'No,' he answered firmly. 'She is either deliberately deceiving you – why, I have not the least idea – or she is genuinely confused and cannot remember. She was sixteen when her mother died and she changed overnight from a carefree child to a troubled young woman with a rather disturbed imagination.'

'I have to say I have never seen evidence of a "disturbed imagination". '

'Haven't you?' he said. 'I have.' He sipped his wine before continuing. 'And then of course came the marriage. You know her husband?'

'I have met Boris Vasilevich once or twice.'

Zinnurov shook his head dismissively. 'An odious little man – vain, pompous, ambitious. A violent temper, too. I could never understand what she saw in him. He's not exactly handsome either. And there are no children, which says a great deal about a marriage, wouldn't you say?'

'Who really knows what goes on between a husband and wife?' I said blandly.

'Does she tell you what goes on in her marriage?' When I did not answer, he asked with brutal and surprising directness, 'Has the marriage been consummated, do you think?'

He peered at me. Again I said nothing. In our early sessions I had asked Anna, as I would any patient, about the state of her relations with her husband. Her answers had given me no reason to suspect the marriage was white.

I said, 'How would you describe your relationship with Anna?'

Zinnurov gave me a sad, wise smile. 'I have not seen or heard from my daughter since last September. It is not my choice. I've tried to get in touch with her. I've tried to get to the bottom of it. When she telephoned this evening I thought it might be because she had forgiven whatever it is I have done wrong. I thought she wanted to see me.'

He searched my face for sympathetic understanding. I did not have to struggle to convey it. The Mountain I detested, the father was myself.

'Have you any idea why she severed relations with you?' I asked.

'There's never a reason. She never accuses me of anything, she doesn't shout at me or blame me for something. She simply . . . withdraws. When a daughter rejects her father, the pain is insupportable. I think about Anna every day.'

'You imply there have been previous estrangements.'

'Many,' he said. 'Then after a time, she comes to see me and she is suddenly once again the loving daughter I used to have. It's as if nothing has happened.' He refreshed our glasses and lit a cigar. 'Does she talk about me?'

'Psychoanalysis is a deep investigation of one's past and present. A patient's father will obviously be discussed in that process.'

He smiled but his eyes were hard. '*Deep* investigation? What does that mean?'

'When the body is sick, the physician will make a thorough physical examination.'

'And you do the same, mentally speaking?'

'Yes.'

Few of us like the idea of being discussed as systematically as my formulation suggested to Zinnurov. 'How does she speak of me?' he asked slowly, doing his best not to appear too interested.

He seemed for a moment quite helpless so that even had I not been bound by a professional code I would have struggled to answer.

'Your expression gives everything away, Spethmann,' he said. He straightened in the chair and cleared his throat, getting himself back under control. 'Give me the name of this police inspector again,' he said, taking a pen and notebook from his pocket.

'Lychev,' I said.

Zinnurov scribbled the name in his notebook. 'And he is investigating the murders of Gulko and . . .?'

'Yastrebov.'

'Who is Yastrebov?'

'Lychev claimed to know nothing about him other than his name.'

'And your daughter is Catherine, yes?'

'Yes.'

Zinnurov closed the notebook and screwed the top back on the pen. He got up. 'I shall call Maklakov first thing in the morning,' he said. 'I can't promise anything but when I explain things I'm sure the minister will understand.'

'Thank you,' I said.

We were in the vestibule and the servants were helping me on with my galoshes and overcoat when a tall, thin old man in the dress uniform of the Household Cavalry entered. With his fine white hair and dull blue eyes he looked grandfatherly and wise, an impression not in the least contradicted by the pale scar that ran from eye to jawbone on the left side of his face, or by the fact that he was head of the secret police. I recognised him at once, for Colonel Maximilian Gan, the famous director of the Okhrana, was as well known to Petersburgers as the tsar himself. The atmosphere chilled perceptibly, as if the door through which Gan had entered could not now shut out the biting cold. The servants, all meekness and uncertainty, kept their heads lowered and their eyes down. Gan nodded tersely to Zinnurov before proceeding directly to the smoking room.

Zinnurov gave me a tight smile. 'I would be grateful, Spethmann, if you would convey to Anna my deepest desire to see her again. Tell her I will see her wherever she wants, under whatever conditions she sees fit to impose.'

A small, bald man in a frock coat approached, a barely subdued urgency about his manner. He whispered in Zinnurov's ear. The Mountain's features darkened. He dismissed the man, turned to me and said, 'The terrorists have struck again. Two dynamite bombs. One they threw into the restaurant at the Angleterre, the other into Irinovka Station.'

'I heard an explosion as I arrived,' I said, 'but I had no idea. Are there many hurt?'

'Four dead, apparently. All at the Angleterre. We live in dangerous times, Spethmann.'

As we shook hands, he fixed me with a look and said, 'I sense that a word from you would carry great weight with Anna. I know you will not let me down.'

He intended me to understand in no uncertain terms that we had made a deal: he would talk to the minister of the interior on my behalf as long as I talked to Anna on his.

'I will do what I can,' I said.

A driver from the club brought me home. The small, dark-blue car followed us all the way. This time I recognised the passenger; Lychev looked pinched and cold. I almost felt sorry for him.

Seven

C atherine kissed me on the forehead and sat down at the table. Lidiya asked what she would like to eat and, as usual, Catherine said she was not hungry. Tea would be sufficient. Lidiya clucked disapprovingly.

'You should eat, child,' Lidiya said.

'I eat when I'm hungry,' Catherine said. 'And when I'm not hungry I don't eat.'

'Breakfast is the most important meal of the day,' Lidiya persisted.

I signalled her to stop: she would get nowhere. Though she had been with us for eleven years, Lidiya still could not accept Catherine's eating habits, and much else besides. Elena had been the same, always trying to get Catherine to eat, or dress, or do this or that, and becoming upset when Catherine refused. From the very start, from the moment she could first say yes or no, Catherine knew her own mind. She was a force of nature and once she said no, nothing in the world could make her change her mind. The trick was never to get into a situation in which the only options were yes and no. It was a trick almost entirely impossible to pull off.

Lidiya accepted my direction with a despairing look – despairing of Catherine, the wilful young woman in sore need of taming, despairing of the father who would never curb her. She poured tea and left us.

'You were out late,' Catherine said.

'I'm sorry,' I said. 'Did I wake you?'

'I wasn't asleep. I was worried about you.'

'Since when do daughters worry about their fathers?'

'When their fathers become old.'

I smiled the weary wise smile of the parent whose offspring still think themselves immune to the passage of time.

'Where were you?'

'I was doing some filing at the office,' I said.

'Really? I telephoned the office three times last night.'

'Then I went to dinner with Kopelzon.'

She threw me a sceptical look. 'Are you sure it was with Kopelzon?'

'Are we in court?' I asked mildly. 'Is this a cross-examination?'

'Were you with that woman?'

'What woman?'

'You know the one.'

'Why have you taken against Anna Petrovna so violently?'

'I know her kind,' she said.

'Really?'

'Shallow society women. All they talk about are shoes and dresses, and who's having an affair with who, and who's had an invitation to tea with the tsarina at the Peterhof. Do you know who her father is? The Mountain. Did you read his article this morning?' She tossed the newspaper across the table, reciting, ' "First shoot the socialists, behead them and make them harmless, if need be through a bloodbath." That's your charming lady friend's father.'

It occurred to me to explain to Catherine that because of the Mountain's good offices she would be spared the trial of presenting herself at police headquarters today.

'I was not at dinner with Anna Petrovna last night,' I said.

'Do you swear it?'

'I have told you where I was and with whom,' I said.

'You swore you would never see her again.'

'I know what I swore,' I said.

I could see she was debating whether to press the matter. She took a sip of her tea. By the time she put the glass down, she had decided to be bored with this.

'I can't eat another thing,' she said.

She had, not unnaturally, a slender figure – unlike her mother, a gorgeous voluptuary. Her face was small and oval-shaped, framed by white-blonde hair which she wore quite short. Her eyes were huge, frank and careless, and vividly blue. Long, dark lashes fell over them. Her teeth were small and white. Altogether the impression was of a doll, except that in her delicate features were obvious traces of a fiercely self-contained and independent temperament: the single, dark unbroken line of eyebrow, the strong jaw-line, the mobile mouth equally capable of expressing burning compassion and withering contempt. She had grown up a great deal since Elena's death. I was proud of her, and would have changed nothing about her even if I could, even if it meant that sometimes she would be more loving of me, or allow me into her life a little more. She lived to herself and most of the time I had no idea what she was doing, whether at the university or in the company of her friends. I did not know who these friends were or anything about their families. I did not know if she had a sweetheart. To ask would be pointless. Just as she used to tell me everything, now she told me only what she wanted me to know, which was very little.

'I'm off,' she said, patting a napkin unnecessarily to her mouth.

'Is everything all right?' I asked. 'At the university?'

'Yes,' she said, with a nonchalant shrug.

'You would tell me, wouldn't you, if there was anything troubling you?'

Most children, I think, would answer yes as a matter of course, if only to effect the quickest possible exit from their meddlesome parent. Catherine, being Catherine, appeared to give the question serious consideration. She pursed her lips. That dark line of eyebrow came down in a frown.

'I don't know,' she said. 'I might. But in any case there's nothing troubling me.'

She was at the door when I said, 'Do you know anyone called Yastrebov?'

'No,' she replied.

I studied her face carefully. She was telling the truth. I knew my daughter well enough to be able to tell.

'Why?'

'Nothing,' I said.

And then she was gone. I smiled to myself. I was in awe of her and, after Zinnurov's promise of last night, I could afford a little sentimentality about my daughter.

I picked up the newspaper. The Mountain's article was in response to the recent wave of bomb attacks. The death toll from last night's, at the Angleterre and the Irinovka Station, had risen to seven; many more had been horribly wounded. There was also an interview with Maklakov, who sounded quite defensive. In spite of the latest outrages, the minister of the interior insisted, the police were having great success in breaking up the terrorist gangs. Only yesterday a senior member of the Bolshevik underground, a Georgian named Dzhugashvili, had been captured in the capital. Although Maklakov would not confirm it, the newspaper attributed the arrest to the Okhrana spy codenamed King who had infiltrated the Party's highest echelons.

I laid the newspaper down and went to my study to collect some books. The telephone rang.

'I spoke to Maklakov just now,' Zinnurov said in a hearty voice. 'Once I'd explained your difficulty and vouched for you, he was entirely sympathetic. You will not be troubled by Inspector Lychev again.'

'Thank you,' I said.

'Tell Anna I will see her anywhere at any time.'

He left a number where I could reach him. I waited a minute before picking up the telephone again. I asked to speak to Madame Ziatdinov.

'I wanted to thank you for arranging the interview with your father,' I said when Anna came to the telephone.

'Was he able to help?'

'More than I dared hope.'

'I'm so glad. I was awake half the night worrying about you and Catherine.'

For some long moments there was only the furred hum and crackle of the telephone line. Though we disguise our hopes with ambiguous meanings, men and women know when what they are really talking about is the thing between men and women.

'I would like to see you,' I said.

Another pause, the business of men and women and its implications working through her mind.

'I have some things to do today,' she said, 'but I'll be free by six o'clock.'

We arranged to meet on Admiralty Prospect. When we said goodbye I was aware of a generalised feeling of pleasure in my groin, as though someone had inadvertently brushed against me. This impulse, this utterly unnerving and commanding impulse. I would be fifty on my next birthday. How little we grow. And how marvellous we grow so little, in this aspect of our lives at least.

I went to the window. Across the river smoke was already rising from the chimneys of the great grey factories of the Vyborg. A gentle snow was falling. I decided to drive to the office.

My first appointment that morning was with none other than Gregory Vasilevich Petrov. As Petrov was champion of the city's poor (and hero to Catherine) so he was reviled as a demagogic opportunist by supporters of the autocracy like Zinnurov and the Baltic Barons. There were plenty of rabble-rousers in St Petersburg at that time, but what made Petrov especially loathed was his combination of oratory, impertinence and scathing quick wit – he was by far the most entertaining deputy in the Duma. His enemies' constant disparagement only enhanced his reputation among the workers and students, in spite of his manifest – and, to some, troubling – contradictions: he professed himself the authentic voice of the destitute and oppressed, yet seemed addicted to expensive restaurants, the theatre and the opera. He dressed in nothing but the finest clothes, paid scrupulous attention to his toilette and revelled in the company of glamorous young women. He had verve and imagination. He was a law unto himself. He was mustachioed, vain, arrogant and clever. He was rarely punctual and often failed to turn up at all for his appointments. I was mildly surprised when Minna announced his arrival, but I was also pleased, for he was never less than interesting.

Petrov collapsed on the couch like a man who has swum from the shipwreck to the shore. Although in public he demonstrated the energy of a man possessed, whenever I saw him he was exhausted. As far as I could tell he never rested. When not making speeches in the Duma, he was leading strikers against the police. When not locked in smoke-filled rooms arguing with comrades as they went line by line through their latest manifesto, he was in the arms of some young lover. He was perpetually in motion as if, like a bicyclist, motion alone kept him upright.

'You missed our last three sessions,' I said.

'I was in Krakow,' he said. 'There was a meeting.'

'With whom?'

'A Party meeting. I can't tell you any more than that, except

56

that it was important and I couldn't miss it. You know there are areas of my life I can't go into.'

Petrov was a member of the Bolshevik faction of the Social Democrats. The Party was notorious, barely legal in Russia and subject to police surveillance and repression. In the absence of Lenin, its exiled leader, Petrov was its de facto chief. The strains involved in this alone would account for his mental and physical exhaustion, but in Petrov's case there was something else. Something tormented his soul. He wanted to tell me, to tell someone, and yet he could not. As with Anna, as with all my resistant patients, I had fallen back on the principal ally of psychoanalysts everywhere – time; I was never in a hurry.

'On the last occasion we met,' I reminded him, 'you said you were at the end of your tether, that you couldn't go on. How do you feel today?'

'The same.'

There was a long silence, which he declined to disturb.

I said, 'Have you been eating properly? Sleeping?'

'It has nothing to do with eating or sleeping,' he answered impatiently.

'What does it have to do with?'

He jabbed a finger at me. 'How would it be if I went to the people I represent and they told me all about their problems – how they couldn't survive on their wages, how they lived twenty to a room and had no clean water, how rats swarmed over their children at night? How would it be if they told me all this and all I could say was: "What colour are the rats?"'

'You have not told me your problems.'

'Are you deaf? I'm exhausted. I'm exhausted and I'm depressed.'

'These are symptoms –' I started to say.

'Enough! Enough!'

His eyes were raging and red, veins throbbed at his temple.

For a moment I think he considered hitting me. Whenever I saw Petrov, I had the sense of wrestling with a violent man made all the more aggressive by his shame at finding himself in a psychoanalyst's office. He was a leader of men, he was openly contemptuous of the very science he hoped would relieve his suffering. Men who have grappled with extreme hardship from their earliest youth – as Petrov had – often armour themselves against the unhappiness that is their lot by developing an omnipotent sense of their own invulnerability. He had always battled his way out of trouble, fighting enemies tooth and nail; but the greatest enemy was in his own subconscious and the battle he had now to fight was with himself.

I stared at him fixedly; with Petrov I had to be firmer than with most of my other patients. He heaved a weary sigh and collapsed again on the couch.

'If . . .,' he began, 'if . . . let us say . . . a man is married and has children. If that man loves his wife, is devoted to her and to their children. And it is a pure love, one built on excitement and enchantment but also on years of shared experience and mutual respect. Yet that same man conceives a similar pure love for another woman. It would be difficult for him, yes? You agree?'

'Go on.'

'He would be torn. Confused. Depressed. Would he not?'

'Are you in such a situation?'

'I feel as if I am.'

'You are married and you have children.'

'So what?'

'Do you have a mistress?'

'I have many women friends.'

'Do you have sexual relations with your women friends?'

'It's no secret,' he said defiantly. 'So what?'

'Is it a secret you keep from your wife?'

'She doesn't ask and I don't tell her.'

58

'How do you think she would feel were she to know?'

'How do you think?'

'You imply she would be upset.'

'To put it mildly.'

'How do you feel about that?'

He sighed and rubbed his tired eyes. 'My dream is to have a little house out in the country,' he said, 'by a lake or a river, where I could fish, and the sun would be shining and the children would play and in the evenings we would sit down together for dinner and there would only be us, the family – my family. Nothing else, no one else. A simple meal, a light breeze, deer and rabbits running over the fields. And I would sleep for ten hours and wake refreshed and content, and the day would start all over again, the sun shining and the children playing.'

'What you are describing is an impossible idyll.'

'I said it was a dream, didn't I?' he answered sharply. 'It's never going to happen. My life is not like that. It never will be like that. But what's wrong with having a harmless little dream?'

'Does it help you solve the fundamental problem of your life?'

'Which is what?'

'I don't know. You won't tell me.'

He stared at me belligerently. 'You have no answers, do you? You can't help me.'

'I can't help you until you trust me.'

'How can I trust you? I can't trust anyone.'

'What about your comrades? Don't you trust them?'

He grunted. 'Are you joking? The Party is a snake pit. Comrades stab each other in the back, they complain, they spread rumours, they manoeuvre against each other. You've heard of "King", I take it?'

'The spy?'

'That's what the meeting in Krakow was all about – who's the traitor, who is King? God knows how many people he's betrayed – Dzhugashvili was arrested yesterday. How many more are we going to lose because of King? There is anger, suspicion, resentment – and that's my life with my comrades. Then there are the factory owners, the police, the government, Okhrana spies, all of whom would like to see me dead. My life is hellish.'

'Then you must live another life.'

'I can't. I believe in what I am doing.'

'What are you doing?'

'What am I doing?' He threw me an indignant look. 'I am fighting against hypocrisy, that's what I'm doing. Russia is a Christian country. As is Germany, England, France, Spain, the Netherlands, Sweden – Orthodox, Catholic, Protestant, but all Christian countries, and yet millions live in poverty. How do we justify this? How do we explain it? Christianity's chief distinction is that it softens the human heart. It urges charity, brotherhood and common cause on believers. Yet it tolerates an economic and political system that runs diametrically counter to first impressions of right and wrong. This to me is utterly repugnant. Destroy Christianity. Destroy capitalism and autocracy. Only when hypocrisy is destroyed can there be justice. This is what I am doing, Spethmann.'

'You have set yourself a very high target.'

'You're a doctor. I want you to make my lives possible.'

'Your *lives*?' I said.

'Life. Lives. It feels like I'm having to live a hundred lives in one body, and it's killing me. I want you to make my life possible. Can you do that, yes or no?'

'Not if you continue to refuse to work with me.'

Before I could say anything more, he took out his pocket watch and drew in a deep, weary breath. 'I have to go,' he said, getting up. He put a hand to his lower back and grimaced with discomfort. 'I have to meet some workers in the naval yards.'

'Minna will make another appointment,' I said, seeing him to the door.

He looked at me with sudden suspicion. 'She doesn't know who I am, does she?'

From the very first, Petrov had insisted on absolute secrecy, fearing the mockery that would result if his enemies discovered he was consulting a psychoanalyst. We used the pseudonym Grischuk in the appointments book and in my notes.

'I have not told Minna,' I said, 'but your face is well known. I can't guarantee she hasn't guessed.'

'But you said she's discreet?'

'She is discretion itself.'

After Petrov, my next patient was a young clerk at the foreign ministry. Addicted to sex with elderly prostitutes, he liked to scour the poorer quarters for the most degraded women he could find for his purposes. He recounted his activities in forensic and scatological detail. I was always relieved when his hour was up.

That afternoon, while I was making up my notes, Minna came in. 'I cannot find Rozental's file,' she said. 'I've looked everywhere.'

'I took it home with me last night,' I lied. 'I'll bring it in tomorrow.'

'The files are a terrible mess. I've been trying to sort them out all day.'

'I'm sorry,' I said. 'I was looking for something and got everything mixed up.'

I wasn't sure Minna believed me and she seemed hurt that I might be holding something back from her.

When she'd gone, my eye fell on the chessboard and I found

myself being drawn into the position. It would be a shame not to play for the win, yet I could find no satisfactory continuation. Exchanging on g5, as Lychev had said, was a dead draw.

What was this?

Spethmann–Kopelzon
After 35 Rg2. Is this any good?

This wasn't the correct position. What was the rook doing on g2? The table must have been knocked and the piece jolted out of place. I was about to put the rook on its correct square – g4 – when I realised there was nothing accidental about its placement. I saw now that it was a very strong move.

How on earth . . .? Kavi. The Cossack must have done it while I was waiting, eyes closed, for the thrust of his knife. There I was thinking he was going to kill me; instead he was considering a chess move.

There was a knock at the door.

'Your daughter is here,' Minna said, looking quite flustered, 'and also –'

Catherine pushed past and entered.

'Catherine? Why are you here?' I said. She had never before appeared at my office without prior arrangement.

'Because I told her to come.'

The voice was Lychev's. The policeman came in behind her, as silently as the breeze. Two uniformed and armed gendarmes followed rather more noisily.

'I have come to ask you and your daughter some questions,' Lychev said in his nasal monotone.

I reached for the telephone but one of the gendarmes intercepted me.

'There will be no calls to your friends, Spethmann,' Lychev said, pushing his fringe out of his eyes. He was holding a leather bag. It gave off a faintly chemical smell.

Eight

L ychev ordered the gendarmes to remain with Minna in the outer office and then heaved the bag on to my desk; it was evidently quite heavy.

'How was the wine at the Imperial Yacht Club?' he asked slyly. 'I hear they keep an excellent cellar.'

Catherine looked at me. The Imperial Yacht Club? What had I been doing at such a place? Sensing her reaction, Lychev went on in the same crafty tone: 'Didn't you know your father has friends in high places? He only has to click his fingers and archdukes, generals and Baltic Barons snap to do his bidding.'

'Don't be ridiculous,' Catherine told him.

Turning his pale eyes on me, he said, 'You didn't tell Catherine about your friendly little chat with the Mountain?'

Catherine turned to regard him. They were about the same height and equally slight, but Catherine seemed to dominate the space between them.

'The Mountain?' Catherine said.

'I understand Colonel Gan himself was also at the club last night?' Lychev continued in the same heavily ironic tone. 'Did you and the colonel discuss ways to stop the terrorist bombings? Did he try to recruit you as an informer for the secret police?'

'Do your superiors know you are here, Lychev?' I demanded.

He ignored me and, getting down to business, addressed Catherine. 'I must ask you if you know a man by the name of Yastrebov?'

'Do not answer him, Catherine,' I said. 'He has no authority to question us. When his superiors find out he is here, he will be in a great deal of trouble.'

'Do you know a man by the name of Yastrebov?' he repeated.

I protested again but Catherine turned to me and asked, 'Is this the same person you asked me about this morning? Because if it is, I've never heard of him.'

'He was a revolutionary, a terrorist,' Lychev said, 'a very dangerous young man.'

Catherine gave a contemptuous laugh. 'In the view of the police, every worker in Russia is a terrorist and every Jew a revolutionary.'

'I have reason to believe you knew Yastrebov,' Lychev went on, ignoring her provocation.

'I can assure you I did not,' Catherine replied.

'Just so there is no mistake . . .'

Lychev turned to the leather bag and slowly undid the two enclosing straps. The chemical odour became more noticeable.

'There can be confusion over names,' he said. 'After all, what is a name? Documents and identities are easily forged. The revolutionary organisations have whole departments dedicated to their manufacture. Names can be changed. Physical features, on the other hand, may be modified and disguised but they are not so easily transformed.'

He needed both hands to withdraw the contents. His back was to us but I glimpsed a large glass jar filled with an opaque liquid together with some solid, dark, unspecific matter. He settled the jar on the desk and stood aside.

'What is the meaning of this?' I demanded.

65

The colour had drained from Catherine's face like water from a sink. We were looking at a human head pickled in formaldehyde.

At that moment, when my thoughts and senses ought to have been focused on the matter in hand, I was nevertheless conscious of the sensations produced by contact with a human body. Other than to shake hands with friends and colleagues or to receive Kopelzon's extravagant embraces, it had been more than two years since I had touched another person. As a child, Catherine had submitted to hugs rather than given herself wholly to them; when I used to lift her up and clasp her to me, the little child became rigid and would bend her knees into my chest to keep us apart. Yet now she was in my arms, her face buried in my chest. I kissed the top of her head. I stroked her hair and closed my eyes, as if the mere fact of our nearness could insulate us against the horror Lychev had brought into our lives.

'Look carefully, Miss Spethmann,' Lychev said, placing the bag on the floor so as not to obscure the view. 'This is the man we know as Alexander Yastrebov. I have reason to believe, however, that this is not his real name. It is imperative that I establish his true identity, and do so as quickly as possible.'

He waited for what he may have considered a decent interval and then said evenly, but with finality, as though refusal were not an option, 'I must insist.'

Catherine kept her face turned away but I sensed her beginning to recover from the shock.

'Do you recognise this man?' Lychev repeated, his patience running out.

By degrees Catherine brought her gaze to the object before us. The glass's convexity distorted the features somewhat, adding to their blood-drained, ghoulish quality.

'No,' she answered in a firm voice, 'I do not recognise him.'

She turned to look Lychev boldly in the eye. It was the policeman who in the end had to turn away.

In the elevator car I tried to regard Catherine not as a father does his daughter, but as a man who must extract the truth from one determined to conceal from him what he needs to know.

'I want you to be truthful,' I whispered to her while the attendant pretended not to listen. 'We are in danger. If you are not completely truthful, we will not escape. Who was the man in the jar?'

'What happened to him?'

'He was murdered a few days ago and his body dumped in the river.'

The elevator car stopped with a jolt. The attendant opened the doors to the lobby.

Though she had rallied well, the ordeal had obviously taken a lot out of her. She was still pale, and unusually placid in both speech and movement, and yet she managed to fix me with a defiant look.

'I never saw him before,' she said.

With the help of the doorman I saw Catherine into a taxi. Before the driver pulled away, I warned her not to leave the house or speak to anyone under any circumstances but to await my return.

When I got back to the office Lychev had dismissed the gendarmes and was replacing the glass jar in the leather bag.

'Was that really necessary?' I asked. 'You must have photographs you could have shown us.'

'You thought my display over-theatrical?' His thin lips spread in a grin.

'I thought it unnecessary and cruel.'

'The times we live in are cruel, don't you think?' he said, closing and strapping up the bag with methodical attention. 'Last month I arrested a man, a member of one of the so-called combat detachments of the Socialist Revolutionary Party. He had poured sulphuric acid over the face of one of his comrades, whom he suspected to be working for the Okhrana. The victim is horribly deformed – his nose is gone, the left eye is gone. The skin on the whole left side of his face has been burnt away. Acid attacks seem to be quite the fashion now among revolutionaries.'

Lychev continued, 'When I arrested the attacker I thought to myself, if you believed your comrade to be a spy why not just shoot him and be done with it? Why pour acid into his face? To borrow your own words, Spethmann, it seemed unnecessary and cruel. I encounter much cruelty, you see, most of it beyond comprehension.'

'I do not envy you your world, Lychev.'

He shrugged and heaved the leather bag to the floor, and indicated the chessboard.

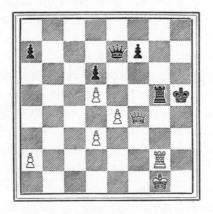

Spethmann–Kopelzon
After 35 Rg2. 'Worthy of a master.' But is it really good enough to win?

'Those backwards moves are always hard to find,' he said, indicating the rook on g2. 'It's worthy of a master. I had no idea you were such a strong player.'

68

'I'm not,' I said.

'You've been getting some help, perhaps?' he said, throwing me a sly look. 'Do you still think Capablanca will win the tournament?'

'I have no interest in discussing this, Lychev,' I said. 'Nor have I any interest in seeing you again now that my daughter and I have answered your questions. I shall of course be making your visit known to the minister of the interior.'

He smiled. 'You are correct, Spethmann. I do not believe either you or your daughter can be of any more help to me. I hope you will understand that I was only doing my duty.'

Was it possible I was seeing the last of him? At the door he bade me good day. Relief flooded into my heart. I waited a minute or two to make sure he was gone before telephoning the number Zinnurov had given me. A secretary answered and asked me to hold. Eventually the Mountain came to the telephone.

'Lychev was here,' I said. 'He came to my office and brought my daughter with him.'

Judging from the pause that followed, it was clear Zinnurov was equally surprised. 'Did he indeed?'

'I understood Minister Maklakov had ordered him to leave me alone?'

'You are correct in your understanding, Spethmann,' he said. 'I will contact the minister at once and find out what happened.'

'What happened is that he came to my office and in front of my daughter produced Yastrebov's pickled head. In front of my daughter!'

'I do hope she was not unduly upset.'

'She was shocked,' I said, outrage growing in my voice. 'It was horrific.'

'Of course, of course,' Zinnurov said smoothly. 'I'll look into it. Either Lychev is acting without proper authority or he has gone above Maklakov's head. Either way, he'll be restrained. I promise you.'

'Thank you,' I said.

'Not at all,' he said. 'We have a lot in common, after all.'

'Yes,' I said uncertainly.

'We are fathers who dearly love our daughters.'

'Yes,' I said, 'yes.'

'Have you spoken to Anna?'

'I'm seeing her this evening.'

'Good,' Zinnurov said. 'Let me know what she says.'

He rang off. I waited another fifteen minutes to give Catherine time to get home before calling.

'She went to bed as soon as she came in, Doctor,' Lidiya said. 'I've never seen her so utterly exhausted. Will you be home soon?'

'I have an appointment,' I said. 'I shall be home by ten, Lidiya. Please make sure Catherine does not leave the house before I return.'

Minna was still in the outer office. It was obvious she wanted to talk about what had happened but I had no time and was rather offhand and impatient with her.

I hurried to my car, which I had left in Sadovaya Street. The Renault was dusted with snow. I cleared the windscreen, cranked the engine and got in. I blew into my hands, pulled on my gloves and pressed the starter. But as I pulled away, I was thinking not of Anna but of Catherine. She had lied to me. She had recognised Yastrebov's pickled face. I saw it in her reaction. And Lychev was too observant of human nature not to have seen it too.

Nine

Anna was waiting at the corner of Admiralty Prospect. She was wearing a long, black woollen coat and black fur hat. The snow was dancing in light flurries, a last hurrah of winter. I pulled up in front of her and climbed out of the Renault to open the passenger door.

'I'm sorry I'm late,' I said.

I felt her eyes on me as I helped her into the car and placed a rug over her lap.

'I thought perhaps you'd changed your mind,' she said, 'about seeing me.'

Why were we seeing each other? The ambiguity was disconcerting and I felt awkward under the frankness of her gaze. She seemed to sense the equivocation in me. I patted down the rug then got back into the driver's seat.

'Where are we going?' she asked.

With everything that had happened, I had not had time to think of where to go. We would have to be careful. Like many big cities, St Petersburg was a small town. I was with a married woman, a patient. The chances of running into a neighbour or colleague were always high.

An idea struck me. 'My favourite place,' I said.

She smiled, pleased at the thought that I was taking her to a place that had significance for me. 'Where?'

'I hope you'll like it,' I said.

I drove to Nicholas Bridge.

71

'Something's wrong,' she said as we were crossing to Basil Island. 'You seem distracted.'

'There's nothing wrong,' I said, summoning a false smile. 'What time are you expected home?'

'Not too late,' she said. 'I'm sorry.'

'No, I have to get back myself,' I said.

She smiled weakly, as did I, neither of us confident enough to express the disappointment we felt that our time together would be short.

We continued north to Apothecary and on to Kamenny and Yelagin. At this time of year a strange, luminous light plays over their cold greys and blues. We left the car near the palace and walked down a long, deserted avenue of leafless great oaks. It was still and quiet but for the waters of the Gulf of Finland gently lapping the shore. The snow continued to fall. There was no wind. We came to the end of the avenue of oaks. Before us there was only sea thickened with snow.

'It's beautiful,' Anna said. 'Thank you for bringing me here.'

'I used to come here after Elena died. I used to come here every day,' I said, not really meaning to tell her this. But the power of this place had a special compulsion for me. 'She used to wear a long dark-red coat. It was so unusual and striking that I would see the coat before I saw her, in the street, in the shops, on the Nevsky. After she died, I looked for the coat everywhere. Wherever there were people I looked out for the red of Elena's coat. Sometimes I would see a similar coat and even though I knew it couldn't be her I would follow the woman until I saw her face. Only when I had satisfied myself that it wasn't Elena could I turn away.'

'You came here because no one else does,' she said. 'Because you wouldn't be tormented by the sight of a woman in a red coat.'

'Even in the summer very few people come to this place,' I said.

She touched my arm. 'Something's happened,' she said. 'Tell me, please.'

'The policeman – Lychev – came to my office this afternoon. Catherine was there as well,' I said.

'My father promised you would be left alone,' she said, with a hint of self-accusation, as though she were the one at fault.

'I believe he tried. Lychev, however, proves not so easily restrained.'

I told her everything, including the visit from Kavi and Tolya.

When I had finished, she said, 'And you have no idea why all this has happened?'

'None,' I said.

'Why should they have taken Rozental's file?'

'It makes no sense.'

'The police must have you mixed up with someone else. With all the bombs and murders, they are arresting so many people. I don't imagine half of them are guilty of anything other than wanting to get on with their lives.'

'When he left, Lychev said he had no further need of me, or Catherine.'

'So, it's over?'

'So it would seem,' I said. Neither of us believed it.

We stared out at the sea, at the great, slow, rolling waves. I stole glances of her. Her lips were red and soft. How hungrily I had kissed as a young man, how insistently my mouth and tongue worked. I could not be satisfied with the mere brush of lips but pressed and sucked and licked and bruised. I wanted then the very breath of my lover, and my kisses were reckless, long and demanding. I wanted to kiss her.

'Your father asked me to give you a message,' I said. 'He wants to see you. He said he would see you anywhere, at the time and place of your choosing, without any conditions on his part.'

73

Anna said nothing for some moments. 'Did you tell him I was under your care?'

'Yes.'

'What else did he say?'

'That he is at a loss to understand why you have severed all connection with him and that he misses you very much.'

She said nothing but kept her gaze fixed on the sea.

'What happened between you and your father?'

'It has nothing to do with my nightmares,' she said.

'You can't possibly know that.'

Touching my gloved hand lightly, she said, 'I had the dream again last night. It was the same as usual. I was in the house, alone. I had a raging thirst and I was going from room to room looking for water. I got to a door. I knew there was water on the other side and I started to pull at the handle. It was stuck fast and wouldn't open. I started to panic. I thought I was going to die of thirst if I didn't get through it. Then suddenly the door swung open and I found my grandmother waiting for me.'

'So it was your grandmother's house after all?'

'I don't know,' she said. 'It may be that I only dreamed it because you had put the thought into my head.'

'What happened then?'

'Babushka was smiling, a big, happy, toothless smile. Then she gave me a glass of tea except it wasn't tea – it was vodka.'

'Go on.'

'I heard a knock. It was quite soft, more like someone tapping at a window pane than at a door, and I heard someone whisper my name. *Anna. Anna.* It was so frightening that I had to wake myself up. Even then, it seemed so real that I lay in the dark listening for the voice again, dreading to hear it. In the end, I had to get up and go to the window, just to convince myself there was no one there.'

'Was your grandmother still in the room?'

'I didn't see her go but . . .' She paused and bit her lip. 'I couldn't get out of my head the idea that she had been . . .' – again, she paused – 'that she was dead.'

'Did you see her body?'

'It was a feeling – a very powerful feeling. I felt guilty, as if I had done something very bad.'

I considered what she had told me, then asked, 'Did you tell your husband?'

'My husband?'

'Last night. Did he not wake when you went to the window?'

'Oh,' she said. 'No. We don't sleep in the same room any more.'

I am not a fool; I can read between the lines – in many ways it is the essence of my profession. But still I was not sure what she was saying, if anything. I should have said something quickly, something honest, simple and direct – and I almost did – but what could I offer her? What was I proposing we do? She had a husband, a home, a life and reputation in St Petersburg. Had she said she loved me, I was not even certain that I would have been physically able to make love to her. I felt disadvantaged – by her beauty, by my lack of the same, and by the years that separated us.

The snow-swollen water slurred like a thick tongue. On the bare branches above us spectral white arms stretched up into the night.

'I suppose we should go,' she said.

I wanted to kiss her the way I had kissed as a young man. Then I would not have cared whether we were in the street or in bed, whether we were overlooked or private. I would not have cared that my lover was married. I would not have cared about professional ethics. And since it would have been beyond my capacities to imagine the power and meaning of bereavement I would have kissed through a whole torrent of grief-tears, hers, mine or anyone else's. I would have kissed her. I had been that man when I was young. He had often been selfish and self-absorbed; he had been capable of indifference, insensitivity, dishonesty and deceit. But he had also been vital. I was no longer him.

'Yes,' I said, my heart heavy. 'I suppose so.'

She lay on her back, head turned slightly to the wall, arms thrown up as if in surrender. I could not but smile at the improbability of this. When had she ever surrendered? When had she so much as entered into a compromise or truce? That will of hers. She made me proud, but afraid. Her eyelids flickered. She had always been a sound sleeper, even when upset or anxious, as though sleep were a safe harbour rather than the raging sea it is when we are at odds with ourselves and the world. But no one, not even Catherine, could sleep through this.

She pitched forward in a violent reaction. Her huge eyes were bewildered and exhausted; she had been crying before she had fallen asleep.

'Where am I?' she asked, blinking; and then, seeing me at her bedside, 'What are you doing? What is that noise?'

The pounding at the front door came again. Lidiya appeared at my side. I had expected her to be thrown into a panic; instead I saw her resolute and unafraid.

'Shall I let them in?'

'I do not believe we have a choice, Lidiya,' I said.

She called quietly on God and his saints to protect the house and all who were under its roof, then descended the stairs.

I heard the door burst open and the stamp of heavy boots in the hall, men storming into my house. There was the sound of breaking glass. I heard Lidiya's voice, stern and rebuking.

Two gendarmes, resplendent in their white coats and

brocade, and armed with carbines, entered Catherine's bedroom. They seemed confused, embarrassed I supposed, to find themselves in the bedroom of a respectable young woman. For a moment I almost thought they were about to apologise and excuse themselves.

Lychev came up behind them. He held a large revolver in his left hand. He looked us over with his baleful, pale eyes and said, 'Get dressed, Miss Spethmann. You too, Doctor. You are under arrest.'

The door to my cell opened and Lychev stepped inside. He sat on the little wooden chair that was, apart from the cot in which I slept and the table at which I read, my only furniture.

'Do you know on what day my birthday falls?' he said.

When I realised I had not misheard him, I said, 'I really don't care about your birthday, Lychev. I want to see my daughter. I want to talk to her now.'

'I was born on the 1st of March, 1881,' he continued, 'on the very day Tsar Alexander II was being driven along the Catherine Canal Embankment to take afternoon coffee with his sister.'

Of course I knew the whole tragic story – which Russian doesn't? – but he went on anyway, eager to make his point, though this was as yet unclear to me.

'The tsar was approaching the Theatre Bridge when the terrorist Rysakov threw his bomb into the imperial carriage. By the mercy of God, the tsar was unhurt, and Rysakov was caught before he could flee. The day should have ended well but the tsar, acting on impulses of kindliness and concern, stepped out of the carriage to offer what help he could to the injured. It was then the terrorist Hryniewicki, the Pole, threw the second bomb. It landed at the tsar's feet and ripped off his legs.'

Lychev paused reverentially. 'My mother was in labour when she heard the explosions,' he continued. 'The disturbance brought on my birth. As the tsar was dying I came into the world.'

'A remarkable coincidence,' I said.

'It was no coincidence,' Lychev said.

For the first time I found myself confident in relation to the detective; his narcissistic delusion reduced him very much in my eyes. I looked on him as I might one who had revealed himself to be Alexander the Great or Ivan the Terrible. It crossed my mind to offer him psychotherapeutic treatment.

Instead, I asked simply, 'What do you want from Catherine and me?'

'I have established that the man calling himself Yastrebov was part of a terrorist cell planning to carry out a spectacular outrage in the near future.'

'What manner of outrage?'

'They intend to assassinate the tsar.'

He allowed the portent of this to lie between us for a moment before continuing, 'You do not seem very concerned, Spethmann.'

'There are always plots,' I said.

'This time the threat is very specific. We have credible intelligence.'

'What intelligence?'

'If I were to reveal the details I would be compromising my sources.'

'Even if this is all true, none of it has anything to do with me or my daughter,' I persisted. 'I had never seen Yastrebov before you brought your hideous jar to my office.'

'Ah, but Catherine recognised him,' he said. 'You saw it too.'

I would have given anything to have been able to contradict him but I could not.

'Obviously she knew him by a different name – probably his real name,' he went on.

'How can you possibly know that?'

'Because Catherine was Yastrebov's lover,' he said. 'I assume you knew Catherine had a lover?'

I knew nothing of the sort but did not want to reveal ignorance of my daughter's life; nor did I want to claim knowledge of something which could be turned against Catherine all too easily.

Lychev went on, 'I need to know what Catherine knows about Yastrebov – his real name, who his friends were, when he arrived in the city, how they met, what he told her.'

'What has Catherine said?' I asked.

'Catherine is being very foolish,' Lychev said wearily. 'She will not co-operate. Every time I try to speak to her civilly she flies into a rage and condemns me as an oppressor. She condemns the government and the landowners. She called the royal family parasites to my face. Did you know your daughter harboured such hatred in her soul?'

'You are being ridiculous,' I said.

'She has betrayed you, Spethmann – your own daughter.'

'In what way has Catherine betrayed me?' I said, laughing in his face.

'On arriving in the city, Yastrebov was at first unable, or perhaps unwilling, to make contact with his fellow terrorists, for reasons I do not yet understand. What I do know is that he had run out of money and had nowhere to stay. Catherine supplied the solution – your office. Your daughter and Yastrebov would wait until you had finished for the day before entering your office and using it.'

'Using it?'

'The first thing Yastrebov used your office for was as a place to hide. The second thing was to make love to Catherine.'

I did my best to keep my expression impassive.

He went on, 'My job is to track down Yastrebov's cell before they proceed with their plan.'

He rose from the little wooden chair. He called to the jailer. As the keys clanged in the lock, he said, 'Your daughter has information I need, Spethmann, and you will stay here, both of you, until she gives it to me.'

He stepped out to the corridor. The door closed behind him and the key turned in the lock. Even then I could hardly believe this was all happening. I lived in a city built on a marsh stiffened with the bones of a hundred thousand serfs who died of starvation, disease and cruelty in its construction. In every part of the empire we lived with the Cossack, the spy and the secret policeman for our neighbours. We passed prisons and fortresses every day. From the window in my study at home I could devise the slums where the poor drudged with their bodies. Catherine liked to provoke me by saying that Russia was a despotism and everyone knew it, though we could pretend not to – a choice open to people like me everywhere, but only for as long as we are personally untouched by the consequences of tyranny.

Ten

T he old jailer was a kindly man. The bread he brought
was fresh, and sometimes still warm, and the butter
sweet. On the third night of my detention he brought a little
chess set. The chessmen were a present from his grandson,
he told me proudly. Naively carved and unweighted, they
were a treasure to him as my Jaques pieces were to me. He
was a cheerful and terrible player. It was everything forward.
Even when down to a couple of pawns against my rook and
bishop, he pushed up the board. 'Onwards!' he would
proclaim, 'advance!' He suffered his defeats with good
humour and declared himself unsurprised by my wins. 'Your
people,' he said matter-of-factly, 'make the best players.
Look at Lasker – World Champion, and Steinitz before
him. Rozental, Tarrasch, Gunsberg, Bernstein and Nimzowitsch – more than half of those who will be playing in the
great tournament are Jews.'

Then he said, following a mental progression of his own
contrivance, 'Almost every single prisoner down here is a Jew.
A few of them are educated but they're not like his honour.
Ruffians, most of them, and filthy. When you ask them why
they murder good Christians, they just laugh. Well, they
won't be laughing when the hangman puts the noose around
their necks.'

I was chewing my bread one night, listening to the prison-
ers call out to each other in Yiddish from their high, barred

windows, and I began to smell – really smell – the sweet challahs and bagels my father used to bake when I was a child. I smelled them as if my father was in the cell with me kneading the dough and setting out the bracelets on the greased tray. *Your people.* Such vivid sensations. When asked, I always said my father was from Riga, which was true in the sense that he lived there before coming to St Petersburg, and that he was German, which was true in that his parents were Germans originally from Kalisz. But he had actually been born in Dvinsk, in Vitebsk, where I still had uncles, aunts and many cousins. He did not move to Riga until he was thirteen. Thirty years later, by which time he was a master baker and had a new young wife, he came to St Petersburg and set up shop in the Vyborg quarter, making coarse rye breads for the working people there. By dint of hard work he prospered, borrowed money, and before long was supplying fashionable establishments like the Donon and the Restaurant de Paris. We moved to an apartment on the Petersburg side, then to a spacious house on Furshtatskaya Street, in which I continued to live after my parents died. The flour became finer as our addresses grew more respectable; eggs were added, the bread became lighter. Father dressed more carefully and modified his speech so successfully he sounded indistinguishable from the city's Russian natives. If my mother let slip a word of Yiddish in front of me she met with a sharp rebuke. We never had challah or bagels in the house on Furshtatskaya Street.

I expected Lychev's return at any hour. But Lychev did not come. Time is a fickle ally. He does not belong exclusively to the psychoanalyst. The policeman used him too. And so the days and nights passed.

But the time will always come when delay serves no further useful purpose and the question must be put. During the sixth night of my detention the cell door opened. Lychev stepped inside and leaned against the wall.

'I had no idea you had such illustrious patients,' he said. 'Anna Ziatdinov, daughter of Peter Zinnurov no less –'

'You have been going through my files – you have no right!' I protested angrily.

'Are you really saying, Spethmann, that when the security of the state is threatened, when the life of the tsar himself is in jeopardy, you would put private files relating to madmen beyond the reach of those sworn to preserve the civilisation in which, I feel it only fair to remind you, you also live and from which you benefit?'

'You put your argument in such ridiculous high terms I cannot possibly answer.'

'Who is Grischuk?'

'I repeat: that you have read these files is shocking and contemptible.'

'It is clearly a pseudonym. A politician, obviously.'

'I refuse to answer,' I said, though I wondered whether Lychev had already identified Grischuk as Gregory Petrov. Petrov was well known to the police.

'A man of dangerous political sympathies to judge from your notes,' Lychev went on. 'Why do you treat such a man?'

'Because I am a doctor,' I said, 'and he is my patient.'

'What is the nature of Grischuk's illness?'

'I am not prepared to discuss it.'

'All I can see from his file is that he drinks too much, eats too much and attempts to fornicate with every woman who crosses his path – often with success,' Lychev said. 'Tell me, please, enlighten me: how can his greed and carnality possibly be termed an illness?'

'I will not speak about an individual patient, but' – I was allowing myself to be drawn but it was impossible to remain silent in the face of Lychev's goading – 'in general terms, such behaviour may be considered a manifestation of psychological illness, in the same way that people scream when they are in physical pain.'

'So Grischuk's drinking, his gluttony and womanising – it is all because he is in pain? Have you discovered the source of his pain?'

'I am not prepared to discuss individual patients.'

'Reuven Kopelzon,' Lychev said, changing direction abruptly.

'I do not treat Kopelzon.'

'Then you will not feel constrained to discuss him.'

'I will not discuss anyone with you, Lychev.'

'Your friend consorts with men who make no secret of their desire to see Russia expelled from her rightfully held Polish territories. How can any loyal subject maintain friendly relations with such a man?'

'I know Kopelzon for his music, not his political views.'

'Are both things not part of the whole man?'

He waited for an answer but I gave him none.

'Avrom Rozental,' he said.

'Rozental is a chess player, as you know.'

'And a friend of Kopelzon's. Why?'

'I have no idea,' I said.

'There are things I do not know either. Though apparently, unlike you, I would prefer to have answers. I still do not know, for example, who murdered Yastrebov or why. Above all, I do not know the identities of the other members of Yastrebov's cell or where they are hiding. These are the things I must find out because the cell will reorganise and press on with its plans. I have to stop the terrorists before they kill the tsar and you are going to help me.'

'Help you?' I laughed. 'After all you have done to us, why would I help you?'

'I hope it would be because you are not one of these Jews

who pretends to be a loyal subject but in his heart despises everything about our Russian civilisation.'

I said nothing to this.

'Catherine still refuses to reveal Yastrebov's identity,' he went on. 'If you can get her to tell me, I will have you both released.'

I searched his features but it was impossible to say if he was sincere. 'How can I persuade her if I'm not allowed to see her?' I said, playing for the time I needed to think his offer through.

'I will arrange for you to see her, if you promise you will try to persuade her.' When I did not reply, he said, 'It's only a name, Spethmann. The name of a man who is already dead.'

'When can I see her?'

'This instant,' Lychev replied at once.

A chance to see and speak to Catherine. I nodded my head and Lychev called the jailer.

Catherine's cell was identical to mine. She was sitting on a little wooden chair, her back perfectly straight, a book in her lap. She looked up as the door opened and, when she saw me, leaped to her feet.

'Are you all right?' I asked, kissing her over and over.

'Yes, yes,' she said. 'I'm fine, I'm completely fine. Don't worry about me.'

Looking past me, she saw Lychev. 'What does he want?' she said, her look implacable and fierce.

'I'll leave you to it, Spethmann. You have ten minutes,' the detective said as he stepped outside to the corridor. The door was pushed to.

Catherine looked at me with suspicion. 'Leave you to what?'

I took a deep breath. 'He says he will release us if you tell him Yastrebov's real name.'

'No,' she said at once.

'Does that mean you admit to knowing Yastrebov?' I said.

A look of annoyance came into her eyes; she was furious with herself for having let her guard down. 'No,' she said. 'It means I won't tell Lychev anything. I wouldn't tell him my own name or yours or even his own if my life depended on it.'

'Catherine, think about this. We are utterly in his power –'

'I have said I will tell him nothing and when I say I'm going to do something that's exactly what I do.'

This I already knew, only too well. Nevertheless, I had to try.

'Why not?' I said, repeating Lychev's own logic. 'Yastrebov is dead. You're not harming him in any way. The only people suffering because of his name are you and me.'

'And who will suffer if I give the name – even if I knew it, which I don't? Who will Lychev arrest then? Who will he throw in prison? Tell Lychev I am content to stay where I am for as long as he wants to keep me here.'

'I am here too,' I reminded her.

Her features softened. I think she may even have been on the point of saying sorry. But then her defiance reasserted itself. She had said no. She would be true to her word. We passed the remaining few minutes reassuring each other as to our health and spirits. I told her I loved her. When our ten minutes were up and the door was once more barred and locked, I stood with Lychev in the corridor.

'She may be content to stay where she is, Spethmann,' the detective said. 'However, she doesn't seem to care that by her stubbornness you also have to stay. How do you feel about that?'

In weighing her alternatives, Catherine had not taken me into account, even for an instant. Though I did not admit it, I felt hurt and angry. Lychev seemed rather impressed.

'Has Catherine had many lovers?' he said. I was completely taken aback. Before I could say anything, he went on, 'There's a fashion among young people of the *demi-monde* to seek refuge from what they consider the depressing reality of Russia by drinking themselves to oblivion and sleeping with whoever will sleep with them. They see it as a form of rebellion, apparently. I just wondered if Catherine was one of these.'

'She certainly is not,' I answered, only just preventing myself from shouting at him.

'She and Yastrebov were practically strangers when they first made love.'

'She denies knowing anything about Yastrebov.'

'We both know she's lying,' he said. 'I was just wondering how promiscuous she is.'

'I do not think that any of your business,' I said sharply.

He looked carefully at me. 'Your daughter is a highly intelligent and very attractive young woman,' he said. 'It would be a shame to see her spend the best years of her life in prison.'

It may be that there is a heaven but even if there is, there is only one life lived on this earth. To have it withheld, to have it stunted, warped and foreshortened by jailers and policemen is a terrible thing. But is it less terrible than a life left unlived through one's own fearfulness? That night when I lay down, I lay down beside Anna. She was in the bed, naked, unashamed and with a gleam in her eye.

Three more days passed. They were not entirely wasted. Using the old jailer's chess set, I analysed the position I had reached against Kopelzon. Kavi had known what he was doing when he retreated the rook. There was no other way to play for the win. I asked for permission to send a postcard to Kopelzon, which Lychev granted on condition that it contained no more than the move – 35 Rg2.

Lychev also allowed me to receive books from Minna. Among these was the Babylonian Talmud, sent at my request.

It amused me that when we played chess the old jailer would eye the sacred text suspiciously, uncertain whether it was safe to be in the same room as so potent a token of alien magic.

I searched the texts from top to bottom, occasionally mumbling to myself as I read, which the jailer, looking in at the observation slit, took as prayer. My father would have been horrified at the sight, even had I been able to reassure him my reading had nothing to do with veneration for the God he had rejected but with concern for the patient I was determined to save.

My father would have been embarrassed to have met Rozental. Rozental was too much like the man from Dvinsk my father wanted to forget he had ever been. Kopelzon wept rivers of sentimental tears when he talked of the poverty of the towns of the Pale. But my father's heart was not moved by the destitution of his people. He was shamed by it, as a son would be shamed by his father falling over drunk in the street. The sight of the *shnorrer* humiliated him; the soup kitchen he felt a personal disgrace. He asked himself a simple question: why were his people so miserably poor and ignorant? Why was there so much vice, prostitution and robbery? Why, among his people, were there so many terrorists and revolutionaries? Kopelzon would have answered him plainly with the words pogrom, Cossack, Pale and the Black Hundreds. But all my father saw was ignorance and backwardness.

My father would never have engaged in debate, with Kopelzon or anyone else. He fell silent when faced with the strong and contrary opinion of others, not so much because his lack of education left him ill-equipped to defend his point of view, but because he took his own beliefs as self-evidently true and therefore in no need of public airing. The answer he had discovered resided in his own people, in their very being. As long as his people were themselves, it could not be otherwise. His success in the world only reinforced his belief. He had the answer, and the answer was to stop being Jewish.

'What is on your head?' I had asked Rozental during a session early in our analysis. He had been scratching his scalp, clawing at it with the nails of both hands.

He uttered a groan. 'It never leaves me alone.'

His hair was very short, practically shorn. I examined it carefully. There was nothing, not even nits.

'It's a fly,' he said desperately. 'Can you not see it? It follows me everywhere. It torments me day and night.'

'There's nothing here.'

'I can feel it crawling over my scalp.'

'Would you like a mirror so you can see for yourself?'

With some difficulty I induced him to stand before the mirror over the fireplace while I held a hand mirror (borrowed from Minna) behind him, as a barber does. Eventually I settled him sufficiently to be able to continue the session.

My approach with my patients was generally the same: I began by asking for as full an account as possible of their life story. Rozental described his early years in Choroszcz, the destitute settlement in which he had lived until he went to yeshiva in Lodz. He was the youngest of twelve children and his father had died before he was born. I asked how his mother had managed.

'My brothers and sisters and I were parcelled out to relatives. I was sent to live with my grandparents.'

'Tell me about your grandparents.'

He hesitated, then said, 'They were good, kind people.'

'Were they religious?'

'Yes, of course.'

'Were you happy in their house?'

'They loved me very much.'

Besides the obvious incompleteness of the answer, I thought I detected a trace of guilt. Here, plainly, was an avenue to explore. 'Are your grandparents still alive?'

'They are both dead.'

'Were they still alive when you became famous as a chess player?'

His reluctance to answer confirmed to me my suspicion that there was something of significance in his relationship with his grandparents.

'Avrom,' I prodded my taciturn patient, 'did they live long enough to hear of your successes?'

'Yes,' he whispered, almost inaudibly.

'How did they react?' He began again to scratch his scalp. 'Were they pleased?'

'Yes . . .' he said vaguely before immediately contradicting himself: 'No – I don't know.'

'Did they approve of your choice of career?'

'How could they?' he retorted, this time forcibly and without vacillation. 'When they sent me to the *heder* they said, "Learn, Avrom, learn! Purses of silver will fall to you from heaven." But instead of learning, what did I do? I played chess. Haran, Padan, Hebron where Abraham buried Sarah? None of this mattered – I was consumed by chess. When the boys were imagining themselves following Moses out of Egypt or fighting with Joshua at Jericho, I had visions of myself a pawn up against Lasker in a rook endgame. How could my grandparents have approved?'

Rozental had not spoken as many words in an entire hour as had just passed between us. I pressed on, 'Were there arguments?'

He did not answer, though I put the question three times.

'Do you feel you disappointed them?' I ventured.

'I just want to play chess!' he burst out. 'I ask nothing of anyone – nothing! I do not interfere with anyone, I do not

90

criticise, I do not condemn. Why can't I be left alone to play chess? Why?'

'Who is not leaving you alone?'

'Everyone.'

'Your grandparents?'

'Everyone wants me to be this, to be that. To do this, to do that.'

'What did your grandparents want you to be?'

'It's not my grandparents, it's not them!' he insisted.

'Who has these expectations you find so onerous?'

No matter how hard I probed, he would not be specific. It was *everyone*.

'They want me to be two things,' he sobbed, 'but I can't be. I just want to play chess. I want to play in the tournament. I want to play Lasker and beat him. But they won't let me!'

' "They" are your grandparents, Avrom, are they not?'

Rozental answered by violently swatting the air around his head. The invisible fly had returned.

The fly was obviously the key to understanding Rozental's illness. But it was not until I was in my cell that I discovered its true symbolic meaning. Between Lychev's interrogations, my reading of the ancient texts led me to this: Beelzebub, the devil, got his name from *ba'al-zevuv* – meaning 'master of the fly'. Searching further, I came upon a Midrash which runs: 'The evil inclination is similar to a fly and sits at the two openings of the heart.'

For someone as thoroughly steeped in Jewish learning and tradition as Rozental, the fly was clearly a manifestation of *yetzer hara* – evil inclination, the impulse to follow selfish desire. It was not difficult to work out the nature of this particular evil inclination. Rozental had told me that, like Benjamin, the beloved youngest son of Jacob, he had been his grandparents' favourite. When I pressed him on his feelings for his father's parents, however, his replies were highly suggestive, for while he never criticised them, never once did he make a positive declaration in their favour. He would repeat, almost formulaically, that they were 'good people', 'kind people', 'simple people'. But they had also been exacting of the promising young student and had entertained ambitions of him both as the economic saviour of the distressed family and as a future religious leader of their community. It was clear that he found these expectations oppressive. 'Everyone wants me to be this, to be that. To do this, to do that', 'They want me to be two things'.

Instead of fulfilling his grandparents' dreams, Rozental became obsessed with chess and quickly aspired to become not a great religious teacher but a great professional chess player – the next World Champion. Whenever I asked him about his grandparents' reaction, Rozental's narrative faltered. Since professional chess would have taken him from their world and their religion, I decided the grandparents were unlikely to have approved, and that Rozental's reluctance to acknowledge this was because of residual feelings of loyalty. In spite of coming up against very strong emotional pressure, Rozental had found the courage to pursue his dream.

But in every corner demons lie in wait for the Jewish soul. Guilt had caught up with Rozental, precipitating his terrible mental crisis. I determined that on my release – assuming that I would, sooner or later, be set at liberty – I would have to bring my patient to confront his true feelings for his grandparents. This was the analysis at which I arrived during my imprisonment. I was both proud and certain of my deductions. At some future time I would write a paper for presentation to Bekhterev and my colleagues at the St Petersburg Psychoneurologic Institute.

*   *   *

More time. And then, at last, Lychev returned. In the pre-dawn light filtering through the high window, Lychev's appearance was cyanotic. It was not the first time I had wondered about the state of his health: a bad heart, I concluded, and time was to tell that in this at least I was not mistaken.

'Catherine still refuses to give me Yastrebov's name,' he said wearily.

'I demand to know what charge you have against us,' I said, rousing myself from the cot. 'I demand to speak to a judge or a lawyer.'

Lychev held up a photograph. 'Do you know this man?'

I was looking at a lean, darkly handsome man of about thirty, heavily moustached with unshaven cheeks and a great tangle of curly hair. Though the chains on his hands were not visible, he was, from the unnatural line of his shoulders, clearly under restraint. His large black eyes stared defiantly back at his captors.

'Of course,' I replied. 'It's Berek Medem.'

Everyone in Russia knew the prison photograph of the Polish terrorist Berek Medem, murderer of innumerable Okhrana agents, policemen, tax collectors, collaborators and spies. Not a week passed without the newspapers reproducing it as they chronicled his exploits with all the ghoulish fascination and horror they typically devote to the activities of such baroque desperadoes. They reported with particular relish his escape from Pawiak prison in Warsaw, after which he went to the house of the woman who had betrayed him. He did not kill her but instead threw acid into her face, and in doing so inspired imitators all over the empire, from Finland to Kamchatka. Many of his sort – the organisers and inciters of terrorism – went to pieces on arrest and revealed themselves as cowards. But one had only to glance at the photograph to see that Berek Medem was possessed of a Robespierrist dedication to his cause. Here was someone who took life and when the time came he would give life. The career of the revolutionary was short, those fierce dark eyes said, and he accepted this without complaint.

'When did you last communicate with Berek Medem?' Lychev said.

It took me a moment to realise he was serious. I laughed. 'Have you taken leave of your senses, Lychev?'

'Answer my question.'

'The answer is I have never communicated with Berek Medem.'

'Why then has Berek Medem been seen in your office building?'

I laughed again in derision of him. Every day there were dozens of supposed sightings. He was seen on a railway platform in Port Arthur. An hour later he was on a boat on the lagoons of Odessa while simultaneously robbing a bank in Kiev.

'Has your friend Kopelzon ever talked about King to you?'

'Your conspiracy grows ever bigger and more fantastical, Lychev,' I said. 'First Berek Medem, now King.'

'Answer the question.'

'No. Kopelzon has never mentioned King.'

'Has Rozental mentioned him?'

'Rozental?' I said, amazed. 'Rozental is probably the only person in Russia who hasn't heard of King.'

'Answer the question.'

'I already have.'

'Are you really so indifferent to the security of the state, Spethmann? You profess loyalty yet you hold the work of the police in contempt. How do you reconcile these contradictions?'

'Your games bore me, Lychev. I will answer no more questions.'

94

'Of course you are above it all – you are the man who has no time for political affairs.'

I froze. I felt sure Lychev would see my heart pounding under my shirt. He seemed to be studying my expression carefully. Was he aware of what he had just said? *The man who has no time for political affairs.* The only occasion on which I had made any such claim was when Tolya was ransacking my files and Kavi was holding his knife up in front of my face.

I was gripped by a sudden fear for Catherine.

'I want to see my daughter,' I said. 'I want to see her now.'

'Your daughter was released last night,' he said. 'Gather your things.'

I was confounded. I wanted to believe him and at the same time I was afraid to. Was it a trick to lower my guard?

The old jailer appeared at the door. 'If his honour would follow me,' he said.

'What is going on?' I demanded. 'Did Catherine give you a name?'

Lychev's look told me the answer was no.

Still scarcely believing this sudden turn of events, I collected my books and few belongings and followed Lychev and the jailer down the dimly lit corridor. We passed through a barred gate into a large room with a low concave ceiling and pillars and arches of brick. From here, I was escorted up a flight of stone steps into a courtyard. The air was frigid, but it was the cold of early spring, not winter, and heartening for that. It stung my nostrils.

We came to a broad, squat gatehouse.

As the bolts were pulled back, Lychev said, 'I need Yas-trebov's real name and I'm going to get it – one way or another.'

He seemed slighter, more insubstantial than ever. I ignored him as one ignores a bore at a party, and stepped outside. The instant the gate closed behind me I had the sensation it had all been a dream.

Ahead was a short bridge. I walked its length, passing a dozen armed guards who regarded me indifferently. Catherine emerged from the back of a waiting taxi and ran towards me.

'You're safe,' she cried, throwing her arms about my neck.

I looked at her in amazement. That fierce will. That it should defeat a doting father is hardly a surprise; that it should have exhausted a Russian policeman was nothing short of astonishing.

'Let's go home,' I said, getting into the taxi.

The driver turned around and said, 'First there is someone who wants to talk to you.'

I turned to Catherine: what was going on?

'Gregory Petrov wants to see you,' Catherine said.

'I don't want to see Petrov. I want to go home.'

'He has something to tell you,' Catherine said, 'something important.'

Eleven

After a complicated and roundabout journey lasting almost an hour, the taxi arrived at the Hay Market. Gregory Petrov was waiting impatiently outside the Church of the Dormition dressed in a heavy overcoat, scarf and hat.

'We weren't followed, Comrade,' the driver said as Petrov opened the door for me.

'I know you want to go home, Spethmann,' Petrov said brusquely, 'but we need to talk.' To the driver, he said, 'Take Miss Spethmann to Furshtatskaya Street.'

I was exhausted but also intrigued. What did Petrov want? I kissed Catherine and promised I would be home soon. The taxi moved off.

We crossed the road to the meat market. It was not yet six o'clock and the butchers were still setting up for the day. White-aproned porters hefting carcasses of cattle, lamb and pig paid us no mind as we made our way along the aisles of the covered market. Every now and then Petrov glanced to the side, or backwards, to check if anyone was taking an unusual interest in us.

'You seem well enough. You weren't tortured?'

'No,' I said.

'You had a gentle introduction to the experience of prison. Next time, it will not be so pleasant.'

I paid little heed to this, thinking Petrov boastful and patronising, the revolutionary showing the intellectual that

97

he takes in his stride the repeating reality of prison; and I remember quite clearly thinking: *For you, perhaps, there will be a next time, but not for me. I am not a man who goes to prison.*

'I was sixteen when I was first arrested,' Petrov said, stopping to inspect some lamb cutlets. He bought six and made a present of them to me. 'My brother, who was a year younger, was also arrested. We were both members of a Party cell among the metal workers at the Stieglitz plant. One of our comrades had been arrested and had betrayed the names of the entire cell. I denied everything, as we had been instructed to do. The police were not gentle. They beat me ferociously during the first three days. They beat us all. The strange thing was that I never felt I was going to break. The more they beat me, the stronger I felt. I thought to myself, if they want to break me they're going to have to do a lot more than this. They kept us isolated from each other so I had no idea how my comrades were doing but I assumed they were handling the ordeal as I was. After a week or so the police came and said the cell's leader had broken and written a confession. I didn't believe them but they showed me the confession and I recognised the signature. They said, "You're the only one who hasn't confessed. You're only making it worse for yourself. Come on, sign this." I didn't care what the others had signed. I wasn't going to do it. Call it stubbornness, call it pride, I simply wasn't going to let them win.'

We had completed a circuit of the meat market and embarked on a second. There were more customers now, mostly servants come to buy their masters' meat.

'In the end, the police came up with a plan. No more beating – they'd tried that and it hadn't worked. No, they came up with something psychological.'

He gave me a sideways glance.

'Most policemen are stupid,' he continued, 'even the detectives. But occasionally you get one who can think for himself. The officer in charge of my case came to me in the middle of the night, at about two or three in the morning, and said, "Your brother is very young. He only joined the cell to please you. We will release him now, this very minute, if you confess and sign." It was a clever stratagem on their part, no?'

I realised Lychev had tried the same thing with me and Catherine: an old interrogators' trick, obviously.

'Anyway,' Petrov continued, 'the officer said, "Your brother has lost his mind. If he goes to prison, he will kill himself. If you want your brother to live, you must confess." I didn't believe them. I thought they were trying to scare me into signing. The officer said, "Come with me." He took me out of my cell and down a corridor to another cell. The jailer opened up and I remember it was almost pitch black. I couldn't see a thing. They fetched a lamp and in the corner I saw my brother Ivan, naked, cowering like a whipped dog. His hair was matted and all over the place, his eyes were big and staring. He was filthy. The cell smelt of shit. The officer turned to me and said, "Now do you believe me?" What could I say? It was true – my brother had lost his mind. The officer said, "If you confess I will release him. Your father is waiting outside. He can take your brother home. If you don't confess, I will charge him with membership of a subversive organisation and he will die in prison."'

'What did you do?'

'I turned to the officer and said, "Charge him."'

Petrov looked at me to check my reaction.

'You think me ruthless and uncaring, don't you, Spethmann?'

'I don't think you are as ruthless or uncaring as you pretend.'

'Then you don't know me.'

We were nearing the end of our second circuit. The market had filled up so that we had to weave in and out of the crowds as we walked.

'Did Lychev ask about me?' Petrov asked.

'No, although he worked out that Grischuk was a pseudonym.'

'Do you think he guessed it was me?'

'It's hard to say with Lychev what he knows and what he pretends not to know.'

Petrov stopped by a stall where pig carcasses had been piled up. He and the butcher exchanged a look. It was almost entirely expressionless and yet had something knowing about it.

'Catherine said you had something you wanted to tell me.'

'I've picked up some rumours about Lychev's investigation,' he said. 'He's an experienced detective with a reputation for thoroughness and success, but he is no nearer catching Yastrebov's confederates now than he was a month ago. The Okhrana have decided to take over the case. Lychev will be allowed to continue his investigation but under the informal supervision of the secret police, who will have their own agents carrying out their own investigations.'

He let this information sink in before continuing, 'The Okhrana will be watching you. They will have your house and your office under surveillance. They will monitor your telephone and read your mail. Be very careful what you say and write.'

'I have no secrets,' I said. 'I have nothing to hide.'

'Everyone has something to hide,' he said, putting out his hand.

I shook it. He said, 'Go home now. Be with your daughter. Eat, drink and rest.'

I was still holding his hand. I said, 'I wish you had told me the story about your brother earlier.'

'I have a million such stories,' he said with a self-mocking laugh. 'Some of them are even true.'

'Is this one true?'

'Possibly.'

With that, Petrov stepped past the low wall of pig flesh, past the butcher and through the stall, and disappeared from sight.

Twelve

The rest of the day was spent receiving visitors and telephone calls from friends and well-wishers. Bekhterev himself called to say he had personally written to Maklakov and Stcheglovitov, the minister for justice, to protest at the arrest of such an eminent member of the Psychoneurologic Institute. There were telegrams and letters from colleagues in London, New York and Vienna. I was desperate to talk properly to Catherine but there was no opportunity. I did, however, find time to telephone Minna, asking that she contact my patients to let them know I would see them again tomorrow.

'Please make sure to contact Rozental,' I said. 'I am very concerned about him. He's staying at the Astoria.'

Minna in turn passed on a number of messages, among which was one from Anna asking me to telephone her. The last of our guests did not depart until well after midnight, and then only at Lidiya's insistence.

The next morning I woke early. I was in my own bed. Everything that had happened since Lychev first came to my office already seemed abstractedly contradictory: definite and imaginary, authentic and unreal – a violent and inexplicable irruption in an otherwise orderly existence.

I washed and shaved and went to my study. Before I picked up the telephone I thought about Petrov's warning. If he was right, someone would be listening. I ran through in my mind what I was going to say, and when I was satisfied that I would be committing no indiscretion, I picked it up.

My first call was to Kopelzon. He had returned the day before from Paris and Warsaw, where he had given recitals, and was full of anger and indignation on my behalf. How was I? How was Catherine? What an outrage!

'Reuven,' I said, interrupting his impassioned flow, 'Lychev asked me about you.'

'What did you tell him?' he said, outrage turning to wariness.

'He wanted to know why you were friends with Rozental.' The silence at the other end lasted so long that I had to say, 'Reuven, are you still there?'

'Why should he be interested in Rozental?' His voice was uncharacteristically reticent.

'I think for no other reason than that you and he are Poles, and in the eyes of the police all Poles are potential terrorists. He even talked about Berek Medem.'

Again there was a long, shocked silence. I understood his anxiety: to be mentioned in the same breath as Berek Medem was not something anyone wished for.

'It was a general question,' I added quickly in an effort to reassure him. 'It felt as though Lychev was throwing out names because he had nothing else.'

My reasoning seemed to ease him. I asked after Rozental.

'I'm seeing him later this morning,' he said. 'If I'd known what was going to happen to you, I would never have left him alone in the city. The tournament is only a few days away. The last thing Avrom needs is to think the police are after him. He is paranoid enough as it is.'

'How could you possibly know?' I said. 'Minna is arranging an appointment.'

'Listen,' he said, recovering himself, 'let's have dinner to celebrate your release – and of course my triumph in Paris. I'll make a reservation at A l'Ours for tonight. Ten o'clock.'

I tried to decline, pleading the need to catch up on my affairs.

'It's important, Otto,' Kopelzon insisted, his tone changing from cheery back to serious all at once. 'We have to talk about Rozental.'

With some reluctance, I agreed.

'Excellent!' he said. 'By the way, I received your postcard with your move. 35 Rg2. Unusual. My reply is 35 . . . Rxg2, if you're still interested in continuing the game.'

Whenever I thought of our game it brought back unpleasant memories of Kavi – not that this had prevented me from analysing the position while in my cell, such is the particular tyranny of the chess player's obsession, even one whose game has been tainted by the unsolicited help of a knife-wielding murderer.

'What makes you think I'm not interested?' I asked.

'It's a draw. Why drag it out? Why don't we just start a new game?'

'I think I can win,' I said.

'Do you now?' Kopelzon said, sounding amused and competitive.

The only reply was 36 Kxg2, which is the move I then made.

Kopelzon said, 'I play 36 . . . Qc7.'

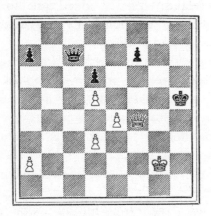

Spethmann–Kopelzon

After 36 . . . Qc7. The rooks are off and
Spethmann has an extra pawn. But now what?

104

I examined the position on the travelling set I kept in my study. I had never been in such a good position against Kopelzon. The clump of central pawns were White's main advantage, while Black's position was cut in two. I had a simple plan: keep him tied down to the defence of his weak pawns, look for a possible breakthrough with e5, and advance the king up the board. If I kept my nerve surely I would win.

'37 Qf5 check,' I said.

'You don't think I'm going to fall for a grubby little trick like that, do you, Otto?' Kopelzon laughed.

It was an obvious trap – if 37 . . . Kh4 Black would be mated after 38 Kf3 and 39 Qg4 – but sometimes such things are overlooked, even by players of Kopelzon's ability.

'37 . . . Kh6,' he said.

Although I had analysed this line in my cell, I did not trust myself to continue without further thought.

'I will let you have my reply at dinner,' I said.

He said he looked forward to seeing me.

Anna, like Kopelzon, was full of concern about what had happened. Once I assured her I was well, I asked how she had been.

'The nightmares have been much worse since you were arrested,' she said. 'I cannot sleep. I feel sick with tiredness.'

'I would like to see you,' I said.

'I want to see you too.'

'Unfortunately, I have a lot of catching up to do with my patients today and tonight I have to see Kopelzon for dinner.'

'I see,' she said, sounding disappointed.

'I could meet you at Filippov's at nine o'clock?' I suggested.

She said she would see me there. When I put the telephone down I reviewed the conversation, trying to imagine what it had sounded like to the secret policemen who, if Petrov was right, were listening. A psychoanalyst arranging an interview with his patient? I told myself I had nothing to hide, but I didn't believe it myself.

At breakfast Lidiya was cheeriness itself. We chatted about ordinary matters: things that needed doing around the house, provisions we required, bills to be paid; it was a strained reaching for normality. The gendarmes' raid was past. I was willing to collude with Lidiya in this illusion but not with Catherine. When Catherine came to the table – refusing all food, of course, accepting only tea – I asked Lidiya to excuse us.

When we were alone I said, 'You lied to me.'

'Yes,' she admitted, to my surprise. 'I'm sorry.'

'Is what Lychev says true? Were you' – here I stumbled – 'were you Yastrebov's lover?'

She wavered only a moment. 'Yes.'

A great wave of sadness broke over me. 'You know that Yastrebov was part of a terrorist cell,' I said, 'that he came to the city to assassinate the tsar?'

'So Lychev says,' she answered.

The features of her little oval face took on a familiar uncompromising cast. I could have thrown so much at her, not least the days and nights I had spent in detention. That I kept my temper had nothing to do with wisdom or patience on my part. In a contest of wills, Catherine would always emerge triumphant. If I were to get from her what I wanted, I would have to come to this interview as I would a session of analysis, teasing the information I sought with neutral questions. I had also to remember that Catherine had suffered a bereavement, that her first lover had been murdered. I had to proceed with sensitivity.

'What did Yastrebov tell you he was doing in St Petersburg?' I said, keeping my voice calm and reasonable.

'He said he was a poet.'

106

'A poet?'

'He wasn't a very good one,' she said with a small, judicious smile. 'He wanted to meet Blok and Akhmatova, to hear them read. He wanted to get to know editors who would publish his poems.'

'How long did you know him?'

'Two or three weeks.'

'Did he tell you much about himself?'

'We talked a lot,' she said, taking a delicate sip of tea.

'Do you know what his real name was?'

She bit her lip. 'What does it matter?' she said. 'He's dead now.'

'Is someone preventing you from speaking?'

'No.'

'Is it because you don't trust me? You know my sole concern is with your safety and happiness.'

She put her hand on top of mine and squeezed it. 'I understand that is your intention.'

'Tell me you are not mixed up in his plot,' I said.

'No,' she said. 'I'm not.'

'Do you swear to me?'

'I do.'

She got to her feet.

'Where are you going?' I asked.

'To the university,' she said blithely. 'I've missed enough classes already.'

Tact and neutrality had got me nowhere. She was more resistant than any of my patients.

I said, 'I would like you to see a colleague of mine, Sukovsky.'

'Why?' she asked, frowning.

'You've suffered a great trauma and I think it would help to talk to someone like Sukovsky.'

'I would hardly call it great,' she said. 'Vera Figner was in prison for twenty years – I was held for less than a month.'

'I wasn't referring to your detention. I meant your loss.'

Her frown deepened. 'My loss?'

'The man you loved was murdered. I think it important that you talk about this with someone who will be able to help you.'

'Are you referring to . . . Yastrebov?'

'Yes.'

'I didn't love Yastrebov.'

'You had physical relations with him,' I heard myself declare.

She looked at me as if I understood nothing. 'That was only sex,' she said as she left the room.

As I drove to my office the car in front of mine ran into a horse. Seconds before, I had been distracted by the sight of a pair of men walking together on the far side of the street. Kavi? Tolya? I was turning to get a better look when I heard the sudden, sharp screech of tyres. Swivelling to the front again, I saw I was almost on top of the other car. I braked quickly but could not avoid a collision. There was a loud bang; steam hissed from the radiator. The owner of the dead horse began cursing the other driver. A gendarme ran over and a small crowd of curious onlookers gathered, the leather soles of their boots crunching on the glass of the Renault's broken lamps. I looked around for Kavi – if indeed it had been the Cossack – but he was nowhere in sight. After half an hour I was allowed to proceed.

I was inspecting the damage to the car outside my building when Semevsky, the new porter, came up. 'Has his honour been hurt?' he asked, all lively solicitude.

'No, I'm fine, thank you,' I answered.

My tone was reserved and probably not very friendly. I had not forgotten my suspicions of the man I had first seen the day Lychev arrived to question me about Yastrebov's murder, and with Petrov's warning still ringing in my ears I was doubly suspicious.

He ran his eye over the smashed lamps. 'If his honour wishes,' he said, 'I will take his car to my uncle's garage. My uncle is a first-class engineer and mechanic. I assure his honour everything will be taken care of.'

Perhaps I had got him wrong. In any case, I could think of no good reason to refuse, unless cutting off one's nose to spite one's face counts as a good reason, and so thanked him.

I was about to step inside when he said, 'I hope his honour will not think me impertinent. I was here the night the police came. They demanded I open up his honour's office. I refused them, of course. They threatened to arrest me but I told them I had only started in my post and so did not know where the keys were kept.'

'You should have let them in,' I said. All at once his expression crumpled. 'Only so as to avoid bringing trouble on yourself,' I hastened to add. 'In future, please, for your own sake, do as the police order. It is the safest way.'

'Sometimes the safest way is not the right way,' Semevsky answered. I made my way to the elevator, berating myself for my earlier ungenerous assessment of the doorman.

Thirteen

There was no evidence of Lychev's raid. The furniture was back in place, the books were precisely arranged on the shelves. Even my Jaques chessmen were set out as I had left them. Minna and her sense of order. Minna was diligent, efficient and reliable. She was tall and pale and her eyes were grey-blue. She kept her hair pinned severely back, and her clothes seemed designed more for the purposes of sexual invisibility than advertisement; she had nothing of Catherine's carnal frankness. Once, shortly after she had started to work for me, she came into the office and took off a light raincoat. As she put her arms behind her to tug at the sleeves, I happened to glance up from some papers and saw her bust strain against the fabric of her blouse. I registered – not quite matter-of-factly but certainly not lasciviously – the simple fact of her breasts. Our eyes met. I thought very little of it but for the rest of the day Minna was unable to look me in the eye. Over the years I had asked about her life, but never found out anything other than that she lived with an unmarried aunt – her mother's sister – in a small apartment near the American Chapel.

'Did you speak with Rozental?' I asked.

'Yes,' she said.

'How did he sound?'

'I'm not sure he had any idea who I was, or who you were, but he said he would be here at seven o'clock.'

I saw two patients between ten and twelve o'clock. After lunch, Kopelzon telephoned to confirm he had reserved a table at A l'Ours. I saw another patient and was trying to catch up on my correspondence when Minna announced I had a visitor, his honour Peter Arseneyevich Zinnurov.

'I owe you an apology, Spethmann,' Anna's father boomed as he took a seat across the desk from me. 'I promised I would get that infuriating little detective out of your hair and instead he breaks into your house and arrests you.'

'And my daughter.'

'Quite,' he said. 'As soon as I heard what had happened I went personally to Maklakov to complain. Sadly, with the way things now are, the minister had no choice but to let the police continue their investigations.'

I doubted whether Zinnurov had done anything of the sort but thanked him anyway.

'Happily, you're free and there's no harm done,' he said.

I smiled frostily. 'What can I do for you, sir?'

His smile was the equal of mine. 'In the last few weeks, since I saw you at the Yacht Club, I have written three or four times to my daughter. I have tried telephoning as well. She will not accept my calls, nor has she responded to my letters.' His smile faded and was replaced by a harder, more implacable look. It was the Mountain who addressed me now, not Anna's father. 'I asked you to speak to her and, if I remember correctly, you promised you would. Did you in fact keep your promise?'

'I did,' I said evenly. 'I saw Anna the night before I was arrested. She would not agree to see you.'

'What did you say, exactly?'

'I told her that you wanted to see her on whatever terms she dictated.'

'And she said no?'

'She said no.'

111

'Did you encourage her to see me? Did you tell her you thought she should see me?'

'Why does Anna not want to see you?'

The Mountain banged his fist on the top of the desk. His ruddy cheeks flushed a deeper red. 'You do not question me,' he bellowed. 'Is that understood?' He banged the desk again. 'You do not question me!'

I was unmoved by this display. Psychoanalysts see much worse every day. I stared at him. Eventually, a look – not so much of contrition but of recognition that a tactic had failed – came over him and he settled back in his chair.

'As you can see,' he began, moderating his tone, 'I am upset by this business, this estrangement. Very upset.'

'If I knew the circumstances behind your quarrel,' I said, 'I might be in a better position to effect a meeting.'

I could tell he was profoundly irritated but was holding his temper in check, for the time being. He summoned a weary smile, 'I have already told you, Spethmann, Anna appears rational but, believe me, she is unstable and sometimes does not know what she's saying.'

'I find that very hard to believe,' I said. 'I've never seen her other than self-possessed and entirely rational.'

'You have no idea what she is capable of,' he said.

'What is she capable of?'

He pressed his lips together and drew in a deep breath through his nose before expelling the air in a heavy sigh. 'There are things that are private and should always remain so.'

'My profession takes a different view,' I said.

'You want everything brought to the surface, is that it, Spethmann?'

'More or less,' I said.

'Then it's a very foolish business you're in,' he snorted. 'Very foolish. In my experience, life runs more smoothly with secrets left undisturbed. I am an old man. I have lived a long

112

life. I have done things of which I am ashamed. Some of them are known. Others stay in here,' he said, tapping his breast, 'and that's where they belong.'

'When she was thirteen, you took Anna on a trip to Kazan, in the summer.'

There was a long silence. He shook his head and laughed in derision. 'Kazan again.'

'Again?'

'What has she told you about Kazan?'

'You took Anna to visit your mother in Kazan.'

'My mother?' He laughed again, then, after he'd composed himself, he declared with some force, 'Anna never met her grandmother.'

'She is certain she did.'

'When she was thirteen, you say?'

'In the summer of 1889.'

'Impossible.'

'Why is it impossible?' I asked.

'Because, Spethmann, her grandmother – my mother – died two years before. I have the death certificate if you're interested.'

Now it was Zinnurov's turn to stare. Was it possible Anna had imagined the trip?

'What interest do you have in this fantastical trip to Kazan, anyway?' he asked.

'From Anna's account, I believed it possible she may have suffered some trauma and that this is at the root of her illness.'

He shook his head as at a deluded imbecile. 'All women tell stories,' he said, adopting the confidential, knowing tone men employ when together they generalise about women. 'They embellish, they exaggerate, they create crises where no crisis exists. It's their nature. They want drama because without it they do not feel alive. Anna is no different.'

His look was pleasant, a man inviting another man to concede the immutable truths about the foibles of women.

'I do not believe Anna made up the story about Kazan,' I said.

At once his look became contemptuous. 'Then you don't know Anna very well – certainly not as well as you think you do.'

He got to his feet in a quick, smooth movement. For an old man, he was remarkably supple. I stood up and went to the door while he gathered his coat and cane. He paused at the threshold.

'Tell me,' he said in a voice full of sly insinuation, 'what is the precise nature of your relationship with my daughter?'

'I am her doctor.'

'I get the impression there is more to it than that.'

It was half-statement, half-question. I had no reply ready, not even for myself. He looked me up and down and, dispensing altogether with the need for formal politeness, said, 'You came to me for help. I said I would do what I could, even though, to be frank, you are not, properly speaking, Russian. You are not to see my daughter again. Do not try to contact her. If you attempt to telephone her or write to her, I will be aware of it.'

'So far as I know,' I said, 'there is no law in Russia to prevent a doctor from treating his patient.'

'Don't underestimate me, Spethmann,' he said, putting on his hat. He smiled and added, 'Don't be a fool.'

When he'd gone, I went to the chessboard and stared at the position. It took almost an hour before I could see the pieces properly. Even then, I could not stop trembling, with anger, with anxiety, and above all with doubt. Was Zinnurov right about his daughter? Had I misread Anna so badly?

Shortly before seven o'clock, Minna entered to say that Rozental had arrived. She also told me that Semevsky had informed her my car had been mended and was parked in its usual place. Then she handed me an envelope.

'A messenger delivered this a few minutes ago,' she said.

I went to my desk and sliced the seal with a letter opener. Inside was a handwritten note.

It read, 'I meant what I said' and it was signed 'P.A. Zinnurov'.

Rozental received my apology for my absence with indifference. Monomaniacally fixated on chess, he was someone for whom nothing had the slightest meaning except as it affected his freedom to play; the existence of others he understood only in terms of their capacity to help or hinder his obsession. If this is to paint an unattractively selfish picture of my patient, I should emphasise that Rozental's character was not in the least manipulative, cynical or grandiose. He was a shy and gentle man, with a pathetic aura of sadness, as though perpetually confused by the world and the people in it. Whenever I looked at him, I was put in mind of a child who has lost his parents in a crowd. Chess was Rozental's life; beyond was a void. To be prevented from playing, whether through illness or mishap or the machinations of others, was as traumatic to him as the loss of a limb to anyone else.

His movements were quick and jerky, he could not sit still. I tried to calm him with some innocuous questions about his hotel and his room (overheated, he muttered) and whether he had any relations with Lasker, Capablanca, Tarrasch, Nimzowitsch and the other participants (he did not). He spent all his time studying the games of his opponents, looking for improvements in his opening repertoire and, his speciality, analysing endgames. I should not give the impression that the information I elicited came easily or conversationally. Again, I was put in mind of a child – one with a very short

attention span and with only a minimally developed aware-
ness of others.

The tournament was only three days away. It was time to
get to the heart of the matter.

'I have been giving a great deal of thought to the fly that so
torments you,' I began. He gave me a wary, doubtful look. 'Do
you recall you told me that everyone wanted you to do this or
that, to be this or that? Do you remember I asked to whom
"they" referred?'

His features took on the suspicious expression of a man who
thought himself being lured into a trap.

'You said "they" were not your grandparents, and yet it is
clear from other things you have told me that your grandparents had extraordinarily high expectations of you. "They"
are your grandparents, are they not?'

He twisted uncomfortably and turned to look directly at
me. It was unusual for him to make eye contact in this way
and, paradoxically, it was a sign in him of extreme distress. At
such critical junctures the psychoanalyst must decide whether
to proceed with the line of inquiry which has produced this
heightened level of anxiety in the hope of a breakthrough, or,
fearing more harm than good will come of it, pull back and
endeavour to calm the patient.

'You disappointed your grandparents, Avrom,' I said, de-
ciding to press on. 'You did not do what "they" wanted you to
do.'

'No, no, no! Not me, not me!' he cried.

'And naturally you experience guilt because you are doing
something they think is wrong.'

'I'm not doing anything wrong,' he mumbled, 'I'm not.'

'Of course you're not, Avrom –'

'It is the other one!' he wailed. 'Not me!'

I was puzzled. The other one? What was this? I pressed on.
'You're not doing anything wrong, Avrom. The guilt you

116

experience exists only because you are aware of your grand-parents' disapproval. The guilt is expressed by the fly.'

'There are two, there are two, there are two . . . ' he muttered.

'Two . . . flies?'

'It's not me, it's not me.' He got to his feet, repeating this senseless refrain. His eyes were distracted. 'I will not do it,' he cried. 'No, I will not do it. Let the other one do it. Not me, not me.'

'Are you talking about a brother, Avrom? Or a sister?'

I was not sure he heard me. Was this what Kopelzon meant when he said Rozental rambled?

'There can't be two, just one,' he muttered, looking around him for the fly.

'How many flies are there, Avrom? What are there two of? You keep saying two, Avrom! What do you mean by two?'

He began to bat the air violently with his hands, as though swatting away a black cloud of flies, all the time crying and moaning. Minna, hearing the commotion, knocked and entered, and together we succeeded in getting him to the couch. He sobbed pitifully for the best part of an hour. When I judged things were again under control I let Minna go for the evening.

Gradually Rozental recovered himself. Unwilling to risk upsetting him further, I said nothing more other than to offer him refreshment.

'I get so confused,' he said at last, his voice exhausted and brittle. 'Sometimes I cannot tell which one is which.'

He was still and rather calm, as one who has suffered a fever after the crisis has passed.

'Would you like to proceed with our session?'

He did not reply. I let some minutes go by.

I said, 'Painful as it may be to you, Avrom, it is essential we continue. I would not suggest doing so if I were not convinced that it will ultimately be of help to you.'

117

He appeared reluctant but willing; he said, 'May I use your bathroom first?'

'Of course,' I said, getting up to show him where to go.

I went back to my office and jotted down on my notepad the word 'Two'. I circled it and put a question mark after it. What did he mean by this? I wrote 'Paranoid Schizophrenia?' I had never personally encountered such a case before. The phenomenon had been only recently discovered and was not at all well understood.

I heard the toilet flush and the tap water run.

Besides my concern for my patient, I felt the stirring of professional excitement. I would write to Bleuler at Burghölzli for advice on how to continue with the treatment.

I waited for Rozental to come in. The sound of running water continued. Many of my patients washed obsessively and I was used to their taking time in the bathroom. I wondered how my interpretation of the fly as the manifestation of *yetzer hara* – the evil inclination that had led him from the centredness of his community and his religion to the life of an itinerant chess player – might be fitted into my new interpretation. The thought that I might be wrong did not even occur to me.

What was keeping Rozental?

I got up and went to the outer office. The bathroom door was open. I turned off the running tap and went out to the hall.

'Avrom!' I called. 'Avrom!'

He was nowhere in sight. Without even locking the office behind me, I hurried down the stairs. Semevsky was standing just inside the door of the lobby.

'Did you see someone leave just now?' I shouted. 'A man? Stocky, with short hair and a moustache?'

'I let him out just a moment ago. Is something wrong, your honour?'

I barged past the doorman into the street.

In the fading light I caught sight of Rozental turning into the Nevsky. I darted after him through the chaotic traffic as he dodged horses and motor carriages to cross the wide avenue at a diagonal, finally disappearing into the crowds outside the Gostinny Dvor.

I was about to give up my pursuit when I spotted him again hurrying into Dumskaya Street. From there, he turned right and continued the short distance to the Griboyedova Canal. His quickness and agility surprised me, for he was physically stolid; I would have almost certainly lost him had he not stopped on reaching the dimly lit embankment.

Not wanting him to take fright at the thought I was following him, I concealed myself in a darkened doorway while I considered what best to do. He too seemed to be taking stock of his situation, looking anxiously around as though trying to decide where to go.

There were no shops or restaurants on this part of the embankment. Apart from the occasional passing carriage, it was completely deserted. I saw him go to the wall and look out over the water. Fearing he might harm himself in his distracted condition, I decided to approach my patient, even at the risk of panicking him. I was about to step forward when I heard a figure coming up behind me.

'Can I be of assistance to his honour?'

I recognised the doorman's uniform – Semevsky.

'What are you doing here?' I said.

'I thought his honour might need help. Is the other fellow a thief?'

He seemed, as always, eager to please.

I said, 'He's no thief. He's my patient and rather unwell. I must see him safely to his hotel.'

As soon as I said this, I realised that the doorman must have seen Rozental come into my office on two or three previous occasions. Something was not right. Before I could say or do anything, Rozental turned away from the canal and started uncertainly towards the footbridge a little further along the embankment.

'You should return to your post,' I said to Semevsky.

He gripped me by the arm. Gone was the ingratiation. 'Let's just see where your patient goes,' he said.

I yanked my arm, attempting to free myself, but he spun me expertly round, simultaneously twisting my arm up my back. Another fraction and it would break.

'Who are you?' I said.

'You don't need to concern yourself with that,' he replied calmly. 'Let's go.'

He nudged me into the street. We were about to cross to the embankment side when a small car came round the corner. As soon as it passed, we crossed the street and moved towards the footbridge. Rozental was already almost on the far side of the canal.

'What do you want with Rozental?' I said.

'Let's see where he goes and who he talks to.'

We were a few paces from the bridge when the same car suddenly swung round and accelerated towards us.

'Who's this?' I heard Semevsky mutter.

The car screeched to a halt and a man in a long coat jumped out. It was Kavi.

For a moment everything was perfectly still. I heard only the approaching stamp of Kavi's boots and Semevsky's quickening breath. Semevsky threw me forwards, the better able to defend himself. I did not fall but recovered my balance in time to see him pull a pistol from his pocket.

'Keep away!' Semevsky shouted.

The Cossack did not break his stride but came steadily onwards. He grinned as he produced his long, bone-handled knife. Semevsky raised the pistol and took aim. Kavi did not even try to get out of the way.

From behind, out of the gloom, a small, nimble figure rushed up. Semevsky heard him, but too late. He let out a groan and slid to the ground. His right leg twitched horribly. Only then did I take in the insubstantial presence of Lychev standing over Semevsky's body. He was holding a knife. Blood boiled from the gash in Semevsky's throat. The twitching stopped.

Without a word, like two men who had spent a lifetime working in concert, Lychev and Kavi lifted the body and hoisted it over the wall into the canal. I could still hear the splash as Kavi bundled me into the car.

Fourteen

Lychev hurled his knife through the open window as Kavi drove up the deserted embankment. The spinning metal briefly caught the light from the street lamps and winked like a star before disappearing over the embankment and into the canal. He lit a cigarette.

We were at the junction with the Nevsky opposite St Catherine's. People were streaming to the theatres, shops and restaurants. Liveried servants with the serious look of men entrusted with sacred tasks rode the running boards of their masters' carriages. Outside an art gallery a double act of juggler and fire-eater performed tricks for the patrons' amusement. At the Gostinny Dvor it seemed that the whole of St Petersburg had assembled to shop for furs and slippers, porcelain and silver, tea and caviar.

I looked from Kavi to Lychev. 'So you two are in league,' I said. 'I knew it.'

'You should be a policeman, Spethmann,' Lychev said. 'There may still be time.'

'Where are you taking me?'

'Where would you like to go?' Lychev said amiably, as if we were driving back into the city from a pleasant afternoon's excursion in the country. 'We can drop you anywhere you want.'

'Why did you kill that man?'

'I was protecting a member of the public,' he said. 'You.'

'Policemen do not throw bodies into the canal. Nor do they consort with thugs.'

Kavi laughed. 'He has a lot to learn about policemen, doesn't he?'

A horse-drawn cab in front of us, which had been going at a sharp trot, slowed as the driver turned left. Kavi braked gently.

This was my chance.

I hurled myself against the passenger door, at the same time grabbing for the handle. Lychev swore and clutched at my coat. I heard the fabric tear as the door swung open.

A second later I was sitting on the wet cobble. I had landed in such a manner that I was facing away from Kavi's car and staring into the oncoming traffic. One of Ivanov's new buses was bearing directly down on me. To my right a tram was coming in the opposite direction. A woman saw me and screamed. I heard the screech of the bus's tyres and launched myself to the left. The onlookers were frozen in shock as I rolled clear and got to my feet. A small crowd was gathering. A man in a bowler hat came forward to assist me. Glancing up the avenue, I saw Lychev hopping out of the car.

'That man is my prisoner,' the detective shouted as he ran towards us. 'Stop him!'

I shook off my confused helpers and started to run. If I could reach the Gostinny Dvor I would be able to lose myself among the shoppers. I glanced back to see Lychev throw the bowler-hatted man out of his way and pull a pistol from his coat.

'Police!' he shouted. 'Stop that man!'

The Gostinny Dvor was no more than twenty *sazheni* away. My heart was pounding, my chest tight. Cold sweat trickled down my back. I dodged blindly right and left, muttering curses at the people who got in my way. Complaints and oaths came after me. I think I knocked down a young woman.

I ran into a brick wall. Or so it seemed, for I staggered backwards, stunned and understanding nothing except that I had come up against something immovable. It was a gendarme, as powerful and solid as Kavi. He threw an arm round my neck and forced my head down almost to my knees. I began to choke.

'I am Inspector of Police Mintimer Lychev,' I heard Lychev pant. 'This man is my prisoner.'

I tried to speak but the gendarme only increased the pressure on my throat. I thought I was going to die.

'Do you need help with him, sir?' the gendarme replied.

'I have him now,' Lychev said, taking hold of me. 'Thank you – well done.'

Lychev yanked me along, brusquely pushing aside the curious pedestrians who paused in our way. I gulped in air and tried not to vomit.

Kavi had doubled back. He pulled up alongside us. Lychev pushed me inside the car.

Lychev ran his finger along his collar, tugging at the front to ease his breathing.

'Why did you kill Semevsky?' I gasped. 'Who was he? Why did you kill him?'

Lychev heaved a sigh. 'Semevsky was a vicious street thug who liked nothing better than to beat up Jews and burn their houses. Three years ago in Moscow, he took an iron gas-pipe to a local Bolshevik leader – Bauman – killed him, then raped his sister. He was arrested but never prosecuted. That's who Semevsky was.'

'I don't believe you,' I said.

'I don't care,' Lychev said, still drawing in deep breaths and speaking with difficulty.

'Why was he not prosecuted?'

'Because by then he was working for the Okhrana.'

'Why would a policeman kill an agent of the Okhrana?' I said. 'It makes no sense.'

Lychev began to splutter and cough. 'Semevsky was recruited personally by Colonel Gan.'

Lychev dropped the name casually. It needed no emphasis for he knew the effect it would produce.

'You know who I'm talking about, don't you?' he said.

I recalled the scarred but grandfatherly figure I had seen at the Imperial Yacht Club, resplendent in the uniform of the Household Cavalry. Colonel Maximilian Gan, head of the secret police, was as legendary as Berek Medem the terrorist was notorious.

. 'After Semevsky was recruited,' Lychev went on, 'Gan continued to make use of his particular talents. He carried out a dozen or more secret murders on the orders of the Okhrana. Gulko's was one of them.'

'You're asking me to believe that the Okhrana ordered Semevsky to kill a newspaper editor?' I said.

'Gan personally ordered the assassination.'

'Why?'

'Gulko obviously found out something the Okhrana wanted to keep secret.'

'What did he find out?'

'I don't yet know,' Lychev said phlegmatically, 'but I will find out. Everything always comes out in the end.'

That Lychev's high-pitched, nasal monotone lent his account such a natural, unforced credibility seemed perverse: the voice should not have been trustworthy, and yet it was. Lychev should not have been convincing, yet he was.

We were continuing along the Nevsky. As we left the shops and theatres behind, the traffic started to thin out.

'Why did Semevsky want to follow Rozental?' I said.

'Gan has had Rozental under surveillance since he arrived in the city.'

'What interest does Gan have in a chess player?'

'This is something else I have yet to find out,' Lychev said. 'But I do know that Semevsky's other job was to spy on you.'

At the Anchikov Palace, Kavi turned on to the elegant, granite-lined Fontanka Embankment, passing on the one side barges and boats and on the other great houses and palaces shaded by lime trees.

The car came to a halt near the old Tsepnoi suspension bridge leading into the Summer Garden.

Lychev lit another cigarette, turned to me and said, 'Gan is trying to take over my investigation into the murders of Gulko and Yastrebov, at least one of which he himself ordered.'

'Are you saying he also had Yastrebov killed?'

'It's a possibility,' he replied. He smiled grimly before continuing. 'I am not without supporters in the interior ministry but if I am unable to show results, if I can't show that I'm getting close to Yastrebov's cell, Gan will get his way.'

'I will miss you,' I said, 'terribly.'

In the front of the car, Kavi guffawed.

'You speak truer than you know, Spethmann,' Lychev said. 'You will miss me – because I am the only person standing between you and Colonel Gan.'

'I've done nothing wrong. I am a psychoanalyst –'

'With no time for political affairs – yes, we know,' Lychev cut in. 'However, your daughter has managed to implicate not just herself but also her father in Yastrebov's plot.'

'I am not implicated. Neither is Catherine. There is not the slightest evidence.'

'The minute Catherine spoke to Yastrebov, the very second, both she and you became implicated. As soon as Colonel Gan gets the chance, he will order your arrest and, believe me, the experience will not be gentle.'

He paused to give me time to take this in.

'I can keep Gan away from both you and Catherine – and I am willing to do so – but only on condition that you help me.'

I looked at him with a mixture of suspicion and loathing. 'How?'

'I need to know everything that Catherine knows about Yastrebov, starting with his real name.'

'Catherine tells me only what she wants me to know,' I said.

'Then you must persuade her that she wants you to know Yastrebov's name,' he said, reaching into a briefcase on the floor between us. He removed what I instantly recognised as Rozental's file.

'I also want to know why Gan is so interested in Rozental.' He looked up at me and smiled. 'Here our curiosity coincides, no?' He tossed the file into my lap. 'I had hoped to learn something from this but it seems you had barely begun your analysis when Kavi and Tolya visited you.'

He drew on his cigarette and said, 'I thought about arresting Rozental and interrogating him – and I may yet have to. But it would be complicated: Rozental is, after all, famous all over the world, and it would not look good to take him into custody with so many foreigners in St Petersburg for the tournament.'

'He would be of no use to you,' I said. 'Rozental's psychological condition is on a knife edge.'

'I came to the same conclusion,' Lychev said. 'That's why you must talk to him.'

'You want me to spy on my own patient?'

'Gan is not interested in Rozental for nothing. He must have a reason. As Rozental's doctor, don't you want to know what that is? Don't you think it might have some bearing on your patient's condition?'

I looked at him with distaste. Lychev knew what I was thinking but seemed unconcerned. Swivelling in his seat, he pointed across the street. 'Do you see that house? Number 16?'

It was a handsome but otherwise unremarkable town house.

'You're looking at the secret headquarters of the Okhrana,' Lychev said, keeping his eyes fixed on the nondescript frontage.

'Colonel Gan is probably in there studying your file,' Kavi said laughing.

I stared at the building and tried to sort out my thoughts.

'I can understand you wanting to think this has nothing to do with you, Spethmann,' Lychev said. 'You would like it to be a game, the kind that children play and when they get frightened all they have to do is say I don't want to play any more. But this game is different and, like it or not, you are involved now. There is no way to stop other than to win or lose.'

He took out a card and scribbled something down.

'When you've talked to Catherine call me at this number at police headquarters. If I don't answer, hang up and call later. Do not leave your name with anyone. And do not use the telephone in your house or your office.'

He rapped the window with his knuckles and commanded Kavi to get on.

'Now,' he said merrily, 'I believe you are expected at A l'Ours for dinner with Kopelzon. This is good. A normal place where the lights are on and people are relaxed and enjoying themselves – it will help you calm down.'

Fifteen

T he lights were on, as Lychev had promised, and through the frosted windows the fashionable after-theatre crowd presented a friendly mass into whose sheltering depths I longed to dive. I reached for the car door, desperate to be out of the dark corners in which Lychev and Kavi dwelled.

The detective took hold of my arm. 'Say nothing to anyone about what happened tonight,' he said.

I made to get out of the car but he did not let go.

'Even if Semevsky's body is swept out to sea and gets lost in the Gulf of Finland, Gan will be missing an agent. The colonel is a thorough man and he will investigate his loss. Sooner or later, he will come to you. Make sure you have your alibi ready.'

I yanked myself free of his grip and stepped out onto Konyushennaya Street. I could hear the orchestra's muted playing from the restaurant as the car pulled away. I did not immediately enter but thought about going to Filippov's where Anna and I were supposed to have met at nine. I checked my watch. It was after ten. Anna would have waited, but not for an hour. As I approached the restaurant, a white-gloved attendant bowed and opened the door for me.

I saw Kopelzon at his usual table but made for the corridor on the left-hand side where the public telephones were and asked the operator to put me through to the Ziatdinov residence. A servant answered and I asked to speak to madam. Some seconds later I heard the telephone being picked up again.

'Anna?' I said.

'Who is this?' a male voice answered.

I said, 'Otto Spethmann. I'm Anna's doctor.'

'I know who you are,' the man said.

'To whom am I speaking?'

'Do you have a message for my wife?'

'I was calling to arrange an appointment.'

'At this hour?'

'I apologise for the lateness. I had meant to call earlier but got caught up in some business.'

'Isn't that why you have a secretary?'

'If you would be kind enough to tell her I called,' I said.

The line went dead. Guilt and anxiety welled up inside me. I needed a drink.

The dining room buzzed with talk and laughter and the cheerful clink of champagne glasses. As I made my way to Kopelzon's table I kept thinking, *As soon as they see me they will know everything. How can they not? How can the inward testimony of murder not be etched in the witness's face?* But no. The maître d' greeted me with the working smile of his profession, declared how pleased he was to see me again and commented on the welcome mildness of the evening. The orchestra continued to play. The diners ate and drank. No one so much as cast a passing glance in my direction as I joined my dinner companion.

Kopelzon embraced me. Brimming over with his own high spirits, he didn't notice my frozen condition. This was not unusual with Kopelzon – his own enthusiasms, feuds, loves and hates always came first. Even when he asked, as a matter of formal course, how you were, you knew he was waiting for you to finish so he could launch into his own latest news. When Kopelzon was in this expansive mood – there were other, darker dispositions – it did not seem ill-mannered. Such

130

was the sheer performance surrounding everything he said and did that quieter, less certain personalities could only sit back and enjoy and envy him. In my present state I was only too happy to be distracted by his bravura.

For the first twenty or thirty minutes I heard him the same way I saw the white-coated waiters, elegantly turned-out diners and the conductor and musicians, which is to say vaguely and generally. Detail was still beyond me. My eyes were unable to focus, my hearing capable only of taking in rhythm and cadence. I do not remember ordering, I do not remember the wine being brought to the table.

While Kopelzon talked I tried to be as logical about Lychev's story as about the variations in a chess game. In chess it is easy to be panicked by a complicated position and the aggressive manoeuvring of an opponent. What is needed always is a cool eye and a clear head. Calculate. Calculate concrete variations. What do I do if my opponent does this? What do I do if he does that?

'Otto?' I heard Kopelzon say.

If I agreed to help Lychev, would Catherine tell me what I needed to know? If I talked to Rozental, what would he tell me? What if Gan's agents questioned me about Semevsky's disappearance? Could I escape by implicating Lychev? Calculate. Where does this go?

'Otto? Are you all right?'

I blinked at my companion. 'Just a little tired,' I said. 'Sorry.'

'Am I boring you?'

'You are never boring, Reuven.'

He smiled, pleased at the compliment. Slowly, words began to take on discrete sounds, and with the sounds came meaning and comprehension. Assured now of his audience's attentiveness, Kopelzon poured forth: he had been in Warsaw where he had given a recital and been praised as a genius. Before Warsaw there had been Paris and the same thing. He had triumphed.

'Otto,' he declared, putting a hand dramatically to his breast, 'I was moved beyond words.'

At the next table a party of glowing youngsters caught Kopelzon's eye and raised their glasses to toast the maestro. He bowed graciously and returned the toast. I saw him mentally pick out the prettiest girls for possible pleasures later that night. Kopelzon inhabited a whole palace of sensuality.

He turned back and, as though only now taking note of me as an autonomous being with independent interests, asked about my arrest and detention. Kopelzon had a melodramatic and somewhat paranoid cast of mind. But even had Lychev not warned me against talking, I did not have the energy for what would have followed had I told him but a fraction of the story. I assured him it had been a mix-up and that everything was now resolved.

'Russia likes to feel the whip – isn't that what the tsarina likes to say? And you felt it, Otto, you felt the whip,' he said grimly. 'Is there anything I can do?'

'I don't think so,' I said, 'but thank you anyway.'

'I saw our friend Rozental. He's improved somewhat, don't you think? He'll never be normal, exactly, but at least when I saw him he had his board up and was analysing Lasker's most recent games – a good sign.'

Couched in this was the implication that he had some right – as a gambler might inquire of the trainer of a horse, or a parent of his child's teacher – to intelligence on Rozental's progress. He refilled his glass and raised it to his mouth.

'When did you see him?' I asked.

'This morning, in his room at the Astoria.'

'I'm afraid he may not be as improved as you think,' I said. 'When he left my office this evening, he was highly agitated.'

Kopelzon put down his glass. His lips were slightly parted, his look more than a little apprehensive. 'He hasn't been rambling, has he?' he said. 'He hasn't been talking rubbish? I told you not to listen to him.'

'He is a divided man. He is in torment.'

'Divided?' Kopelzon said warily.

'He feels guilty because he's a chess player. He feels he has betrayed his grandparents.'

This analysis seemed to come as a relief to him. 'I see,' he said, nodding sympathetically.

'When did you meet Rozental?' I asked.

'A year or so ago, at the chess club in Lodz.'

'Are you good friends?'

'I believe so. I hope I'm good a friend to him.'

'How well do you know him? I mean, his background, his interests?'

'He never talks about his family. As for interests I don't think he has any, apart from chess.'

'Is he interested in other sports or games?'

'Not that I know of.'

'Theatre, music?'

Kopelzon turned down the corners of his generous mouth. 'He's never mentioned it.'

'Religion? Politics?'

Kopelzon gave me a look. 'Politics? Why on earth do you ask that?'

'I'm trying to build up a picture of my patient.'

'I've never heard him venture anything remotely resembling a political opinion,' Kopelzon said. 'Look, Otto, is he going to be ready to play or not?'

I hesitated, knowing how much what I was about to say would anger my friend. 'I believe it essential for Rozental's psychological well-being,' I began slowly and carefully, 'that he take no part in the tournament.'

Kopelzon slammed his glass to the table. His brow came down in a glower. The transformation from companion to

133

adversary was instant and total; Kopelzon never knew degrees. There was either calmness or rage with him, ecstasy or despondency. There were not opponents but enemies born out of blood feuds. From his friends he demanded uncritical allegiance to his person, commitment to his views and acceptance, always, that his wants came first. He took rejection of any of these things badly.

'He will play! He must play!' he shouted.

I stared into his large brown eyes. They were not soft. He pursed his lips and looked around the restaurant. Had I not known him better, I would have thought he hated me.

'You have to understand the importance of this, Otto,' he said, striving but not entirely succeeding in making his voice conciliatory.

I answered in the same tone. 'I am his doctor and I must advise my patient as I see fit.'

'You are his doctor only because I brought him to you,' he snapped, 'and I can just as easily take him away.' He thought for a moment, then said, 'Do you know what it would mean for a Polish Jew to win the St Petersburg tournament? Have you any idea? The Russians think us barely human, the rest of the world doesn't give a damn. We are despised, Otto, twice over – first as Poles, second as Jews. Can you imagine it? Rozental beating Russians, Americans, Germans, Cubans, Englishmen? Did you know the winner will be invited to the Peterhof for a personal interview with the tsar? A personal interview during which he will receive a title specially designed for the winner of this tournament – Grandmaster of Chess. What can they say about us then? A Polish Jew in the Peterhof, presented to the tsar and tsarina!'

'Do you think Rozental going to the Peterhof will stop the pogroms?' I asked.

'Of course not,' Kopelzon replied, irritated. 'But it would be a powerful message: it would say we are human beings. It would say we are as good as anyone else.'

We said nothing for some minutes but endured a difficult silence. We had started on the *sakuska* and the waiters had filled our glasses with champagne before Kopelzon spoke again. He did so carefully and earnestly, for evidently he wanted me to understand that what he was telling me went very deep with him.

'I've lived in St Petersburg the whole of my adult life,' he began, 'and, if I'm truthful, my sense of Polishness, my true national and cultural identity, was in danger of being lost. Little wonder – for nearly twelve years I didn't set foot on Polish soil. It was only last year, on my way back from Paris, that I visited the city of my birth. I can hardly tell you what emotions it produced in me. To walk the streets I grew up in. To speak the language I learned as a child. To hear the voices of the women in the market and see the children coming from the *heder*. I tell you, Otto, whenever I go back I feel ashamed. Here I am, living well in the land of the people who have conquered, partitioned and oppressed my country. You know the saying the *goyim* have – "Since the partition of Poland, Europe has been in a state of mortal sin"? I feel I also have committed a sin, a terrible dereliction of duty.'

He had a mobile face, capable of expressing in quick turns excitement and mournfulness, rage and despair, devotion and disappointment. With Kopelzon, nothing was trivial, he had an opinion about everything: women, wine, houses, horses, war, chess and politics.

'What do you conceive your duty to be?' I asked.

I heard a voice say, 'His duty is to play like an angel so we mortals may hear the music of heaven on earth.'

It belonged to one of the young women at the adjacent table. Her face was flushed from the heartiness of her friends' company and the vodka and champagne she had consumed. She had found the courage to approach her idol. It was a frequent occurrence. I scratched my ear and played with the crumbs on the tablecloth as she introduced herself as Kopelzon's sincerest, most dedicated admirer. Kopelzon took her hand and kissed it and the two flirted, he congratulating her for her charming conversation, she for the beauty of his playing. At last, having extracted a promise that Kopelzon would join her and her friends for a drink, she returned to her table, from where she continued to send silent, doe-eyed pleadings to her hero.

'You take no side in these things,' Kopelzon said, taking up our conversation again. 'That's entirely your affair. But you have to understand, Otto, that not all men are made like you.'

'How do you think I'm made?'

'You see things calmly, from above, with a third eye. I'm not criticising you. But what I see cuts me to the quick. I can't help it – that's how I'm made. Every time I cross the border from Germany and pass through Ciechocinek and Wloclawek and on to Warsaw, when I travel through the great plain of Poland, I am horrified by what I see. Miserable villages made of wood so weather-beaten and faded it is as grey as the half-starved people who inhabit them. Jews, Otto. Jews like us. Except here I am in St Petersburg playing my caprices and sonatas while you listen to the ravings of madmen.'

I made a face to show mild disapproval.

He smiled collusively and went on, his tone lightening. 'Is it not right to speak of *duty* when we see these things? When we see our brothers forced to live as beasts? What should we do then? This is the question, Otto. It is the question for men like you and me, comfortable, well fed and successful. What do we do for our brothers?' He drained his champagne in a single gulp. 'Madmen and fanatics are killing us every day,' he said, 'murdering us.'

'We have our own madmen and fanatics,' I said. 'Berek Medem, for example.'

At the mention of the name, Kopelzon hunched his shoulders and looked around to see if anyone had heard.

136

'Why do you say that name? Why?'

'The name is notorious, Reuven. Everyone knows it.'

'You know the reason they know it? Because the Russians will never let anyone forget it. What better way to tarnish us than by chanting his name, over and over and over?'

'Lychev claims he was seen in my office building.'

'Berek Medem?' he whispered.

'That's what he said.'

Kopelzon considered the news for a moment, then shook his head. 'The police are obsessed by him. They see him everywhere, or pretend to. It suits their purposes. Why do you think he keeps escaping? It's because the police want him out there setting off his bombs and throwing his acid. It suits them to have a bogeyman – that way they can slur the cause of Poland. I'm telling you, Rozental winning the tournament will do more for us than a whole army of' – he could barely bring himself to utter the name – 'Berek Medems.'

I had upset my friend. He stewed for some moments, shaking his head and glowering around him.

Spethmann–Kopelzon

After 37 . . . Kh6. The black king is exposed
but does White have enough resources to win?

Eventually he said, rather sullenly, 'Do you have a move for me?'

'I'm not in the mood,' I said. 'I'll let you have it tomorrow.'

'Come on,' he said, 'you're so confident you can beat me. Let me have your move.'

I dragged my thoughts back to the position. '38 Qf6 check,' I said.

He threw me a hard look. 'Do you really think you can beat me, Otto?'

'I'm not sure I want to, if this is how you behave when you're losing.'

He let out a small dismissive laugh. 'To win an endgame like this requires considerable technical skill, Otto. I've seen better positions than yours ruined in an instant by a single inaccuracy: 38 . . . Kh7.'

Provoked, I responded quickly, 'In that case I play 39 Kg3.'

'39 . . . Kg8,' he replied at once, affecting a nonchalant air, as though nothing I could do would hurt him.

I had analysed this line at home but his bravado made me hesitate. I tried to visualise the position. Did he have something? I could not see it. Surely my plan remained viable: march my king up the board and break with e5 at the appropriate moment. The only thing I had to worry about was Kopelzon getting in behind my king and finding a perpetual check. My heart began to thump – ridiculous after what I had witnessed on the embankment only a couple of hours earlier. But chess produces extraordinary levels of anxiety, never more so than when a player is on the point of realising an advantage but knows that a single wrong move can destroy his prospects.

'40 Kh4,' I said.

Had we been at the board moving the pieces, he would have seen my hand tremble.

'40 . . . Qb6,' he said, fixing me aggressively with his dark eyes, telling me again, *You think you have me, but you don't.*

He could check me at f2 on his next move and harry my exposed king. I had to be careful if I was not to let the win slip through my fingers.

'I'll need to think about this,' I said.

'What's there to think about?' he said sharply. 'If you're so confident, why don't you see it through?'

'I'd rather think about it,' I said, 'if you don't mind.'

He made an approximation of a smile. 'Of course,' he said with an expansive wave of the hand.

My uncertainty seemed to lift his mood. Calling for the bill, he poured vodka into a little glass, then looked over at his besotted young admirer and raised it in a toast to her. Her features lit up at once. Her friends turned in our direction. Kopelzon inclined his head gallantly, much to their delight.

'Let me pay,' I insisted.

'I wouldn't hear of it,' Kopelzon said.

Whatever his other faults, he was a generous man; he spent money with an attractive recklessness.

'Why don't you join me and my new friend?' he said with a mischievous grin. 'She has companions – beautiful ones, too.'

'I leave the women in your expert hands, Reuven.'

We parted with the fulsomeness of friends who had had a disagreement but wanted to demonstrate the survival of their mutual affection. And yet neither of us could entirely over-look the hard edge of what had passed between us. I slipped on my coat, bade the maître d' goodnight, took a last look at Kopelzon with his new young friends and went to the door. To my astonishment, Rozental entered. I had already started to greet him before I realised it was not Rozental after all, but a sturdy, crop-haired man of about the same age who was only superficially similar.

'I'm sorry,' I said. 'I mistook you for someone else.'

The man seemed to think I had intended disrespect, for the look he gave me was stiff with reproach. He turned to the maître, his manner fretful and impatient, and said, 'I must speak at once with Mr Kopelzon. He is dining here tonight.' The accent was Polish.

'I have just left Reuven Moiseyevich,' I said, pointing to Kopelzon's new table. 'He's over there.'

The man walked briskly to the table. I saw Kopelzon rise as though looking at a ghost. Recovering himself, he made an excuse to his companions and came forward to meet his obviously unexpected visitor. Though I could not hear what passed between them, it was clear from their gestures that their business was fraught. Then Kopelzon noticed me by the door. He forced a smile to his lips and waved weakly.

I waved back and stepped outside. The air had cooled and it was threatening to rain. I was about to set off up Konyush-ennaya Street to get a cab when I heard my name called. A figure stepped out of the shadows and came towards me.

'I got worried when you didn't come to Filippov's,' Anna said.

I was so surprised, and pleased, I could say nothing.

'Then I remembered you said you were having dinner here with Kopelzon,' she said.

'I'm sorry,' I said, not knowing how to explain my failure to keep our assignation. 'Have you been out here all this time?'

'Yes,' she said.

There was a strange look in her eye, full of intensity but at the same time vague and slow. I was reminded of Zinnurov's dark hints about her. But then a heavy fat raindrop suddenly struck the brim of her hat with the force of a pebble. It was followed by a second. Ten seconds later we were drenched to the bone. Her look became carefree and amused. She started to laugh.

I pushed up the limp brim and kissed her.

Sixteen

U nwrapped, she was a surprise. I had always had the impression her frame was slight but, freed from her dresses and stays, her figure was revealed as fuller. I loved it. Her breasts were plump and soft. There were tiny hairs on her nipples; I felt them on my tongue. Impatience got the better of me. I wanted to touch every part of her all at once. No sooner had I put my lips to her breast than I wanted to kiss her belly. Then I wanted to admire her face and would raise my head to look at her.

'You are so beautiful,' I murmured.

'I'm happy you think so,' she said with a smile.

Impatience again. I turned her over, she laughing, amused, I think, by my ardour. I had strength in my hands and arms and shoulders, and the only aches now were from desire. I licked the sweat from the small of her back and, my free hand reaching round to her breast again, I began to nuzzle between her legs. She stiffened, clenching, telling me I thought, *No, not that*. I was about to come away when she reared and pushed energetically into my mouth and started to moan. 'That's gorgeous,' she sighed.

When I came up, she said, 'That always leaves me tingling all over.'

I licked between her shoulder blades. I swept the thick black hair from her ears and kissed her lobes. Impatience! I went back between her legs. There was a slightly bitter outer tang; inside was sweeter.

Gradually impatience gave way to purpose. I was behind her and above her. I wrapped her hair around my right hand and with the left took hold of my cock. I brought it gently to her and rubbed its way into her. She exhaled slowly and cried out a filthy word. I smiled to myself, thinking of her in her formal gown as I had seen her at so many soirées, the elegant society hostess, and I imagined her circulating among the generals and princes and their ladies, responding to their politenesses not with her customary decorousness but with the words she was moaning now: 'Oh my cunt, my cunt.'

'I worry I am a lazy lover,' she said. 'Let me do something for you.'

I have always been in awe of women's capacity for pleasure. So much of my own pleasure came from pleasing and this was pleasure. This glorious heat and sweat and sour, heavy smells, the sight of Anna's flushed cheeks and the sound of her groans. The air in the room was dense.

'There is nothing I want but this,' I said.

I tightened my grip on the rough braid I had made of her hair and began slowly to move against her. I soon found her rhythm. The pace quickened. I heard that joyful slap of groin and thigh against buttock. Pushing herself face down into the pillows, she raised her behind up so that I had to get to my feet to stay inside her. After that it was frenzy. It could not last long. With Elena, I could usually choose the moment of my own orgasm – age, a long marriage, the repeating patterns of kind and loving sex. But not now. With a gasp, I folded over on top of her and we collapsed, ending up on our backs, side by side. My nostrils filled up with more earthy smells. I felt a bead of sweat trickle down my neck. She reached out for my hand. I felt recklessly unin-hibited. Had Minna or Kopelzon or Lychev walked in at that moment, I do not believe I would have pulled the sheets around me in shame. I would have said, Look, here is a man and a woman. This is what men and women do. Look or look away, the choice is yours.

In the tournament hall there were half a dozen games in progress. Mine was a rook and pawn endgame, the kind of game in which Rozental's skill was unsurpassed. With sudden blinding clarity I saw the way to win. I put my hand on my king and shifted it one square to the right, to h1. Zinnurov leaned back in his chair, stupefied by the unexpectedness and brilliance of my move. Lasker and Capablanca interrupted their game to come and look at the position. Lasker, grey, grizzled and ashy, relit his cigar and said, 'Zugzwang, my dear Zinnurov. You are in zugzwang.' The smooth and graceful Capablanca said, 'There is only one thing for it, Zinnurov – resignation.' The Mountain swallowed the dense French red wine in his glass, then turned the king on its side. 'Congratulations,' he said with a forced smile, rising from the table. He left the ballroom with Lasker clapping me on the back and Capablanca shouting 'Bravo, bravo!'

The childish dreams we dream when we are happy. I was but a few days short of my fiftieth birthday and here I was, a small boy again; I could not boast to my dead parents, but I could still boast to myself.

I came half-awake to find that we were kissing. We were on our sides, facing each other. My right hand rested on her hip, her little fist worked on my cock. I began to masturbate her.

'What will you tell your husband?' I said. 'How will you explain being out all night?'

She turned on her back, urging me with a look to fuck her.

I held her hand. Her bare upper arm lay against mine. She rose up and licked my nipple. This time she refused to let me be active, putting her hand to my chest and pushing me down on the bed when I tried to sit up. In contrast to my impatience, she was unhurried and feline. This time the pleasure was from being pleased.

She kissed my chest as she straddled me. At the undersides of her breasts were fine white stretch marks, little slivers of imperfection. I put my hand up and touched them with my fingertips.

I was not ready, but she was open and wet and once inside her I soon became fully hard again. The urgency was gone. I lay almost perfectly still while she moved slowly on top of me. She continued her slow work, occasionally using her own fingers to excite herself. I told her I loved her. She took her hand away from her cunt and lowered herself down on me. I pressed my nose into the sweat and perfume of her hair and kissed her ear and listened to her breathing. Her heart beat against my chest.

I moved my hand up to cup her behind, slipping my fingertips between her buttocks, stretching her a little. I slipped a finger inside her. She arched and tensed. She moved her face so she could kiss me. Our tongues pushed through the veil of the strands of her hair that had fallen between us.

'More fingers,' she whispered.

More and deeper. She let out a little cry and ran her tongue over my teeth. She screwed her eyes shut.

'I don't want to hurt you,' I said.

'You're not hurting me.'

She sucked my lower lip between her teeth and moaned; then, releasing me, lowered herself so her forehead was resting against my chin.

'How many fingers now?' she gasped.

I dozed for a little while but lightly, aware that she was awake.

'Can you remember anything more about your trip to Kazan?' I whispered.

'Why do you keep going on about Kazan?'

'Something happened to you there,' I said, 'something that has affected the rest of your life.'

'How do you know that?' she asked with a playful smile.

'It's my job,' I replied lightly and seriously at once.

She pulled the sheet back, complaining of the heat, and lay unselfconsciously naked while we talked. Occasionally she would rub away the sweat from her breast or between her legs.

'Are you sure your grandmother was there?'

'Of course.'

'Had you met your grandmother before you went to Kazan?'

'No, it was the first time, which is why I remember her.'

'Did you see your grandmother again after the trip? Did she come to St Petersburg? Did you go again to Kazan?'

'No.'

'What happened to your grandmother?'

'She died.'

'When?'

She reached over and took hold of my cock. It was limp but still thick. She thickened it some more.

'When did your grandmother die?' I asked again.

'I don't remember,' she said with a grin.

'What about your mother?'

She propped herself up on her side the better to work on me. She laughed dirtily and, admiring her handiwork, said, 'What are you going to do with this?'

'You told me your mother died when you were fifteen.'

'If someone were doing this to me,' she said, 'I wouldn't want to talk about ancient history.'

I put my hand on hers, stopping the movement.

'You were fifteen, is that right?'

She snatched her hand away and gave me a peevish look.

145

'Yes, I was fifteen.' She sat up and pulled the sheet around her in a show of petulance. 'Why are we talking about this? First my grandmother, then my mother.'

'I'm trying to help you.'

'You *were* helping me,' she said, 'a few minutes ago.'

'Your mother died of pneumonia?'

'She killed herself,' she said brutally.

'You told me in our first or second session that she died of pneumonia when you were fifteen.'

Her attitude was defensive and fixed. She pursed her lips in annoyance. 'I didn't tell you because I hardly knew you. It's not something one tells a stranger.'

'But later, when you'd got to know me, why didn't you tell me then?'

'I didn't want you to think that I'd deceived you,' she said. She stretched out a hand to take mine. 'I'm sorry,' she said. 'I should have, I know. But I didn't want you to think badly of me.'

I wanted to continue but her patience was exhausted and my resistance was low. She leaned forward and took my cock in her mouth.

Semevsky entered the room. His hair was matted, his clothes sodden. He leaned over the bed on which Anna and I lay. Freezing foul water gushed from his nose and mouth. It would not stop. Anna got up and said she had to go back to her husband. The bed started to rise up until it was perpendicular to the floor. I grabbed for something to hold but all I found were pillows and bolsters, which tumbled down with me into the night-dark sea. Elena rowed by in a boat. She wore a straw hat and was singing an aria from *Manon*. She waved at me and blew me kisses. She sang, *No! pazzo son!* as I drowned.

It was still dark when we left the house. I half hoped Catherine would find us together when I would have had the opportunity to tell her it was only sex. Except of course it was more than that. I had not just fallen in love, but fallen in love with the woman she hated.

'Your father warned me not to try to see you again,' I said as we walked in search of a taxi.

'I think you already know how pleased I am that you ignored him,' she said lightly, seemingly unconcerned.

'He says there was no trip to Kazan.'

She bit her lip. 'It's not true. He took me there. We went on the train.'

'Why does he say the trip never took place?'

'There are many things my father would prefer to keep hidden.'

'He says you never met your grandmother, that she died two years before the trip.'

'He's lying,' she said, her eyes ablaze. 'He doesn't want anyone to know.'

'Know what?'

She was becoming agitated. 'During the visit. He doesn't want people to know what happened.'

'How much do you remember about Kazan?' I said, suddenly uneasy about what she was saying.

She put a hand to her forehead. 'I really can hardly think. I'm so tired. I don't think I slept at all.'

I took her by the arm. 'What happened?' I repeated.

She looked at me in alarm. This was not the gentle, patient psychoanalyst she was used to. She tried to pull away from me.

'Anna?' I said. 'Tell me what happened.'

'There was an argument,' she said. 'My father and my grandmother started screaming at each other. It was horrible. They had both been drinking. Then my father . . .'

She hung her head.

'Your father? What happened, Anna, tell me?'

147

'He hit her. He picked up a knife and . . .' She was sobbing, unable to go on.

'He killed her?' I said. She nodded. 'You saw your father kill your grandmother?'

She nodded again.

'You saw it with your own eyes?'

She looked up at me sharply. 'Yes! I saw him kill her. I saw him do it with my own eyes.'

I could not say anything for a minute or more. Eventually I managed: 'Why did you not tell me this before?'

She didn't reply, but dabbed her eyes with a white lace handkerchief. 'I tried to forget it, I tried for so long,' she said. 'But then, once you'd started asking me about Kazan, it all came back to me. It was horrible, so horrible.'

She put her head to my chest and I held her. After a while, when she had recovered herself, we walked on.

She said quietly, 'Am I going to see you again?'

'What do you think?' I said with a smile.

'When?'

'I don't think you should come to my office again. Or here. Your father may be having us watched.'

She thought for a moment. 'I think I know somewhere we can go,' she said with a smile.

We found a taxi. We kissed as she got inside. I waved as the car pulled away.

Imagine yourself a hermit. You emerge from your cave only to discover that during the twenty years of your isolation a huge metropolis has been built on your doorstep. Instead of the loneliness of the mountains you are confronted by the helter-skelter of a great modern city. So it was that morning for me. I was suddenly exposed to the assault that life makes on the senses. Motor cars flew past. Satin horses, with battery lights on the carriages, liveried servants, soldiers in uniform, cavalry officers, civil servants, students, and well-to-do young men walking past well-to-do young women, flirting with them, turning to look at the faces of the objects they fancied from behind. The noise, the colour, the smells of the street. Flurries of wet snow blowing up every now and then and vanishing as quickly as though a tap had been turned off.

I was beginning to see clearly again. And one thing I saw was that Anna was not telling me the truth, or at least not the whole truth. I had worked with patients who had buried traumatic experiences, some for the best part of a long life-time. But none recovered their memories as readily as Anna had.

Seventeen

R eturning to the house, I telephoned Minna to say I would not be in until midday.

'Telephone Rozental to confirm our appointment. He may be reluctant to keep it, in which case, Minna, try to persuade him.'

'I will do my best,' she said, sounding slightly puzzled. 'Mr "Grischuk" called twice this morning already. He wants to see you today.'

Petrov. It was highly unusual for him to ask for an appointment.

'Does he want to come to the office?' I asked, remembering what he had said about the Okhrana.

'No,' Minna said, sounding even more puzzled. 'In fact he was quite vague about where he wanted to meet. He said to tell you he would see you at four o'clock "where the pigs are". He said you would understand.'

'See that I can get away for two o'clock,' I said, 'even if it means moving another patient.'

I had smuggled Anna in and out of the house without Catherine knowing. Lidiya was another matter. She said nothing, but her look was full of disappointment and reproach. I asked her to make some tea, which I took to Catherine in her room. Catherine was coming out of a deep sleep but smiled sweetly when she saw me. Since our release, we had hardly spent more than a few minutes alone together. I sat on the bed and kissed her.

'Good morning,' I said.

She made a contented, sleepy sound. 'You were out late,' she said.

'I was dining with Kopelzon.'

'Did you have a nice time?'

'Very nice,' I said. 'I've brought your tea.'

She sat up and rubbed her eyes while I arranged the pillows behind her. 'What time is it?'

'Almost ten o'clock.'

She sipped her tea, leaned back on the pillows and closed her eyes.

'We are not yet out of danger, Catherine,' I said.

Her eyes moved to meet mine. 'I'm so sorry for the trouble I've caused you.'

I reached for her hand and squeezed it. Catherine never apologised for anything. She embraced me, fierce and tender all at once.

'Tell me about Yastrebov,' I said.

On occasion Blok, Akhmatova, Gumilyov and other famous writers dropped into the Stray Dog and sometimes read, but the club was mainly the resort of students and the *demi-monde* who wanted to bemoan the woes of Russia, discuss symbolism and the approaching apocalypse, listen to poets, get drunk and have sex. One night in February, Catherine noticed a thin young man with sad eyes, high cheekbones, long, wild hair and the brave, anxious look of the young lost. Catherine, always attracted to strays, started talking to him. He was shy, friendly and serious. The atmosphere between them quickly became intimate and, in the way of young people, they were soon exchanging their life histories. Catherine's was true – at least as she recognised it – his only partly so.

151

His name, he told her, was Leon Pikser. He had left his small village beyond the Urals two years before to go to Moscow, driven by a passionate desire to do something meaningful with his life, which for him meant writing poetry. But things did not go as he had hoped: his poems were rejected by every editor he sent them to. He decided to travel to St Petersburg to solicit help from his heroes, Blok and Akhmatova. He had not been able to make contact with them, however, and had soon run out of money and been reduced to the doss-house and soup kitchen.

Catherine, charmed by his romantic idealism, poverty and good looks, proposed temporary solutions to two of his most pressing problems: a friend of hers worked at Leinner's on the Moika Embankment and, she was certain, would be able to find him a job there as a waiter. As for somewhere to stay, she could get the key to an office which, after eight or nine o'clock at night, was always empty.

After leaving the Stray Dog, Catherine smuggled Pikser into my office building through a back door. They made love on the couch and stayed together until dawn. Before they slipped out again early next morning, Catherine took one of my *cartes de visite* so he would be able to find his way again to his provisional sanctuary. They used the office on three or four occasions only and were meticulous about leaving everything exactly as they found it.

'Did you love him?' I asked.

'It wasn't love,' Catherine said after some moments. 'Or maybe to begin with it was. I liked him, but after I'd seen him a few times I started to like him less. When I told him I wouldn't see him any more he started to cry, and that's when he told me about the other things.'

'What other things? You have to tell me, Catherine. This is more important than you know.'

'Leon did write poetry – in fact, he showed me some of his

poems. They weren't very good. But he'd lied when he said he came to St Petersburg to meet Blok and Akhmatova. I think he would have liked to meet them – who wouldn't? – but what had really happened was that in Moscow he'd fallen in with a group of anarchists. He implied they were serious revolutionaries and that he'd learned things from them.'

'What sort of things?' I asked.

She shrugged. 'Practical things of use to the revolutionary, he said, but he never revealed exactly what.'

'Go on.'

'One day, in Moscow, Leon met this man. He was obviously in awe of him. He described him as "the true revolutionary".'

'What did he mean by that?' I asked.

'Someone who didn't waste time with words and arguments – just got on with the job.'

'Did he tell you his name?'

'I'm not sure Leon ever knew his real name.'

'What happened then?'

'This man, this revolutionary, persuaded Leon to come to St Petersburg where, he said, he would arrange for him to be put in touch with other serious comrades. He gave Leon the name and address of someone he could stay with, until the man himself could join him, that is.'

'What was the address, did he tell you?'

'19 Kirochny Street, near the Preobrazhensky Barracks.'

'Did he go to the address?'

'He said it was being watched by police spies, that he was walking into a trap. He asked me to go with him and we posed as a courting couple so as not to attract attention. We strolled past it. I didn't see any police but Leon was convinced they were watching. I don't know if they were – I think he just lost his nerve.'

'What did this mysterious man in Moscow want him to do?'

'Leon just said that it was very important, the most

153

important thing that would ever happen in my lifetime. I didn't know if any of it was true or if he was making the whole thing up, including the house on Kirochny Street, to impress me. By then I was getting a little scared of him. I wanted him to go and leave me alone. I didn't want him in your office any more.'

'Did you ever see him with guns or dynamite?'

'He always carried a big, heavy bag. But I never saw what was inside and assumed it was his clothes and books. I never saw guns or anything like dynamite or chemicals, in the office or anywhere else.'

'Did he ever mention the name Berek Medem?'

Catherine's eyes widened. 'Berek Medem the terrorist? No, never.'

'When did you last see Leon?'

'The day before he was murdered. He was on his way to Leinner's to start his shift. He was very excited. He said he'd had word from the man from Moscow and he was going to meet up with him that night. But I wasn't interested any more. He got upset and started shouting at me. He said, "Soon the whole world will know my name."'

'What do you think he meant by that?'

'I have no idea,' she said.

We sat together for a while, both of us thinking about Leon Pikser and the trouble he had brought into our lives. The question now was how to extricate ourselves.

I drove to Yegorov's. Undressing in the Moorish tent, I smelled Anna's smell all over me. I took a steam bath, then went to float in the pool. After half an hour, feeling somewhat refreshed, I got dressed and went to Café Central. I lit a cigarette and ordered pastries and coffee. The smoke in my nostrils did no more to dislodge the scent of Anna than the steam or the pool. She was in my throat, on my tongue and my fingertips. She was under my nails. I did not want her to go. The heyday was past, but the blood was not yet humble.

I scanned the faces of those around me. If there was an agent among the patrons, I could not pick him out.

I concentrated on two specific variations, two lines. One: co-operate with Lychev. Tell him what Catherine had told me of Pikser/Yastrebov and the house on Kirochny Street. It seemed simple enough. Pass on the information. If I got anything from Rozental, pass that on too. What were the likely consequences for Catherine and me? Would Lychev leave us alone?

The second line: refuse to help Lychev. What would be the consequences? The detective's investigation is taken over by Colonel Gan. There would be another raid, more time in the cells of the Peter and Paul fortress. The interrogation would be more brutal. There was more to hide: my knowledge of Pikser; Semevsky's murder; Gan's involvement with the Gulko assassination.

What line to choose?

I ordered a second cup of coffee and lit another cigarette. For distraction, I went to the newspaper rack and selected *The Orator*. There had been another bomb, this time the Bronze Horsemen was the target. According to the account, the device was small and amateurish; there were no casualties and it had inflicted only superficial damage to the monument of the city's founder. In a separate, prominently displayed item, the German ambassador had complained to the foreign minister about reports that Russia and Great Britain had agreed closer naval ties, something the ambassador could interpret only as an act of hostility towards Berlin. In the newspaper's opinion it was not a question of *if* there would be war but *when*. I folded the paper and pushed it aside.

What line to choose?

155

I checked my watch. It was almost time to go to the office. I finished my coffee and went to the telephone booths in the short corridor leading to the bathrooms. I called police headquarters. Lychev answered at the first ring.

'I will do what you want,' I told him, 'but first you have to do something for me.'

There was silence from the other end. The policeman said, 'I wasn't offering to bargain with you.'

'I want you to find out about something that may have happened in Kazan in 1889.'

'This is beginning to sound a little vague,' he said sarcastically.

'I want to be quite clear about this, Lychev. I've made up my mind. I will co-operate with you only if you help me find out about this episode in Kazan.'

'You are wasting time, Spethmann,' he hissed with angry irritation. 'I need to know Yastrebov's real name and I need to know now.'

'I talked to Catherine,' I said. 'She told me his name.'

Lychev could not conceal his excitement. I imagined him sitting forward at his desk, leaning into the telephone. 'She told you Yastrebov's name?'

'And an address Yastrebov was told to go to on arrival in the city. I'll tell you both when you have something for me from Kazan.'

'Tell me now, damn you,' he said.

I said nothing. The silence continued.

Eventually, he said, 'All right. Kazan – what may have happened there?'

'A murder,' I said.

'Who was the victim?'

'Peter Zinnurov's mother.'

There was a long silence, but even so I could tell he was intrigued. 'And do we know the murderer?'

'Peter Zinnurov.'

Another silence, though briefer. 'Where did you come by this information?'

'If there was a murder,' I said, 'there will be a police report, correct?'

'*If* there was a murder.'

'All you have to do is check the records from Kazan.'

'Have you any idea how difficult that is going to be?'

'That's your problem,' I said.

He muttered an oath. 'When did this murder occur? What date?'

Anna had been very precise. She was thirteen and two months when she made the trip. From her records I knew her birthday to be 16 June. 'August,' I said. 'More than likely during the second half of the month.'

'Meet me at seven o'clock this evening in the St George's Gallery,' he said.

I put down the receiver and walked out to the street. The day was bright and clear.

There were no police at the office building, no detectives asking questions about Semevsky. A uniformed doorman greeted me formally as I entered. Another Okhrana agent, a replacement spy? It was impossible to know. I took the stairs to the third floor.

'Just a minute,' Minna said into the telephone she had been about to put down as I entered, 'he's here now.' Covering the mouthpiece, she said, 'It's Kopelzon.'

I went into my office while Minna put the call through. I thanked him for dinner.

'It was my pleasure,' he said warmly; he was in an expansive mood after his night of revelry.

I did not need to ask but did so anyway, 'Did the night continue enjoyable?'

157

'Very enjoyable,' he said. 'The young lady proved most charming.'

'I can imagine,' I said. 'Did your other friend also enjoy himself?'

'Which one?'

'The one I mistook for Rozental.'

'Ah yes. He was most flattered, though I have to say he was just as surprised as I. Do you really think there's a resemblance? You're the only one.'

'It must have been a trick of the light,' I said. 'He seemed worried about something.'

'No,' Kopelzon replied with a faintly exaggerated airiness. 'He's often like that. Excitable.'

'Have you seen Rozental?' I asked.

'Actually, that's why I called you. I saw him at the hotel. He's definitely over the worst.'

'I seriously doubt that, Reuven,' I said. 'When he left me last night he was highly disturbed.'

'So you said. But I can assure you, Otto, he's fine now.'

'I'm seeing him later today –'

'He doesn't want to continue the treatment,' Kopelzon said quickly. 'Don't feel bad. It's not a comment on your expertise. It's just that he feels perfectly well and, to be honest, he really needs to concentrate on preparing for the tournament.'

'You are jeopardising Rozental's mental well-being,' I said frostily.

'It was his decision, Otto,' Kopelzon replied evenly. 'I had nothing to do with it, but, I have to say, I really didn't think when I brought him to you that you'd dredge up these things from his past. All this stuff about his grandparents – you were making him even worse.'

'What did you think a psychoanalyst would talk to him about?'

'Otto, you just have to accept that some people can't be

helped. As long as Rozental plays and plays well, what does it matter what's going on in that mad head of his?'

'That's precisely the point: I doubt very much whether he will play well. In my view, he should withdraw.'

'No!' Kopelzon snapped. 'I've told you – he's perfectly fine.'

'All so you can boast that a Polish Jew takes coffee with the tsar and tsarina at the Peterhof?'

He breathed out with annoyance. 'You may not think it important, others do.'

A harsh silence followed. Struggling to affect an amiable tone, he eventually said, 'Speaking of chess, you owe me a move.'

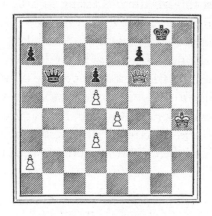

Spethmann–Kopelzon
After 40 . . . Qb6. Should White play 41 e5 in
an attempt to break through Black's defences?

Our games were always competitive but they had never been spiteful. I went to the table and quickly brought the position up to date. Here I would take my anger out on Kopelzon. An aggressive move, something to tear open his position and demolish his defences at a stroke. 41 e5 was the

159

move. This would be his punishment. I stretched out my hand to take the pawn forward one square.

But then I saw his reply – 41 . . . Qd4+. After the king moved, say to h5, he would play 42 . . . Qxd3, and if then 43 exd6 he would play 43 . . . Qe2+ and my king would hardly be able to escape perpetual check. My move wouldn't work.

'Come on, Otto. What's keeping you? Are you losing your nerve?'

I had to find something else. But what?

'Otto? I'm getting this feeling you know you can't win.'

'41 Kh5,' I said.

The pause that followed suggested he had expected me to make the pawn move. After a moment he said, '41 . . . Kf8.' He sounded as though he was trying to hide his disappointment.

Again I thought about playing e5. Much later, long after our game had concluded, I analysed this line. It turned out it would have brought me victory but at the time I did not trust myself. So I played 42 Kh6, confident that the queen check at e3 would bring Black no advantage. Now it was my opponent who asked for time to consider his next move.

We tried to end the call on a friendly note but it was a strain, for both of us.

Eighteen

Shortly after three o'clock I left the office by the back entrance, avoiding the new doorman. Once among the crowds on the Nevsky, I started west. As far as I could tell I was not being followed. I continued past the Stroganov Palace and almost as far as Admiralty Prospect. I ducked into an alley and concealed myself in a doorway for some ten minutes. Judging the coast to be clear, I emerged and once more set off, this time taking side streets and alleys to the Moika Canal. Near the Yusupov Palace I found a taxi. I got to the Hay Market a little after four. It was quiet. A few peasants were selling leftover vegetables from their carts and some drunken horse-dealers were arguing over their animals. I entered the covered market, passing a swineherd with his squealing piglets, and made my way to the stall where I had last seen Gregory Petrov. It was meatless and, apart from the butcher who was clearing up at the end of his day, deserted.

'I'm looking for Grischuk,' I said to the butcher.

His look was dully belligerent. 'I don't know any Grischuk,' he said.

'I am Otto Spethmann,' I said.

The butcher cast a lazy look around, continued with his sweeping for a moment or two, then said, 'Wait here.'

He returned a minute later. 'Were you followed?'

'No,' I said.

'You're sure?'

'I'm sure.'

After another quick glance to confirm that I was alone, he beckoned me forward and led me to a storeroom. Inside, on a simple wooden chair, sat my patient. He was more exhausted than I had ever seen him. His eyes were small and red, his cheeks sunken, his skin grey. The starched collar of his shirt was limp and rimmed with dirt. His suit, usually so immaculate, was crumpled and stained. There was about him a faintly faecal odour.

'I hope I haven't put you out, Spethmann, dragging you all the way over here,' he said when the butcher was gone. 'But I had to talk to someone.' He uttered these last words as though admitting something shameful.

'You haven't put me out at all,' I said. 'What can I do for you?'

He buried his head in his hands and mumbled, 'Is everything all right with you? You haven't had any more trouble with Lychev and the police?'

'Thank you for asking,' I said, 'but we're here to talk about you. Has something happened?'

'You mean, has something worse than usual happened? Is my life even more hellish?' He looked up at me blearily. 'You can't tell anyone about any of this.'

'Of course not.'

He had said he needed to talk to someone, but that did not mean he got straight to the point. Instead he treated me to a polemic on the growing anger of the workers in the factories and naval yards, and the crisis with Berlin. He talked about his stomach, which he feared was getting flabby, and his children's pet cat which had gone missing. His wife's mother was in poor health. I listened without interrupting him or seeking to lead him. He would get to where he needed to arrive when he was ready.

He took out a silver cigarette box. I declined his offer of a

162

cigarette. He lit one, drawing the smoke deeply into his lungs, and ran a hand through his uncombed hair.

'Have you ever heard of a man named Sverdlov?' he asked.

'I read something in the newspapers – wasn't he arrested recently?'

'Yes,' he said, swallowing more smoke. 'An important comrade. He had been sentenced to ten years' exile but he escaped in January. He made his way across Russia and arrived in St Petersburg a week ago. I found him somewhere to stay in the apartment of a friend, someone not connected with the Party and in whom the police have no interest. He was going to rest for a few days before continuing to Krakow to join Lenin.'

He stubbed out the cigarette and lit another. He pinched a stained trouser leg from his thigh as though it were unpleasantly damp. Perhaps it was.

'Somehow the police found out where Sverdlov was hiding,' he continued. 'They raided the apartment and arrested him. He's on his way back to Siberia. It was King – the spy. He's betrayed us yet again.'

Petrov scratched at his unshaven chin and neck and tore at the stud in his collar as though he were being choked. Loosening his tie, he threw his head back and gazed at the ceiling.

'I don't know if I can keep going,' he said.

'Because of the constant risk of betrayal?'

'Because of everything.' His hand trembled as he brought the cigarette again to his lips. 'The Party leadership has ordered an investigation. They want to know how and why Sverdlov was arrested,' he said slowly. 'Only three other people knew where I had hidden Sverdlov. They will be interrogated by the Party's security department. Believe me, you do not want to cross those people. By comparison, the Okhrana are gentlemen.'

'Are you saying you are one of those under suspicion?'

'I was one of those who knew where Sverdlov was hiding. I have to be investigated. But if I'm the traitor then the Party might as well give up now. I'm Lenin's deputy in Russia. I'm the leader of the Bolshevik delegation in the Duma.' He shook his head at the absurdity of it all, then sighed with exhaustion. 'Anyway, it seems the Party's security department have their man.' He looked at me with rheumy eyes. 'A friend of mine, a good friend – Delyanov. No one suspected him. He's a bit of a plodder but he was a good comrade. The Party was all he lived for, or so he led us to believe.'

'What will happen to Delyanov?'

'He's still denying everything but there seems little doubt. And when the case against him is proved . . .'

He blew a smoke ring and let the conclusion of his sentence hang in the air with it.

'Are you saying he will be murdered?'

Petrov threw me an aggressive glance. 'Have you ever done anything, Spethmann, of which you were deeply ashamed?'

'Yes.'

'I mean, utterly, profoundly ashamed? Ashamed to the depths of your soul?'

'Yes.'

'How did you live with yourself afterwards?'

'There is always guilt. But we can resolve to avoid repeating the act that gave rise to the shame.'

'It's that easy?'

'On the contrary.'

He ran his hand over his moustache and mouth. 'What if you cannot avoid repeating the act?'

'Are you saying we are without choice?'

'We go around in chains – chains of debt, of need, responsibility, dreams. All of us. Choice is only ever a chimera.'

164

'Are you talking about your complicity in Delyanov's murder, when he is killed?'

'I haven't said I will be complicit in anything,' he snapped as if I were a policeman or a journalist trying to trap him into a damaging admission. He eyed me knowingly. 'You were an adulterer, weren't you, Spethmann? That's your guilty little secret, the deed of which you are so ashamed, isn't it?'

'I have not come here to discuss my deeds or my shame.'

'Do you think I am remotely interested in discussing them?' he said with a dismissive wave of the hand. 'Your boring, petty deeds? I'm talking about real shame, the enormity of which you cannot imagine.'

'I think I can imagine what complicity in murder means.'

'Stop calling it that!'

'Why do you object to the word?'

'It's not what I'm talking about now.'

'What are you talking about?'

He stubbed out the cigarette and lifted his gaze again to the ceiling. Tears welled up in his eyes and were soon streaming down his broad face.

'Why can you not tell me?' I said.

He shook his head and began to sob. His whole body was soon convulsed. 'Help me, Spethmann, help me,' he cried. 'I can't go on like this.'

I stretched out my hand and put it on his shoulder. His coat gave a false impression of bulkiness for all I felt was skin and bone. Inconsolable, he wept like a child. At one point, he clutched my hand and held it fast, lowering his head to it; hot tears ran over my fingers. I could do nothing but wait for his sobs to subside.

'I want nothing more than to help you, Gregory,' I said when the worst was over, 'but I can do nothing until you are honest with me.'

He wiped his eyes roughly with the palms of his hands. 'I

165

want to be honest. Believe me, Spethmann, that's exactly what I want.'

'Perhaps the thing of which you are ashamed is not as despicable as you think.'

'Oh, it is. It is every bit as despicable.'

He stood up.

'Are you going?' I said.

'I have a meeting.'

'Please, a moment longer. Tell me more about this shame you feel.'

Tears sprang again into his eyes but this time he succeeded in getting himself under control.

'I've said too much already.'

'Where is Delyanov now?' I asked.

'At home.'

'Aren't you afraid he will go to the police?'

'He's so ashamed of what he's done he will wait at home until the time comes.'

'The time for his own murder?' I said.

Petrov made no answer but went to a small, cloudy mirror which hung from a nail on the wooden planks. He scrutinised his features with the despairing objectivity of an ageing actor.

'I would like to change this face,' he said. 'I can't bear to see it any more.'

'There are many who admire you, Gregory Vasilyevich,' I said, 'for all your self-loathing. Try to remember that.'

'My God,' he said, summoning a grin, 'I haven't turned you into a Bolshevik, have I, Spethmann?'

'After what you have just told me about Delyanov?' I said. 'No.'

'When the stakes are so high,' he said, taking his hat and coat and going to the door, 'such things are unavoidable.'

'What happened to your brother?' I asked as he was about to leave.

'Which brother?'

'The one who was arrested with you – Ivan.'

'Oh that?' he said, attempting to laugh it off. 'I made that story up. I'm surprised you took it seriously.'

'I don't believe you.'

'Thank you,' he said. 'Just talking like this – believe it or not, it helps.'

'If I doubted that I would close my office tonight and find a new profession.'

I took the direct route back to my office along Sadovaya Street and was there in fifteen minutes. Minna made me some tea and I went to the window and stared out to the street. When Catherine was ten I met a woman. She was unmarried, pretty, lively and flirtatious. On social occasions, she always sought out my company. One day I asked her to go for a walk on the French Embankment. In the Tavricheski Gardens I kissed her. We met again the following day. There were more kisses.

And then there was shame.

'I don't understand,' she said when we bumped into each other at a party some weeks later. 'When you asked to see me – why did you do that? Be honest with me. Why did you ask to see me?'

'I cannot continue with this,' I said.

'Then you are not being honest – to me, or to yourself.'

'I do not dispute you.'

'You pull and you push. Is that a trick you use when you want to ensnare a woman? You pull her to you and, just when she thinks she is close, you push her away again.'

'That was not my intention.'

'Wasn't it?'

'I assure you.'

She fixed me with a look. 'I am going to ask you something now and I want you to be completely honest in your reply.'

She paused, waiting if not for my assent then at least for a confirmatory silence. 'Imagine a dacha. It is in the forest, far from the city. No one will see you arrive, no one will see you leave. You come to the door and it is open. You go inside. The dacha is not large but there is a fire to keep you warm and there is good, simple food to eat. You become sleepy. You undress and go to bed. The bed is big and comfortable, the linen is fresh. There is a telephone beside the bed. It starts to ring. You hear a voice at the other end of the line. Are you following this?'

'Yes,' I said.

'It is my voice,' she said. 'I tell you that I am free of all engagements and can come to the dacha. This is my question to you: Do you want me to come to you in your dacha?'

'To my dacha in the forest?'

'Do you want me to come to you – yes or no?'

'There is no such place.'

'There is,' she said.

'We can all have dreams,' I said. 'We can imagine ourselves alone in the forest. But there is a reality in which we must live. I am a husband and a father.'

'The dacha in the forest exists –'

'It does not.'

'– if you want it to, and since you seem unable to find your way I shall have to help you to it.'

I went to the dacha. I should have known better, for there was no such place. However much we dream, there is always a reality.

I telephoned Kopelzon at home.

'Are you resigning?' I said.

'Don't be conceited, Otto. And be very careful you don't fall flat on your face,' he said. 'You still have a long way to go: 42 . . . Ke8.'

168

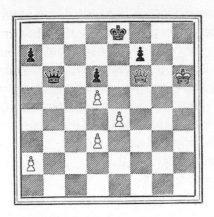

Spethmann–Kopelzon

After 42 . . . Ke8. Spethmann is clearly better but to win
he needs to capture the pawn at f7. How can he do this?

I played 43 Kh7.

'You're going after my f-pawn, aren't you? You can attack
with two pieces, I can defend with two pieces. You won't win
it. And if you can't win it, your extra pawn means nothing.
You won't win the game.'

'Are you going to move?' I said. 'Or do you need more time
to think?'

He played, as I had expected, 43 . . . Qc5. I responded with
44 Qg7.

'I'll give you my reply at the opening ceremony,' he said.

'Reuven,' I said before he put down the telephone.

'Yes?'

'I just wanted to say how much I value your friendship. I
would hate to think something has come between us.'

'Despite the boorishness you have displayed during this
game,' Kopelzon said with a laugh, 'I send you a thousand
kisses.'

I went to the outer office where Minna was getting ready to

go home. As she pulled on her coat, I saw a red-brown bruise on the left side of her neck which her high collar could not quite conceal. A love bite? I saw too that she was not wearing one of her usual, rather shapeless, blouses but something altogether more fashionable and expensive, and very flattering to her figure. Her hair was still pinned back, but she had allowed golden ringlets to fall by her ears.

'You look different,' I said.

'Oh?' she said, a little warily.

'Is that a new blouse?'

She pulled the coat to. 'I've had it a while,' she said.

'It's very nice.'

'Thank you.'

'A present?'

Her cheeks flushed. 'No,' she said, 'I bought it myself.'

Turning from me, she did up her coat buttons. I glimpsed again the bruise on her neck. Seeing that I was still looking at her, she smiled awkwardly.

'Well, it's very nice,' I said. 'Goodnight.'

'Goodnight.'

As I was leaving the building, the new doorman handed me an envelope. Usually messages were delivered directly to my office and, suspicious of the man, I asked why he had kept it.

'The messenger was very insistent it be held here for his honour,' he said.

'Where is Semevsky?' I said, taking the envelope.

'He did not report for work this morning.'

The note was in Anna's hand. It gave an address on Bolshoy Prospect and a telephone number. I slipped it into my pocket, stepped out to the street and made for the Neva Quays.

An ice-breaker was coming in to harbour, passing a French warship under way for Kronstadt. I pulled up my collar against the wind coming off the river and walked the length of the huge gallery looking for Lychev.

'Keep walking,' he said, materialising out of nowhere and falling into step beside me. 'You said you have Yastrebov's real name?'

'Did you find out anything about Kazan?'

'Yes,' he said. 'You go first.'

I hesitated; even after calculating the variations several moves deep, the chess player always reviews the position one last time before committing himself to the actual move. Was I doing the right thing? I could see no alternative.

'Yastrebov's real name was Leon Pikser.'

'So Catherine knew all the time,' he said, 'and she didn't reveal it, even in prison.' He sounded more impressed than angry. 'Pikser,' he repeated. 'Where was he from?'

'Somewhere beyond the Urals – Catherine doesn't know exactly. He moved to Moscow to write poetry. While he was there he met a man who persuaded him to come to St Petersburg – to do something very important, so the man told him. Yastrebov didn't say who the man was, nor did he say what they were going to do.'

'It has to be Berek Medem,' Lychev said.

I laughed. 'So you're another of these people who sees Berek Medem everywhere?'

Lychev ignored this. 'What else did Catherine tell you?'

'Yastrebov was supposed to go to a contact. But he got cold feet and never went.'

'You said you had an address?'

I had made my move; there was nothing for it but to follow through. '19 Kirochny Street,' I said.

Lychev fell silent as he thought things through, then said, 'How is Rozental?'

'He cancelled his appointment.'

'You like Rozental, don't you?'

171

'Yes, I do,' I said. 'Away from the chessboard, he's an innocent. He doesn't understand the world he lives in. I can't help feeling that he is always in danger of being harmed by it.'

'If I were you I would keep a friendly eye on him,' Lychev said. 'The world Rozental inhabits is more dangerous than he knows.'

'What did you find out about Kazan?' I said.

'I telegraphed my colleagues in Kazan, asking them to check their files for a murder committed in August 1889. A detective responded this afternoon.'

'That was quick.'

'My name has a certain cachet,' he said bluntly, 'in certain quarters. There were five murders that month. Four victims were male. Two were killed during drunken arguments. Their killers – family members or friends in both cases – were apprehended and convicted. The third was a railway clerk strangled by his father, who then committed suicide. The fourth victim was an intruder who broke into a house during the night, presumably with robbery in mind. He attacked the occupants, seriously wounding two of them, before he was himself overpowered and killed. A rather curious case.'

'How so?'

'The intruder was never identified and the house he broke into was apparently quite humble. If robbery was the motive, he should have been quite desperate. And yet he was, according to the police report, well dressed and had in his pocket a first-class railway ticket for Moscow. Curious, as I say, but nothing to do with your supposed murder.'

'And the fifth victim – the woman?'

'A female, yes,' Lychev said, 'but her name was not Zinnurov.'

'That means nothing. No one knows if Zinnurov is the Mountain's real name.'

'Of course. But the victim was aged forty-four.'

172

Too young to be Zinnurov's mother at the time of Anna's visit.

Lychev stared at me with pale eyes. 'Whoever told you Zinnurov murdered his mother was having you on.'

I suspected he knew only too well the source of my information and was trying to provoke me. I struggled to fight them down but I could not prevent doubts about Anna surfacing again. She had been so certain: *I saw him kill her. I saw him do it with my own eyes.*

We walked on in silence, each digesting the information he had received. Lychev was by far the more satisfied.

At length he said, 'I hope you have your alibi ready.'

'Do you think I will be questioned?'

'About Semevsky? You will certainly be questioned. Do you think when one of Gan's agents disappears the colonel simply shrugs and hires someone else?'

'Who are you, Lychev?'

'My name is Mintimer Sergeyevich Lychev and I am a detective of the St Petersburg police.'

'Police detectives do not murder agents of the Okhrana. You and Colonel Gan are on the same side. You uphold law and order.'

Lychev sniffed, took off his hat, swept his fringe back and patted his hair before carefully replacing his hat. 'I like to think I uphold law and order, and I also like to think I am a servant of justice.' He threw me a sideways glance. 'You think that sounds pompous?'

'It sounds ridiculous and hypocritical after what I saw you do last night.'

'I am disappointed, Dr Spethmann. If I may say so, you are making a very superficial judgement. Surely such a respected psychoanalyst would understand that what lies on the surface is never the full story.'

'I saw you kill an Okhrana agent,' I said deliberately.

173

'And in your view that renders my claim to be a servant of justice invalid?'

'Unless murder and justice are now compatible.'

He smiled as at an inward joke. 'Colonel Gan planned and ordered Gulko's murder. Don't you think justice dictates he be brought to account?'

'Policemen are usually aware of the value of a blind eye, particularly when it involves the misdeeds of the powerful.'

'I commit murder while Gan commits "misdeeds"?'

'That's not what I'm saying.'

Lychev stared out at the ships on the water. 'In the twenty years he has run the Okhrana,' he began, 'Gan has ordered more murders than you can possibly imagine – politicians he thought dangerous, trade unionists, teachers, doctors, journalists, even policemen who took an undue interest in his affairs. You'd have to gouge out both eyes not to see what was in front of you.'

'So you are determined to take on one of the most powerful men in the empire?'

'Exactly.'

'Why?'

'I think I have already answered that.'

'I forgot: you are a servant of justice.'

Lychev laughed thinly. 'I admit it does sound pompous.'

'You can't win,' I said. 'You can't beat Gan.'

Lychev shrugged. 'Gan is powerful, as you say, but he has enemies in the government and at court, especially among the pro-French faction. If I can produce evidence that he was behind Gulko's murder, Gan will fall.'

'Only if Gulko was innocent.'

'There are many good reasons to kill journalists,' he said with a sly, sideways look, 'but Gulko's only crime was to discover something Gan did not want made public.'

He stopped and put his hand out. I took it, but not just out

174

of politeness. He touched a finger to

'Please give my compliments to your cha.

I watched the strange little man as he made

way we had come. His footsteps were delicate

stride short. It was odd, but I found myself be

respect him.

Nineteen

The apartment on Bolshoy Prospect belonged to a friend of Anna's who had gone to the Caucasus to be with her husband, an artillery officer. The living room was spacious enough but rather overstuffed with heavy furniture. Deep reds and blues dominated in the velvet drapes, the ottoman rugs and wall-hangings; an entire wall was covered in a mosaic of gilt-framed photographs. Altogether there was an almost suffocating sensation of constriction.

The same was true of the bedroom, but here constriction was welcome. I took Anna's right nipple between my lips and licked it with my tongue. We had already made love and she was lying on her back. I widened my mouth and brought my fingers up between her legs. Her head was all the way back, her chin pointing almost at the ceiling. She cupped her left breast with her hand, the thumb running back and forth over the nipple. I sucked more of her breast into my mouth.

'Slowly,' she said.

She lay with her head in my lap. I wanted nothing more than to stay under the spell of intimacy and contentment our love-making had cast. What did it matter what happened in Kazan all those years ago? What if Zinnurov had killed his mother? I was no detective, I was no servant of justice. Some secrets, Zinnurov had said, were better left undisturbed, and I was afraid that in disturbing this one I would be doing more than

176

going over dangerous ground. I was afraid of what I might find out about the woman I had fallen in love with.

'Are you sure you were thirteen when you went to Kazan with your father?'

I felt her stiffen.

'Anna?'

'Yes, I'm sure,' she said. 'Why are we talking about this?'

Because, although I was afraid, I had to know the truth.

'I told Lychev.'

She sat up suddenly. She stared at me. 'You did *what*?'

'I told him there was a murder of an elderly woman in Kazan in August 1889. I did not tell him how I found out. I did not mention your name.'

'Lychev? But he's the man who's been persecuting you!'

'He's not entirely what he seems,' I said.

'What's that supposed to mean?' she shot back, incredulous.

I could have said it meant that I saw him kill a man. What I did say was 'I know it sounds ridiculous but I think he can be trusted, in some things.'

'But why did you tell him about Kazan?'

'Because if you are to get well we have to get to the bottom of what happened there.'

'I am well,' she said. 'I'm better now, really. Much, much better.'

'Anna, no one recovers from a trauma like the one you witnessed just like that.'

'You're making too much of it.'

'I'm making too much of a murder?'

My tone was scolding and sarcastic. I had slipped. I was not the good father now. She responded by turning away and refusing to talk.

'Anna, please. Trust me. I know the pain it causes you to talk about this, but for your own sake – for our sake – we must.'

She turned to me. Her face was ugly with anger. 'I made it up,' she said brutally. 'I made it all up. Everything. Saying goodbye to my mother at the station, the cavalry officer on the train, the people staring at us as if we were a married couple. None of it happened. I made it all up.'

'Why would you do that?'

'It was a dream I had, a fantasy. My father ignored me as a child. I wanted nothing except to be with him and for him to take notice of me, but he was always too busy. He never had time. And so I used to imagine us on a long trip together, alone, without my mother, so I could be with him. I used to imagine it when I went to bed at night, going over the same thing night after night, embellishing the details, until the journey was so real I began to think it had actually happened.'

'Why would you imagine he had killed your grandmother?'

'To punish him,' she said. 'To punish him for ignoring me.'

Psychoanalysts usually interpret dreams as disguised forms of wish fulfilment but with Anna I had proceeded as if the dream were the literal truth, not a secret code, and that she had been dreaming real events as they had really occurred. Perhaps in this I had been in serious error. Perhaps I should have followed known theory.

'You made it all up?'

'Yes,' she said defiantly. Then she said, 'Do you believe me?'

I looked into her eyes. They were fierce with challenge, pride and anger.

'Yes,' I said. She looked back at me, unflinching. 'I believe you,' I said.

She lay down. I drew the sheet over her shoulders. She turned on her side, her back to me, her knees drawn up, a carapace against me. I turned the Tiffany lamps off and in the darkness fell profoundly asleep.

*   *   *

She wasn't in the bed. I sat up. It was still dark.

'Did you hear that, Papa?' I heard her whisper from somewhere in the room.

I reached over and turned on the lamp. She was by the window, naked, crouching by the drapes. Her voice was strange and remote.

'Someone's calling my name, Papa. Listen.'

There was, of course, nothing. I got up and led her back to bed. I checked her expression: it was vague and frozen. Her eyes were open but unblinking; if she saw anything it was not her present surroundings.

'I'm thirsty,' she said.

'Why don't you go to the kitchen and get some water?'

'They're talking.'

'Who's talking?'

'Babushka and Papa.'

'They won't mind. Are you still thirsty? Shall we go to the kitchen?'

'They're shouting.'

'Are they having an argument?' She did not say anything. 'What are they arguing about? Can you hear them?'

'Make them stop, please!' she cried. 'Make them stop!'

I put my arms around her. She was stiff, resisting in a way that reminded me of Catherine as a child, all knees and elbows and torque, but eventually she became still. She blinked and looked about, determining where she was.

'Have I been dreaming?' she said. 'I think I heard voices.'

'There's no one here,' I said. 'Just us.'

'I was in my grandmother's house,' she said, sounding amazed and apprehensive.

'Tell me about it,' I said, guiding her head to the pillow and pulling up the covers.

Anna's account was confused and incomplete, and it took

179

the rest of the night and much of the following morning to piece together the story of what had happened that night in Kazan. Even then there were gaps. Even then I could not be sure if it was true. Was she making it up? Was it the fantasy with which she had consoled herself as a child? I had no idea. I don't think Anna did either.

In Anna's story, she and her father arrived at the railway station, tired after the long journey from St Petersburg to Moscow and on to Kazan. At her grandmother's house, on the northern outskirts of the city, Anna remembered being greeted by her grandmother with kisses and hugs. Between mother and son, the atmosphere was affectionate though restrained, as if the old woman was afraid of doing or saying the wrong thing around the only child she had brought into the world.

She recalled a small garden at the back of the little wooden house. There were vegetables and hens. She remembered her father setting out a table. They had supper as the sun went down. The adults drank some vodka and Anna pleaded to be allowed to try it. Her father gave in and poured her a glass. She listened to her father and grandmother talk about things from the past. She could remember no details but she did remember being fascinated, for at home her father never talked of his childhood and all of this was strange and thrilling.

Menstruating for the first time, Anna felt bloated and barely ate. The vodka did not help. She went to bed early. It was stiflingly hot, even with the window open. Her father sat on the edge of the narrow bed and tucked her in. He told her this used to be his bed. She claimed she smelled his smell on the sheets. He was a handsome man in his prime.

She fell asleep as soon as he'd gone but woke with a desperate thirst. She could hear voices from the kitchen. Her grandmother and father were still up.

She went to the door, but just as she put her hand to the latch she heard a crash, as though a door had been broken open. It was followed by shouting. She did not move, not wanting to interrupt the argument between her father and grandmother. But she was terribly thirsty. She put her hand again to the latch.

At that very moment she heard a bang. She did not understand what was going on. There was a second explosion. Someone screamed. She heard banging and clattering, like pots and pans falling to the floor. The wooden walls shuddered. And then there was silence.

Anna could not bring herself to raise the latch. It was still dark. Morning seemed a long way off.

She forced herself to open the door. It swung inwards on crude, creaking hinges. Squinting into the darkness, she could just make out the sack of corn stored at the top of the stairs. She inched forward, crouching as she went under the low roof. The heat was even worse and sweat poured down her face. She called for her father but he did not come. She descended the narrow staircase that led to a storeroom, off which was the kitchen. For a long time she was unable to bring herself to open the door.

She remembered it was so dark she had to put a hand to the wall for a guide. She had gone only a step or two when she stumbled and fell over something. Somewhere in the darkness someone was breathing roughly. Then there was a sharp exhalation – like the air released from a balloon – and then silence. Her hands felt sticky and wet where she had touched the floor. So was the side of her leg. She found a lamp and somehow managed to light the wick.

The first thing she saw was the blood on her hands. Then she saw the blood on the wall in front of her. There were thick, uneven smeared trails on the floor.

She was suddenly grabbed by her ankle. Looking down she

saw a long, thin figure stretching out his hand and looking up imploringly at her. Blood flowed from a deep wound in his left cheek where there was a flap of skin turned back like a sheet, exposing bone and tissue.

Slowly, her senses disordered and chaotic, Anna looked around the room.

Her grandmother lay on the floor by the back door in a heap, like a coat shrugged from the shoulders. A second man lay face down and partially across her. The clothing on his back was in ribbons and the skin beneath was raw and bloody.

The man at her feet tried to speak but only gurgled and choked. The last thing Anna remembered was asking him what he had done with her father.

We sat at the breakfast table. I made tea for Anna. She sipped it periodically, but I could not persuade her to eat anything.

'Is there anything else you can remember?' I said.

She looked past me for some moments, then shook her head.

'When did you see your father again?'

'I remember a hospital. He was lying in bed. But I don't know if it was St Petersburg or Kazan or Moscow.'

I poured tea for myself and drank it.

'Why did you tell me that your father killed your grandmother?'

'I was angry,' she said. She looked worn down and contrite. 'I think I have always blamed him for what happened to my grandmother.' She reached for my hand. 'You don't believe me,' she said. 'I can tell from your face.'

Thirteen-year-old Anna had tried to wipe the trauma from her memory, and she had succeeded. But only for a time. Trauma cannot be held at bay indefinitely or completely. Dreams may be disguised and censored but they cannot be banished. The body also responds, in Anna's case with head-

182

aches and, especially, numbness: numbness in the same hand that opened the door to reveal the slaughter in her grandmother's kitchen in August 1889. This was one reading of the story she had told me. It was the reading I wanted to believe.

'According to the police records in Kazan there were five murders in August 1889. None of them involved an elderly female victim.'

She leaned her head against my shoulder. We were both very tired. 'I'm telling you the truth,' she whispered. 'Why would I make it up?'

'I believe you,' I said.

'What are we going to do?' she said softly.

'I don't know.'

'Does Catherine know you have been seeing me?'

'I think she has probably guessed,' I said.

'She hasn't said anything?'

'No,' I said.

'Have you said anything?'

'No.'

'Why not?'

'She wouldn't be interested,' I lied.

'I think she would be very interested.'

'I didn't say anything because after Elena died she was insecure and unhappy. She's much better now.'

'Then you could tell her,' she said, raising her head from my shoulder. She took my hand and kissed it. 'If she's better now, you could tell her.'

'Why do you want me to tell her?'

'It will make us closer. I want to be close to you. I want to be with you, always.'

'Are you going to tell your husband?'

She let go of my hand.

'Why are you being horrible?'

'Let's talk about this later,' I said.

183

I got up and went to the telephone. I called Minna and said I would be in late, again, and asked her to shuffle the appointments as best she could.

'Did you get hold of Rozental?' I said.

'I telephoned him at the Astoria three times,' she said, 'but he didn't answer.'

'Try again,' I said. 'I'm worried about him.'

I went back to Anna. 'You're punishing me,' she said.

'I'm not.'

'It feels like it. You think I'm making up the whole story about my father and you're punishing me for it.'

'I have to go,' I said.

'Will you come to me tonight?'

'I have to go to Saburov's house for the opening ceremony. Rozental will be there and I have to see him.'

'Will you come when it's over?'

'It will be late,' I said.

She gave me a key to the apartment and we kissed briefly. It was almost midday by the time I left.

Twenty

I crossed to the left bank over Nicholas Bridge and stopped in at the Architects' Club to use the telephone. Lychev answered at the first ring.

'I'm looking at young Leon Pikser as we speak,' he said. I heard a sound like a pencil tapping on glass and thought of the jar Lychev had brought to my office. 'I don't think he was anything like as handsome as Catherine says, do you?'

'He wasn't at his best when I saw him,' I said.

'Was Catherine in love with him?' he said. 'I mean, really in love?'

'What does that mean?' I asked.

'Good question,' he said with a thin laugh. He went on, 'Pikser published some of his own poems in Moscow. They suggest he believed indulgence in vodka and sex was an act of political rebellion. His other theme appears to be that art's first duty is to reflect the great issues confronting society. There's a poem called *Manifesto for the Soul* – an aesthetic disaster, of course, but he takes his argument a step further: writers not only have a responsibility to speak out, they must participate. It's all very tedious and juvenile.'

'Is this the sum of what you have learned about Pikser?'

'Not at all,' he said, unperturbed. 'Some very interesting people have been going in and out of the house on Kirochny Street.'

'Anyone I know?'

'As a matter of fact, yes. Your friend Kopelzon.'

I leaned back against the booth. 'Kopelzon?'

'Yes.'

'What was he doing there?'

I turned around in the booth and looked out over the lobby, trying to gather my thoughts. A man dressed in a dark-blue suit and wearing an old-fashioned Russian collar took a seat in one of the armchairs. He unfolded a newspaper and began to read. I turned away again.

'I'm not in a position to answer that yet,' Lychev said. 'But it is intriguing, don't you think? It proves a link between Pikser and Kopelzon.'

'Pikser never went to the house on Kirochny Street.'

'The link is not negated. That they both knew of the house demonstrates the connection.'

'Are you sure?'

'I have men watching the house from an apartment across the street. Kopelzon arrived this morning, stayed an hour, then left. Shortly afterwards a second man came out. I had him followed, but all he did was buy bread and cigarettes before returning to the house.'

'Do you know who he is?'

'No.'

'What did he look like?'

'Average height, rather sturdy, short dark hair, moustache, about thirty-five years. Average in just about every way. Why do you ask? Do you know him?'

I thought immediately of the anxious Pole who came to A l'Ours to find Kopelzon.

'No,' I said.

'I strongly advise you to stay away from Kopelzon, at least for the next few days. Goodbye.'

'Wait!' I said before he ended the call. 'Is it possible that the police records from Kazan are incomplete?'

'Incomplete in what sense?'

'Could they have missed out, for whatever reason, the murder of an elderly woman?'

'Theoretically anything is possible. Policemen are human, after all. They make mistakes. Files are put away in the wrong place. Names are forgotten. Why?'

'The fourth male victim, the intruder killed while breaking into the house.'

'What about him?'

'Is it possible an old woman was killed, or perhaps seriously injured, during the break-in?'

'Do you have reason to think there is more to this incident than the report suggests?'

'I have information about a very similar event which occurred in Kazan, also in August 1889. It seems too much of a coincidence.'

'I'll look into it,' Lychev said.

Turning again to look out to the lobby, I saw the man in the blue suit still in the chair. He was making very little effort to pretend he was reading the newspaper.

'I think I'm being followed,' I said.

'Where are you?'

'At the Architects' Club. There's a man in the lobby. I'm certain he's watching me.'

'Do you have your alibi ready?'

'I don't want anyone to have to lie for me.'

Lychev let out a grunt of irritation. 'I advise you to come up with something fast. Keep it simple and stick as closely to the truth as you can,' he said, ending the call.

I stepped out of the booth and crossed the lobby to the main door. The man in the blue suit folded his newspaper, got up and followed me out. He rode the same tram to Sadovaya Street and got off at the same stop. Only when I turned left to go to my office did our paths diverge.

*   *   *

Opening the door, I saw Minna at her desk. She was wearing a new lilac-coloured blouse with a bow. I was about to say good morning when she indicated two men sitting on the bench to the side, where my patients sometimes waited.

'These men wish to speak to you, Doctor,' Minna said, fidgeting with her collar.

I knew exactly who they were but had to go through with the performance. 'Yes?' I said. 'How can I help you?'

'We have some questions for you, Dr Spethmann,' the taller of the two replied. 'About the doorman – Semevsky.'

'Semevsky? I don't understand,' I said.

The taller man's smile intended no warmth. He said, 'Semevsky's body was pulled out of the canal yesterday.'

'How terrible,' I said. 'You must be police officers?'

'Similar,' the taller man said, his smile fading.

I offered them tea, which they declined, and showed them into my office. As I went to my desk, the taller man said, 'Do you have a certificate of political reliability, Dr Spethmann?'

'My political reliability has never been in question,' I said.

'It is now,' the taller man's colleague said, removing his overcoat and folding it over his lap.

I said nothing.

'When did you last see Semevsky?' the taller man said.

'I saw him' – I had to be careful not to overact – 'let's see. It wasn't yesterday . . . The day before. Yes, that's right. My car suffered a minor accident as I was coming into work and he very kindly offered to have it mended.'

'What time was that?'

'In the morning – I can't remember exactly.'

'You are certain that was the last time you saw Semevsky?'

'Yes. He brought the keys up after the car was fixed and gave them to my secretary, but I was with a patient and didn't speak to him then.'

The two men exchanged a look. The slighter man took over. 'What time did you leave the office?'

I went to my desk and made a show of checking my diary to refresh my memory. I saw Rozental's name entered for the seven o'clock appointment. 'I had a patient at seven,' I said. 'Usually I see patients for an hour but I remember this session being more difficult. It ran over by another thirty or forty minutes.'

'What did you do then?'

Again, with carefully measured hesitation, as though trying to recollect the ordinary, I said, 'I had a dinner appointment at ten o'clock. At A l'Ours, with a friend. There was no point in going home first. So I stayed here and made up my notes.'

'What time did you leave to go to the restaurant?'

'Around ten o'clock.'

'Did anyone see you leave?'

'I don't know what other people saw.'

'Did you see Semevsky?'

I paused. 'No,' I said, 'now I come to think of it, he didn't let me out.'

The two men exchanged a glance.

'How did you get to the Donon?'

'It was A l'Ours.'

'How did you get there?'

'I walked.'

'Why did you walk when your car had been repaired?'

'I wanted the exercise.'

'Is there anyone who can corroborate this?'

'I can't think of anyone,' I said, 'not at the moment.'

'At what time did your secretary leave the office?'

'Shortly after my last patient arrived.'

'You're certain of that?'

'Yes.'

They exchanged another glance. 'Your secretary says she did not leave until you did, shortly before ten.'

I frowned, genuinely puzzled. 'She's mistaken.'

I could not work out what was going on. What had Minna said? Were they trying to catch me out?

'Who was the patient?'

I hesitated. 'There is a matter of confidentiality –' I began.

'This is a matter of murder,' the slighter man interrupted. 'What's the patient's name?'

'I cannot divulge that,' I said.

The slighter man stood up in a smooth, deliberate motion, put his overcoat on the seat and came over to the desk. 'I am ordering you to hand over your diary,' he said.

I closed the book and put my hand protectively over it. I was completely unprepared for the rapidity and violence of his reaction. My head was suddenly on the desk, yanked violently down by the hair. Almost simultaneously I received a shuddering blow to the back of my neck.

He took the diary, opened it and ran a finger down the page. 'Rozental,' he said to his colleague when he came to the entry.

He tossed the book contemptuously back onto the desk. I sat up slowly. The back of my head was numb. There was bile in my mouth.

'Is there anything else you think you should tell us?' the taller man said. 'Think very carefully.'

'No,' I said. 'I have nothing more to say to you.'

The taller man turned to his colleague. 'Bring the woman in.'

I protested. 'What do you want with Minna?'

My interrogator gave me a contemptuous look. 'Sit down, Spethmann, and keep your mouth shut until I tell you otherwise.'

Minna was ushered in. She gave me a look and then guiltily hung her head.

The taller man addressed her. 'What time did you leave the office?'

190

Minna replied in a small voice, 'Shortly before ten o'clock.'

'Dr Spethmann says you left just after seven. He's quite certain about that.'

I searched Minna's face for some kind of clue: why was she saying this?

'No,' she said, returning my look. 'We were here together until ten.'

'Why does the doctor not remember?'

She paused. 'He probably wishes he could forget,' she said; then she added, 'Because of what happened . . . between us.'

The taller man studied her carefully, then turned to me. 'Were you carrying on with your secretary, Dr Spethmann? Is that what you were doing?'

'I refuse to answer that question,' I said, 'or any others from you.'

The taller man scratched the bridge of his nose with his left index finger, sighed and got to his feet. At the door, he said, 'You shall be hearing from us again, Dr Spethmann.'

Minna stood where she was, facing me. We heard the outer door open and close. She turned to go.

'Minna,' I called after her.

But she ignored me and left the room.

Whether he admits it or not, every psychoanalyst has patients who bore him. It was my bad luck that day to have to listen to the young foreign office clerk as he regaled me with his depraved exploits as he scoured the Vyborg for his victims. My next appointment was with the wife of a timber merchant. A vicious snob, she complained chiefly of her husband's lack of refinement. Perhaps I should have been grateful for the distraction they offered but all I really wanted to do was talk to Minna. Why had she lied for me?

It was not until I'd hurried out the last of my patients that I

191

had an opportunity to talk to her in private. She was at her desk, bringing the diary up to date.

'I tried Rozental again but he's not answering the telephone,' she said, as if nothing had happened.

I sat on the bench to the side of her desk. 'What's going on, Minna?' I said.

She pursed her lips and shook her head. Nothing.

'Why did you lie to those men?'

'If you will forgive me, Doctor, I have to finish some correspondence before I go.'

She pushed back her chair, lifted a sheaf of papers and went to the cabinet. She pretended to concentrate on sorting the papers. I got up and stood behind her.

'It was a very dangerous thing to do,' I said.

'I did it to help you,' she said, enunciating each word carefully so that I could not possibly misunderstand.

I put a hand on her shoulder. She froze and spun round, her eyes wide and startled as if I were about to assault her. I snatched my hand away.

'I'm sorry,' I said. 'I just don't want you to get into any trouble on my account.'

The papers filed away, she pushed the drawer shut, went back to her desk and picked up a pen.

'I do not want to talk about this again,' she said.

Twenty-One

B y the time I arrived at the opening ceremony, Saburov, as president of the St Petersburg Chess Union,
had already started his speech. Manoeuvring through the
throng to the French windows at the far end of the
ballroom, I scanned the faces around me. Of the players,
I glimpsed Capablanca and also Bernstein, but I could not
find Rozental. Saburov was thanking the organising committee for their hard work and the benefactors for their
generosity. At the mention of Tsar Nicholas's subscription
of one thousand roubles, there was a burst of reverent
applause.

'This tournament,' Saburov intoned, 'which marks the
jubilee of the St Petersburg Chess Union, is the strongest
ever seen in the history of chess. The committee decided to
invite only the first-prize winners in great international masters tournaments, that is, masters who have triumphed in
open contest with the very strongest of their peers.' Saburov
smiled, obviously enjoying every second of his time in the
limelight. 'Thus we are delighted to welcome Dr Lasker, the
reigning World Champion.'

There was another, less restrained burst of applause. I
caught sight of Lasker, bowing in acknowledgement. It was
the first time I had seen him in person. Although quite short
and unremarkable-looking, he projected a determination that
could not but command attention.

'From Cuba,' Saburov went on through the roll, 'the man already being talked of as "the chess machine", Senor José Raul Capablanca.'

The audience clapped and cheered, and the suave Cuban inclined his head graciously. Lasker was World Champion, but Capablanca was the true celebrity. He glanced at Lasker, the young lion eyeing the old; it was well known the two hated the sight of each other. Extraordinarily handsome, with sleek black hair and burning dark eyes, he gave off an astonishing confidence. Surrounded by awestruck admirers with fixed and silly grins – they included a large number of women – he was irresistibly suited to glory in a way Rozental never would be.

Saburov continued, 'Five years ago, here in St Petersburg, many of you will have been present at a now legendary game. It was one of Dr Lasker's rare defeats but I'm sure, great sportsman that he is, the World Champion will not object to my reminding you of his epic encounter with Avrom Chilowicz Rozental.'

The applause started up but soon faltered when Saburov failed to locate Rozental in the crowd.

'Is Avrom Chilowicz present?' he asked somewhat plaintively.

People craned their necks and turned to their neighbours with the question in their eyes.

'I could not prevail on him to come,' a voice next to me whispered. It was Kopelzon. 'Nothing to worry about. Avrom never attends these things.'

Saburov made a little joke about Rozental's legendary modesty and went on with his speech.

'How is Avrom?' I whispered to Kopelzon.

'Well enough,' he whispered back. 'He'll be able to play, that's the important thing.'

Saburov next introduced the American, Marshall.

194

'Avrom's first game tomorrow is with Marshall,' Kopelzon said. 'He's a tricky player, but tactical, and shallow. Avrom should beat him comfortably.'

We clapped each of the remaining competitors as they were introduced: Tarrasch, Alekhine, Nimzowitsch, Blackburne, Janowski, Bernstein and Gunsberg.

'Only Lasker and Capablanca present any real difficulties,' Kopelzon said, raising his voice as the applause climaxed. 'The rest are cannon fodder.'

Saburov signalled for quiet.

'I have one final but very important and very exciting announcement,' he said, making his voice grave. 'As you know, the scheme of play is that there will be a preliminary tournament in which each of the eleven competitors will play one game with every other. The five leaders of the preliminary tournament will then play off in a double-round final section. The winner of the final section, the winner of the 1914 St Petersburg tournament, will have the inestimable honour . . .' Saburov paused for dramatic effect. 'Of being presented at the Peterhof to His Imperial Highness Tsar Nicholas II to be created the first Grandmaster of Chess.'

There was a frenzy of cheers and applause. Kopelzon was in good form, beaming smiles at friends and admirers, but it was hard for me to look at him without feelings of anger and hurt. If he knew about the house on Kirochny Street, then he knew about Yastrebov, which made his pretended concern for me and Catherine and his outrage at our arrests a hypocritical fiction.

Oblivious as always to others' moods, Kopelzon said cheerfully, 'It seems the appropriate moment to give you my move, Otto. I play 44 . . . Ke7.' He checked my reaction, then said, 'We each have king and queen. I can protect the f-pawn with as many defenders as you have attackers. I really don't see how you think you are going to make progress.'

Spethmann–Kopelzon

After 44 . . . Ke7. Kopelzon says it's a draw. Is he right or is he bluffing? Can White make further progress?

Perhaps he was right but I didn't care; I wanted to win. Or, rather, I wanted to beat him. I concentrated on visualising the position. If I played 45 Kg8 to attack the pawn, he would respond simply with 45 . . . Qc8 +, so I played 45 Qg5+. It didn't help me with the f-pawn, but there was a trap.

Kopelzon grinned amiably. 'Really, Otto. Aren't you embarrassed to play these cheap tricks? Did you really think I was going to allow you to checkmate me on the back rank? I play 45 . . . Ke8.'

'46 Kg8.'

'Still going after the f-pawn, eh, Otto? You won't get it. 46 . . . Qc7.'

Chess without sight of the board, at least for more than a move or two, was beyond my powers. Even with so little material remaining I was having trouble keeping track of the pieces, as Kopelzon knew only too well.

'You'll be here for Rozental's opening game tomorrow, won't you?' he said rather patronisingly. 'Give me your move then.'

196

A waiter came round and refilled our glasses with champagne.

'Come and meet Lasker,' Kopelzon said. 'Saburov introduced me earlier – and guess what? Lasker congratulated me on my performance in Vienna last summer. Can you believe it? The World Champion came to see me perform. He said my playing moved him to tears.'

'Your fame knows no boundaries, Reuven.'

'Apparently not,' he said without irony. 'Let me introduce you. He's a fascinating man. There's not a subject under the sun he can't talk about – philosophy, politics, economics, religion. He'd love to meet you.'

'Perhaps later,' I said.

'As you please,' he said, sounding disappointed. 'By the way, are you coming to my recital at the Mariinsky next week? I'm going to be playing a selection of Bach's Partitas and Sonatas. I'm told the tsar himself is coming. Don't tell anyone – they don't like these things to get out too far in advance. All very exclusive' – he jabbed me jocularly in the ribs – 'but I'll get them to make an exception and allow you in. Put it in your diary. The 26th. I'll arrange the tickets.'

He clapped me on the back and made me promise not to go before he could effect an introduction to Lasker.

For an hour I made uneasy small talk with acquaintances from the St Petersburg Chess Union. I exchanged a few pleasantries with Herr Tarrasch when we were briefly introduced, and with the Englishman Blackburne who, it turned out, had been to Yegorov's and found the experience wonderfully invigorating.

I asked a servant if I could use the telephone. I dialled the number of the apartment on Bolshoy Prospect but the telephone bell just rang and rang. I thought about calling Anna at home, but I did not want to risk having her husband answer. I dialled another number.

'Where are you?' Catherine said.

'At Saburov's. It's the opening ceremony tonight. Has anyone called for me?'

'No. Were you expecting someone?'

'Not especially,' I lied. 'What have you been doing?'

'I had a visitor,' she said.

'That's nice. Who was it?'

'Mintimer Sergeyevich.'

'Who?'

'Lychev. That's his name – Mintimer Sergeyevich Lychev.'

'What did Mintimer want?' I asked acidly.

Catherine was unexpectedly serene. 'Nothing – just to talk. It wasn't anything to do with Leon or the murders. It turns out he's really quite unusual, for a policeman. To hear him talk about the conditions of the workers in the Vyborg you'd think you were listening to Petrov.'

'Catherine,' I said. 'Listen to me. He had no right to call on you. If he tries to talk to you again, you must refuse to see him. Do you understand?'

There was a long silence. I imagined her mouth setting and that single dark line of eyebrow coming down.

'You always accuse me of never telling you anything,' she responded sharply. 'And what happens when I do? You immediately start to interfere and order me around.'

'I am not ordering you around,' I said. 'But Lychev is a very dangerous man. I forbid you to see him.'

'And who are *you* seeing?' she asked, a note of triumphal vengefulness in her voice.

'Catherine, this is about your welfare. It is about your safety.'

'Did you think I wouldn't find out?'

I was in no mood to take a scolding from my daughter. 'We

198

can talk about Anna Petrovna later if you like, but I am telling you: stay away from Lychev.'

'You swore to me you would never see her again but she has been your patient for almost a year –'

'Enough, Catherine. This doesn't concern you.'

'And the fact she is your lover? Does that concern me?'

Even good fathers become exhausted. 'No,' I said with harsh finality, 'it does not.'

Catherine put down the telephone.

As I waited to collect my hat and coat I became aware of someone standing next to me. Turning, I saw Peter Arseneyevich Zinnurov.

'What gives you the right to dig around in other people's lives, Spethmann?'

I was in no mood to take lectures from the Mountain either. With my coat over my arm and my hat in hand I made to push past him. He put a hand up to my chest.

'Kazan is in the past. No one cares. We have enough problems in the present. We have terrorists and revolutionaries. Germany and France threaten war. The people are hungry. What is Kazan compared with this?'

How did he know about Kazan? He read my thoughts at once.

'You really don't know my daughter at all,' he said. 'She told me everything. Yes, Spethmann, she came to see me. She told me how you wore her down and bullied her and put words in her mouth.'

I didn't know what to think but I knew I had heard enough. This time when he tried to stop me I pushed him away. He staggered backwards but recovered quickly. The servants looked over, ready to intervene.

'Goodnight, sir,' I said.

'Goodnight, Dr Spethmann,' came a deep, soft voice from

my left. The speaker wore the uniform of a colonel in the Household Cavalry. He extended his hand.

'We haven't been introduced,' he said. The old soldier's grip was precise and strong. 'But I believe you knew one of my employees.'

'Really?' I said. 'Who?'

'Semevsky,' he said.

For a moment, even though I knew who I was speaking to, I thought he was about to tell me he was the building's owner.

'I hope you enjoy the rest of your evening, Dr Spethmann,' Colonel Gan said with a bow before continuing upstairs to the ballroom with Zinnurov.

I set off for my car, which I had parked in a yard behind Saburov's house. It was almost ten o'clock and not yet fully dark. Soon we would have our beloved white nights. I was about to climb into the driver's seat when Kopelzon hurried up to intercept me.

'I thought you wanted me to introduce you to Lasker?' he said with an aggrieved air.

'I think it was you who wanted to arrange the introduction,' I said, getting into the car.

Kopelzon clutched at the door. 'What could be so important that you'd pass up a chance to meet the World Champion? He's the man Rozental has to beat, after all.'

'What have you got yourself mixed up in, Reuven?' I said. Kopelzon frowned as if at a simpleton and attempted another smile. 'What are you on about, Otto?'

'You're a grown man so I suppose it's your own business,' I answered him, 'but what I cannot forgive is that you've dragged Rozental into it as well.'

A flash of alarm crossed his face. 'You don't know what you're talking about.'

I stared at my friend. 'I hope to God nothing happens to

200

Rozental because of you. I don't believe you would want that on your conscience.'

'Don't talk to me about conscience, Otto,' he spat back angrily. 'My conscience is alive and well. Yours is another matter.'

I let out the clutch and the car started to pull away. Kopelzon ran alongside for a little way, hanging onto the door with one hand.

'Stay away from Rozental, Otto!' he shouted. 'I'm warning you.'

I pressed the accelerator, the car speeded up and at last Kopelzon let go. I caught sight of him in the mirror breathing heavily and staring after me.

At the corner of Liteiny Prospect I saw a poster advertising Kopelzon's forthcoming concert at the Mariinsky. The last time I had seen him there his performance had been electrifying. Bouquets rained down on him. Like the playing of all truly great musicians, Kopelzon's spoke to the higher instincts of men and women. That night I had the sense that I could be a better person and live the rest of my life without pettiness or spite or envy. Kopelzon enjoyed his triumphs in a way that was, perhaps, not quite as elevated as the sentiment he produced in his audience. I never held his pride or vanity against him. But now all I could think of was the scale of his betrayal.

Twenty-Two

I t occurred to me that among those milling about the lobby of the Astoria there might be someone waiting to see who turned up to visit Rozental. I did not have time to worry about the possibility. I hurried to the elevators and rode to the fourth floor.

I started down a long corridor, lit by bright electric wall lamps. Mahogany tables with vases of white roses were set out at intervals; on the walls hung copies of Vereschagin's battle scenes, as well as amateur watercolours of the city's land-marks, including – I could not help but note – one of Politseisky Bridge, where Gulko was murdered.

I got to Rozental's room, number 442. I knocked and waited. There were shuffling movements from inside, but the door remained firmly shut.

'Avrom Chilowicz,' I called, rapping loudly. 'It's me, Dr Spethmann. I must speak with you.'

After some moments the door opened to reveal a blinking, unshaven Rozental. He was wearing the trousers and waist-coat of a stained, dark-blue suit and a collarless shirt open at the neck. He was barefoot. His skin was puffy and had the sweaty pallor of a prisoner. He squinted, as though trying to place me.

'May I come in?' I said.

He shuffled back to allow me entry, more out of passivity and ingrained habits of deference than curiosity or politeness.

The room was overheated and in the stale air lingered a cloying mixture of cigarette smoke, leftover food and the odours of unventilated night and sleep. Clothes and towels were strewn over the divan, the gilt furniture and the oriental rugs on the floor. On an ornate, claw-footed table was a small chessboard and, beside it, scribbled notes on a spectacular disarrangement of dog-eared pages.

'Have you been eating, Avrom?' I asked, indicating a tray of cold, untouched food on the bed. He glanced at it uncomprehendingly. 'I was at the opening ceremony at Saburov's house,' I went on, trying a conversational gambit. 'I thought you might be there.'

He gave no sign that he'd heard me and wandered back to the chessboard. I had interrupted him and he was going to get back to work whether I was there or not. I recognised the position – it was from Marshall's famous victory over Capablanca the year before at Havana and had been in all the chess magazines.

'Avrom,' I said, 'I have to ask you about Kopelzon.' He reached out to move a rook but seemed to hesitate. 'Has Reuven Moiseyevich asked you to do something for him?'

He took up the rook and started to scratch at his scalp.

'What did he ask you to do, Avrom?' I pressed, coaxing him as gently as I could. 'I won't tell anyone anything that you say. It will be strictly between us.'

Rozental hung his head and started to mutter while his fingers raked his dark, close-cropped scalp.

'Tell me, Avrom,' I said. 'What does Kopelzon want you to do?'

Suddenly, like a child seized by a tantrum, Rozental hurled the rook at a standard lamp in the corner of the room, provoked, I assumed, by my questioning. But then he muttered, 'Why exchange the rook here?' He looked at me with a desperate plea in his eyes, as though begging me to solve a mystery that had been tormenting him all his life. 'Why?'

I looked again around the stuffy, disordered room and made my decision.

I said, 'Avrom, I want you to come with me. Don't be alarmed. I'm going to take you home, to my house. I'm going to see that you're properly looked after. You need to eat and rest so that tomorrow you will be ready for Marshall.'

I don't know if he understood what I was saying, but he did not resist as I guided him to the bed and, sitting him down, got him into his socks and shoes.

'I'm going to pack your clothes now,' I told him. 'Why don't you put away your chess set?'

He watched, inert and bewildered, as I retrieved his valise and went around the room gathering up his clothes. Eventually, as though he had only just grasped what I had asked him to do, he went to the table and started to put the chessmen into their box.

'There's a rook missing,' he said, looking about anxiously.

'You threw it over there, Avrom,' I said, indicating the lamp. 'Remember?'

He got down at once on his hands and knees to search. I was by the dresser, emptying out the drawers. That was when the door opened.

Kopelzon was first to let himself in. He expressed no surprise on seeing me but stood aside to allow entry to a heavily built man of medium height. He had filled out somewhat from the notorious police photograph so beloved of the newspapers, and age had tamed and thinned his unruly hair. His thick moustache and respectable clothes gave him a solid, burgher appearance. Had I not had him in mind, I doubt I would have recognised the empire's most wanted terrorist. Berek Medem was holding a gun in his left hand.

His gaze fell on Rozental, still scrabbling around on the floor in search of his lost rook, oblivious to the new arrivals. Then he turned to examine me.

'This is Spethmann, I take it?'

Kopelzon nodded slowly. 'Why did you have to come here, Otto?' he said. 'I warned you not to. Why couldn't you just leave well alone?'

'Because it wasn't well, Reuven,' I replied.

Medem turned to Kopelzon. 'If you hadn't involved him in the first place he wouldn't be here. What did you think you were doing, bringing Rozental to see a psychoanalyst?'

The Polish terrorist's voice was rather beautiful; it was sonorous, deep and confident. His Russian was perfect, without a trace of the usual gutturalness of Yiddish speakers. I would have taken him for a well-educated St Petersburger instead of the tough raised in Smocza Street in the Warsaw ghetto, the graduate of Pawiak prison, the murderer of so many policemen, tax collectors, informers and spies.

'Rozental was going to pieces,' Kopelzon protested indignantly. 'You were in Moscow and I had to do something.'

'Well, you did the wrong thing,' Medem said matter-of-factly. He pinched his trousers at the thigh and sat down, resting the gun in his lap. 'And now I am going to have to tidy up.'

'Tidy up?' Kopelzon said.

'In case you haven't understood, Reuven,' I said, 'he's going to kill me.'

'Don't be ridiculous,' Kopelzon snorted, turning to Medem.

Medem shrugged. 'He knows. He's worked it out.'

'Impossible!' Kopelzon shot back.

'The only reason I didn't see it from the very start –' I began.

'Don't say any more, Otto! You don't know, you don't know.'

'Pretending I don't know isn't going to save my life, Reuven. Your friend here has already made up his mind.'

Kopelzon threw his head back and let out a melodramatic groan.

'The only reason I didn't see it earlier is because it's so implausible and outrageous,' I said.

'Those are the plans that tend to succeed,' Medem said smoothly, a smile playing around his lips. 'They take people by surprise.'

'Whose idea was it?' I said, looking between them.

Kopelzon was the first to speak. 'When I heard the tsar would be receiving the winner of the tournament at the Peterhof,' he said, 'it set me thinking. The winner all alone in a room with the great tyrant? It's the perfect opportunity.'

'And did you think you were going to turn Rozental into an assassin?'

We looked at the chess player, now reaching under a dresser to pat blindly for his missing piece; he had begun to whimper in distress.

'We thought about asking him – he's a Pole and a Jew, after all,' Medem replied. 'And we sounded him out, without being too specific, suggesting it as a joke almost.'

'No doubt he jumped at the chance to embrace martyrdom for the cause of Polish freedom,' I said.

'No, actually,' Medem replied with a straight face, 'he became rather upset. I hadn't realised he was so highly strung.'

'Fortunately, you had prepared for the eventuality,' I said, 'with a double.'

Medem permitted himself a smile. 'Not too hard to find. There are hundreds like Rozental in the ghetto – stocky, dark types, remarkable only for their uniformity. I myself have two or three uncles who look like him. In fact, one of my aunts bears more than a passing resemblance.' He chuckled at his own joke. 'The guards at the Peterhof won't be suspicious of a mere chess player. Our man will get past them easily. I heard you yourself mistook him for Rozental, at a restaurant?'

'Rozental found out there was a double, didn't he?'

'It was an accident,' Kopelzon said defensively. 'I arranged for him to be taken out to dinner so the double could come here and try on his clothes. But then Rozental suddenly walked in and found his twin standing in front of him, dressed in his own clothes, his hair and moustache cut exactly the same way. He got terribly agitated. That's when I brought him to you.'

Rozental let out a cry of frustration and the three of us turned again in his direction.

'What's he doing?' Medem asked.

'He's looking for a chess piece,' I said, 'a rook.'

Medem studied the scrabbling, prostrate figure for some moments.

'For your plan to work,' I said, 'it needed Rozental to win the tournament. That's an awful lot to leave to chance.'

Kopelzon answered vehemently, 'It's nothing to do with chance. Chess is a game of pure logic and Rozental is at the peak of his powers. For the last two or three years he's been virtually untouchable.'

'Things go wrong in every tournament,' I snapped back at him. 'Upsets happen. Strong players lose to weaker ones. If you need proof, look at our game. I've never beaten you before, Reuven – you're a much better player than I – but I'm winning, on this occasion at least.'

'I've said before you've overestimated your position, Otto,' Kopelzon replied. 'That much should be clear to you by now.'

Berek Medem stood up. I did not move. He said, 'Put up a fight, if you want. By all means shout for help. All that will happen is that anyone who intervenes will die. And of course you will die with them, an hour or so before your time.'

Certain of my senses were sharper – smell, for example – and others duller – hearing and touch. I remember that my vision was blurred at the periphery; I saw only straight ahead

207

and narrowly, as though looking through the wrong end of a telescope. Berek Medem seemed to be addressing me from a faraway place.

'I want to write a note to my daughter,' I said.

Berek Medem considered my request but shook his head, with some regret it seemed to me. But I could see there was no point in asking again. 'At least let me say goodbye to Rozental.'

'Be quick,' Medem said.

I went over and got down beside my former patient. He turned to me momentarily, his eyes large and vague.

'I can't find it anywhere,' he said.

As a child, Catherine was always misplacing the things she wanted most – a book, a colouring pencil, a favourite toy – and wailing to the heavens that they were lost forever. I reached behind the base of the standard lamp and quickly located the missing rook. Rozental took it from me, examining it the way Catherine used to inspect the things I retrieved for her, as if some magic inhered in them. How else could the vanished thing reappear? Relief flooded into his eyes. I helped him to his feet.

'Good luck tomorrow, Avrom,' I said. 'Try to get some sleep.'

I hugged him, which only confused him, the way we are disconcerted when a nodding acquaintance embraces us with sudden sentimental warmth.

'Don't worry about him,' Medem said. 'You forget that I need him to be at his best.' He turned to Kopelzon. 'See that he eats and gets to bed. Bring him to the tournament tomorrow yourself. Make sure he arrives on time.'

I took a last look at Rozental. He was already back at the board, setting out the pieces.

Kopelzon stood aside to let me pass. 'I'm sorry we never got to finish our game. Let's call it a draw,' he said. He put out his hand. 'I'm sorry, Otto. You may not believe me, but I am – very sorry.'

He took on a self-pitying and harassed look. In that instant I came to despise him. Anger welled up inside me.

'If you were sorry you wouldn't stand by and let me go to my death. If you were sorry you wouldn't let these people destroy Rozental. Because whether your attempt works or not, the police will arrest him. They will throw him in jail. They will torture him –'

'Shut up!'

'They will put Rozental on trial,' I continued with heat. 'They will take him to the gallows. They will put a hood over his head and a rope around his neck and they will hang him – that man!' I said, pointing at the pitiful figure bent over the chess board. 'You're going to kill him just as surely as if you were to cut his throat with your own hand. Tell me now that you are sorry, Reuven.'

'For the greater good, sometimes sacrifices must be made,' he said, reining in his instinct to shout me down. 'Despite what you say, I am sorry – but what's one man's life weighed against the future of a whole nation?'

'It won't be just one man,' I said, clenching my fists in pure rage. 'The Black Hundreds will rampage through the villages and towns of the Pale. Thousands – tens of thousands – will die. Jews will die lynched and defiled – and you, Reuven, and your friends, will be responsible.'

'We die every day, Otto. What's new?' Kopelzon said, turning away.

For all that I hated him at that moment, I could not bring myself to hurt him. I unclenched my fists and dropped my shoulders.

Berek Medem indicated the door and said, 'It's time to go, Dr Spethmann.'

Twenty-Three

T here were two men waiting in the corridor, both younger than Medem but with the same ferocity of purpose written into their features. After a terse exchange in Polish, which I only half-understood, one of them took my arm and we started to march away from the elevators towards the stairs at the back of the building. The deep carpet was springy underfoot. My heart pounded in my chest.

Medem walked beside me, holding his gun so the barrel was parallel to the seam of his trousers and pointing at the floor. The casual observer would notice nothing out of the ordinary.

'The double will never escape,' I said. 'He will never get out of the Peterhof alive if he makes an attempt on the tsar.'

'He knows that,' Medem replied.

'You are prepared to commit suicide to achieve your goal?'

'Is it somehow more repugnant to your sense of morality that the doer of the deed should die as he strikes?' Medem countered.

'No,' I said. 'The repugnancy lies in the imagination that can contrive such a thing.'

'What does the just man do, Spethmann? This is the question we cannot avoid. What does the just man do when there is injustice all around him? You know that Poland has been invaded, occupied and partitioned?'

'I know my history,' I said.

The sign for the stairs indicated that we should turn left at the end of the corridor.

'So how do we improve the lives of our children and those of the unborn generations? What is the way forward?'

The door to one of the rooms opened and a large man in a grey overcoat and hat stepped out. I did not shout for help. What was the point? The man would die. I would die. The few minutes of life I could yet live were mine only so long as I colluded with my abductors. Indifferent to what he undoubtedly took to be a group of hotel guests either returning to their rooms or leaving them, the man bent to lock the door behind him.

'What is your answer?' Medem said. 'What is the way forward?'

'I am not a politician,' I said. 'I do not have an answer.'

'That is your defence?' Medem whispered as we approached the man, who seemed to be having trouble with his key.

'Of what am I accused?'

'You are accused of apathy, Spethmann,' he said. 'You are accused of opportunism, selfishness and cowardice.'

The man in the grey overcoat straightened as we were about to pass. I felt the grip on my upper arm tighten and Medem moved closer to me, ready to block any attempt to flee.

The brim of the man's hat was pulled low and the collar of his coat concealed most of the lower part of his face, but I had recognised him. His shape and bulk gave him away.

There was a moment – a split second, no more – when the five men in the corridor, positioned so closely together that each could have put a hand out to touch the rest without even having to stretch, knew what was about to happen before it happened. Then it was a simple matter of who moved fastest.

A bullet leaves the barrel of a pistol at a velocity in excess of a thousand feet per second. The human eye cannot see it.

Perhaps a muzzle flash, perhaps smoke; and then, if the aim is true, the projectile strikes. Once the shock has subsided, the primary senses are no longer concerned with vision but with pain. But I saw the bullet. I saw the tiny disc the colour of tarnished silver erupt from the barrel of Kavi's gun in a white-grey cloud and come spinning towards me.

And I remember thinking, *So this is what it's like to be shot.*

An age later a deafening bang followed in the bullet's wake, as though someone had let off a firework a fraction from my ear. I felt the grip on my arm suddenly relax as the man who had been holding me collapsed to the floor.

The door from which Kavi had appeared swung violently open and a second gunman materialised, crouching as he came. Lychev! He fired twice.

Simultaneously, Kavi swivelled to turn his gun on Berek Medem. There was another deafening report by my ear and I felt myself yanked back. The last shot was from Medem's own gun. He locked his arm around my throat to use me as a shield.

There were more shots. Pops and bangs, wilder, more random than the first. I was aware of blood on the walls. The corridor filled up with smoke that gave off a horrible, sharp stench. Someone was shouting but it came to my ringing ears as an echo. I stumbled. Medem pulled me up as we retreated to the stairs. I was choking. I brought my hands up to fight his hold, to fight for the air I desperately needed.

The shooting stopped. I saw Lychev's lips move to shout commands my ears could not hear. He and Kavi were half-crouching near one of the mahogany tables, their gun arms outstretched, their faces taut, eyes wide.

Something new, some new sensation. Something hard pressed to my temple and from behind I now heard words and curses and threats.

'Let him go . . .'

'I will kill him . . .'

'Let Spethmann go and we won't come after you . . .'

'Stay back . . .'

'We don't want you. You can go. As long as you don't hurt him . . .'

Immobilised and suffocating, the barrel of the gun at my head, my feet barely on the carpet. Lychev and Kavi inching forward with wary half-steps, manoeuvring past the bodies of the two men they had killed. A terrified guest opening the door and closing it in an instant. Broken glass from an electric lamp. Spilt water from an overturned vase. A white rose petal stuck to my left shoe.

Medem grunting with the effort.

'I will kill him . . .'

I brought my hands up and pulled at his arm to ease the pressure on my throat. Medem tightened his grip and pulled me back.

It would be too much to say it was a conscious decision. Perhaps it was nothing more than the instinctive recognition of a momentary advantage. Or perhaps simple desperation. Sensing Medem off-balance, just for a second, I tensed my left leg and heaved with all my strength, driving him into the wall. There was another loud crack. Dust and fragments of plaster showered us from the ceiling where Medem's bullet had struck.

I spun round and, bending low, rammed him in the chest, trying at the same time to pull him down. He managed to step back and fire over my back at Lychev and Kavi, forcing them down behind a table.

Unbalanced now, I was thrown aside by Medem. I went crashing to the floor. He turned and sprinted to the door for the stairs.

Before he reached it, the door flew open and Tolya appeared, his pistol trained on the terrorist. Berek Medem was faster and more ruthless. Tolya went down as though his legs had been kicked from under him. Medem fired again before leaping over Tolya's body and disappearing through the door.

Kavi raced to where Tolya lay. He looked to Lychev and shook his head. Dead.

'What a mess,' I heard Lychev mutter as he surveyed the devastation. Then he said to Kavi, 'Disappear. Now!'

Kavi kneeled down beside his dead friend. I heard him say, 'Goodbye, Comrade,' before getting to his feet and going through the door to the stairs.

Lychev helped me up. 'Are you all right?'

'What are you doing here?' I said.

'We've been keeping an eye on Rozental. Tolya saw you in the lobby and telephoned me. I came as soon as I could. I had an idea you were getting yourself into trouble.'

A guest opened the door to his room a fraction and poked his head out.

'It's all right,' Lychev said. 'I'm a policeman. There's been an attempted robbery. Close the door and stay inside your room until you're informed otherwise.'

The frightened guest was quick to oblige.

'Attempted robbery?' I said.

'There's no need to panic people even more,' Lychev said. 'Is Kopelzon still with Rozental?'

We hurried to Rozental's room, Lychev repeating his orders as more guests hesitantly emerged into the corridor.

Rozental's door was ajar.

'Is Kopelzon armed?' Lychev asked.

'I don't think so.'

Nevertheless, when Lychev burst in it was with his pistol at the ready. I followed, only to find Rozental still staring at his chessboard. He had once again set up the critical position from the Marshall–Capablanca game. This alone had meaning for him.

Lychev searched the bathroom and closets. Kopelzon had fled. 'The police will be on their way,' he said. 'Stay here until I come for you.'

'Won't the police want to talk to me? To ask me questions about Berek Medem?'

'Some thieves were trying to break into a room. Unfortunately for them I happened to be in the hotel at the time. Do not say anything different. Do not mention Berek Medem.'

'Who are you, Lychev?'

'I've already told you my name, I think.'

'Your name is not in doubt. Your priorities and loyalties are not so clear.'

I tried to push past him but he blocked my way. 'Where are you going?'

'There's someone I have to see,' I said.

'Not now,' he said, pushing me back. 'I mean it. Do not come out of this room until I come for you.'

He left without another word.

'Why did he exchange the rooks?' Rozental mumbled, shaking his head. 'It makes no sense.'

I found a bottle of vodka and poured myself a tumblerful. I poured a second. None of it made sense.

Every now and then policemen knocked to check that we were safe. The hotel's manager arrived, mortified, to apologise in person for the unfortunate events, and offering food and drink and assurances that nothing like this had ever happened before and expressing his hope that it wouldn't spoil the guests' stay.

I used the telephone to call the apartment on the Bolshoy. There was no answer. I called home. Again there was no answer. I began to get very worried. Where was Anna? Where was Catherine?

There was a high-pitched whine in my ears. I tried pressing

a finger to them and blowing my nose. After a while they began to ache.

Shortly after 2 a.m. Lychev returned. I had just got Rozental to bed; he had fallen asleep instantly and was already snoring lightly.

'I'll drive you home,' he said.

'I said there's someone I have to see,' I said.

'Who?' When I did not reply he said, 'I have just saved your life, Spethmann. I had hoped that would convince you I have your welfare at heart.'

'I'm going to see Anna Ziatdinov,' I said.

He considered for a moment. 'I'd better take you.'

Twenty-Four

T he streets were all but deserted and we were soon on
Palace Bridge. The black water of the Neva sparkled in
the moonlight and the electric lights shone all along the
embankment.

'Did Medem escape?' I asked.

'Apparently,' Lychev replied.

'You don't seem very concerned. Why did you tell Kavi to
disappear?'

'There was no reason for him to stay.'

'Kavi is not a policeman, is he?'

'No.'

'He's a Bolshevik.'

Lychev cast me a sideways look.

'And so are you,' I said.

He shrugged, a nonchalant acknowledgement.

'A Bolshevik spy in the St Petersburg bureau of detectives,'
I said. 'I seem to recall you telling me you were born the same
day Tsar Alexander II was murdered? You came into the
world to prevent such a thing happening again, so you said.'

'If one is to play the part,' Lychev said with a shrug, 'one
must learn the lines.'

'A servant of justice?'

'That line is for real.'

'I seem to be surrounded by just men,' I said, 'which is odd.'

'Why odd?'

217

'Because I find just men utterly terrifying.'

We had turned on to University and were passing the Academy of Science. We would be at the apartment in less than five minutes.

He said, 'How would you characterise this plot of Berek Medem's?'

'I would call it amateurish,' I said.

'Go on,' he said.

'Kopelzon is an amateur,' I continued, 'so it doesn't surprise me that he came up with something so unlikely. But Berek Medem is a professional. He's also ruthless and, from what I saw of him, highly intelligent. I find it hard to believe he ever really imagined it would work.'

Lychev smiled as if at a promising student, and, helping me to the correct conclusion as a good professor does, he asked leadingly, 'But if he didn't think it would work, why did he go to so much trouble?'

'I have no idea.'

'Because someone wants him to succeed,' Lychev said. 'Someone powerful whose interests coincide with his, on this issue at least.'

'Who?'

'Where do you think the Okhrana have been all this time? Do you think they don't know about Kopelzon and his political opinions? Or his sudden friendship with Rozental? Why do you think Colonel Gan placed an agent in your office building? Why do you think Semevsky was following you and Rozental that night?'

I was lost.

'It isn't Kopelzon's plot. He didn't dream it up. Gan did.'

It was a moment before I could take this in. 'What are you saying? Why would the head of the Okhrana want to kill the tsar?'

At the Imperial Academy of Art, Lychev turned right.

Ahead was the junction with Bolshoy Prospect. We passed a droshky, the driver whipping the little pony briskly. Apart from that there was no one on the streets.

'Gan is a pro-German reactionary,' Lychev went on. 'He is conspiring with his friend Zinnurov and the Baltic Barons and their pro-German allies to kill Nicholas, who is pro-French and who, in their eyes, isn't up to the job of defending the autocracy. It doesn't matter how many mistakes Kopelzon and Medem make. They are being given a free hand.'

'Does Medem know he is being used by Gan?'

'Medem is highly intelligent and it's possible he's worked it out. It wouldn't change things. Either way both he and Gan get what they want – to kill the tsar.'

'What about Kopelzon? Does he know?'

'Your friend has known from the start.'

'Then why hasn't he told Medem?'

'Because he doesn't want Medem to know that he's an Okhrana agent.'

I spun round to look at him. He flicked a careless glance at me.

'Kopelzon has been spying on Polish émigré groups in Paris, Berlin and London. Wherever he goes on tour he makes sure to meet Polish exiles. He's a hero to them and naturally they're talkative. And when he comes back to St Petersburg Kopelzon goes to meet Colonel Gan and tells him everything.'

'Why is he doing it? What does Kopelzon get out of it?'

'Money,' Lychev said simply. 'Your friend likes to live well – or hadn't you noticed?'

I thought of all the expensive meals we'd shared at A l'Ours and the Contant. Kopelzon was recklessly generous. Did he give away his money out of guilt?

I directed Lychev to turn left.

'After the assassination,' Lychev went on, 'Gan and his friends will install a puppet on the throne. They'll close the

Duma, break the alliance with France, ally with the Kaiser and unleash a patriotic crusade. You have to admire their creativity: Gan is plotting a coup which they will pass off as a revolutionary uprising.'

'Are you going to let this happen?' I said.

Here Lychev dropped the offhand tone he had deployed until then. 'It's not my decision,' he said with a hint of bitterness. 'The Central Committee of the Party has of course been kept informed of everything. They are analysing the likely consequences. When they make their decision, I will receive the appropriate instructions.'

'The consequence will be a bloodbath,' I said.

'There are two schools of thought within the Party leadership. One is against letting the plot go ahead. They say if the country is panicked by an assassination, Gan will be free to clamp down with an iron fist and set the revolution back by a generation.'

'And the other school?'

'They say that objectively we have reached the limits of what we can achieve in the present climate. They say our organisation is riddled with traitors and spies like King. They say we will only break through in an atmosphere of chaos.'

'And you?' I said. 'What is your opinion?'

'My opinion is whatever the Central Committee decides,' he said.

What to make of such a man, for whom every moral choice was bent wholly to the needs of a machine?

'The Central Committee's decision may yet be irrelevant,' I said. 'If Rozental doesn't win the tournament, someone else will be going to the Peterhof – Lasker or Capablanca – and Medem's plan will fall apart by itself.'

The apartment block came into view. 'Stop here,' I said.

Lychev ignored me and continued for another block before making a right turn into a side street.

'What are you doing?' I said.

'There was a car parked across the street from the apartment block,' he said. 'Let's just be careful.'

We walked back the way we had come. The motor car stationed opposite the apartment building appeared to be empty.

'What floor is the apartment on?' Lychev asked.

'That's it,' I said, pointing to a darkened window on the first floor.

Lychev took a last look around and then approached the entrance. We climbed the stairs to the first floor. Nothing stirred. Lychev held his gun the same way Medem had held his, the barrel pointing down, parallel to the seam of his trousers. He was taking no chances.

'When did you last see Anna?' Lychev asked.

I had to think for a moment. A very long time ago – this morning.

'Is she expecting you?'

'She asked me to come.'

He took the key and, beckoning me to stand to the side of the door, quietly slid it into the lock. The tumbler clicked, loud enough to wake the dead. The apartment was in darkness and the only noise was the sleepy ticking of a grandfather clock. Without waiting for our eyes to adjust to the gloom Lychev crept forward, disappearing into the kitchen on the left.

I inched forward, trying to recall the layout of the room and the placement of the furniture. There was a clear path, I remembered, from the front door across the length of the drawing room to the short corridor leading to the bedroom.

I bumped into something and fell awkwardly on what I immediately knew, though I still could not properly see, to be the legs of an overturned wooden chair.

Lychev sprang into the room, pointing his gun.

'It's me,' I said quickly.

He turned on the light. I looked at the chair. Why was it here? Why was it lying on its side?

Getting to my feet, I saw it was not the only thing out of place. There was a broken teacup on the floor by the table, and a small writing desk had been upended; papers and pens were scattered everywhere.

My heart filled up with fear. I ran to the bedroom and turned on the Tiffany lamps. The heavy drapes were open and the bed was unmade. Anna's clothes were strewn everywhere. I whipped aside the blankets, as though Anna might be concealed beneath.

'They've taken her,' I said. 'Zinnurov has taken her.'

Suddenly, Lychev put a finger to his lips. Be quiet! I looked around but could not see what he had obviously seen.

'I'm going to the kitchen,' he said, making his voice distinct. But instead of moving to the door he sidled up to a full-length closet to the right of the bed. Raising his pistol to head height, he reached for the handle and, in a rapid, simultaneous movement, pulled open the door.

The man inside was also armed and he fired once before Lychev, displaying more physical strength and agility than I had imagined he possessed, wrenched him out and threw him to the floor. The man's gun skidded to a stop at my feet. By the time I took it up, Lychev had dropped his right knee onto the man's chest, pinioning him. I dropped the pistol into my coat pocket.

'Where is she?' Lychev shouted, pressing his pistol into the man's throat.

'Don't shoot me! Don't shoot me!' the man pleaded, making no effort to resist.

'Where is Anna Petrovna? Tell me, you bastard, or I will shoot you dead.'

'I swear I don't know. She got away.'

222

'What do you mean, she got away?'

'This morning Zinnurov sent two men to get her but she got away from them. He told us to wait here in case the Jew came back.'

Lychev looked up at me then back at his prisoner.

'Us?' Lychev said. 'How many are you?'

The man swallowed nervously. 'Three.'

'Where are they?'

'Outside.'

'In the car?'

The man nodded.

There was a piece of paper on the pillow. Thinking it must be from Anna I picked it up. The note read:

My daughter has told me everything. You took advantage of an unhappy woman made vulnerable by illness. Your aim was to defile her, and you succeeded. Outwardly you pretend to be a Russian but you cannot disguise the stink of your race. You are despicable and revolting beyond measure. You will learn the lesson that your kind must ever be taught, and sooner than you think.

The brain does not take in such messages at a stroke. We get to the end without really having read the beginning or middle: single words only come off the page, a matter of tone and insinuation. *Stink. Defile. Despicable.* I started again. The words had not changed. 'You will learn the lesson that your kind must ever be taught, and sooner than you think.'

I handed it to Lychev. He read it quickly, then said, 'We have to get out of here now.'

He looked down at the man on the floor. Without warning he fired once into the man's head.

'Let's go,' he said, starting for the corridor.

Transfixed by the sight, I hadn't taken a single step when

the window suddenly exploded, showering me with glass. I felt a sliver fall under the collar of my shirt and, instinctively putting a finger to my neck, I remember thinking, *I will have to be careful trying to get that out if I'm not to cut myself.* Then I noticed a cobblestone lying in the middle of the bed. I turned back to the window. A huge shard hung like a dagger from the top of the frame.

I heard Lychev shout, 'Get out now!'

Through the broken window a second cobblestone now sailed as gently and gracefully as a leaf borne by the breezes. The huge shard dropped to the floor and shattered. The second cobblestone also landed on the bed, up by the pillows. It had a fuse and the fuse was burning. It was not a cobblestone.

I scrambled as fast as I could to the corridor. Lychev was ahead of me, half-running, half-throwing himself to get clear.

Someone picked me up and propelled me through the air and a great hot wind whooshed past me. There was a blinding flash of light. I passed through a furnace. I felt the hair on my head shrivel. There was a strange smell, like burnt wool. Then came the deafening roar.

What was I doing like this? It was desperately uncomfortable. I was upside down and in a very constricted space, my head pushed forward into my chest. Dust fell into my mouth and eyes and nostrils, it settled on my lips. My mouth was parched. Someone was trying to double me up. I thought my back would snap. I couldn't breathe. Then I began to slide a long way down.

Twenty-Five

I n the beautiful White Hall of the Mariinsky, Kopelzon was
playing Bach's Partita No. 3. How I loved his playing, the truth
he brought to the music, the way he released and controlled its
loveliness and melancholy. What a gift he had, what sublime
comprehension. He followed the lines that drove the music but
was never unbending. Flexibility – and cunning! – this was how
Kopelzon made beautiful music his own. The tsar and tsarina
were in the audience, and so were Zinnurov and Gan. Rozental
suddenly jumped to his feet and said, 'You are all in zugzwang,
ladies and gentlemen. You cannot save yourselves.' One of the
magnificent chandeliers fell from the ceiling, crashing on top of
Kopelzon. But when I went to dig my friend out of the mountain
of diamonds I found not him but Yastrebov's pickled head. I
picked it up, put it in my pocket and brought it home to Catherine.

Every now and then the bed tipped up violently, sometimes
feet first, sometimes head first. Bile surged into my mouth. I
wanted to wake up. I wanted to wake up very badly. But I lost
my footing. I would have fallen into the pit had I not flapped
my arms and started to fly. It was not the soaring, effortless
flight of dreams but precarious and treacherous, and several
times I almost crashed. I was a novice, really, at flying. Worse
than the nausea was the awful confusion in my head, a reeling
drunkenness that sleep did nothing to cure.

*   *   *

I could not stop thinking about chess. At first it only made the dizziness worse, but after a time things settled down. A single position came into focus and the visualisation without sight of the board that I had always found so difficult suddenly became possible.

Spethmann–Kopelzon
After 46 . . . Qc7. Can Spethmann win the all-important f-pawn?

I had to be utterly precise and utterly ruthless. Everything depended on the f-pawn. If I could win the f-pawn I would win the game. But how to do it? I had king and queen to attack it, he had king and queen to defend it. If I played 47 Qg7 Kopelzon would reply 47 . . . Qe7, and the f-pawn was still defended. As long as he kept his queen on the seventh rank he could defend against all my threats. If I then played 48 d4, he would play 48 . . . Qxe4 49 Qxf7 + Kd8 50 Qxa7 Qxd5+ 51 Kf8 Qe6 – and it would be a draw. I had never been in such a good position against Kopelzon and I so wanted to beat him, for many reasons.

It all hinged on the f-pawn.

And then suddenly I saw it. I had my answer.

*   *   *

I opened my eyes. Gregory Petrov was standing by the bed. With him was Lychev.

'So, you've decided to rejoin us,' Petrov said. There were crumbs on his moustache.

'Catherine?' My voice was hoarse. Lychev gave me water to sip.

'Safe,' he said. 'She's been here several times to see you.'

'And Anna?'

'Don't worry,' Lychev said. 'She's also safe.'

'What happened? Where is she?'

'Zinnurov sent two men to the apartment to kidnap her. They thought she'd go meekly but she didn't. She managed to escape and eventually made her way to your house. She was in a terrible state. She told Catherine everything. It was late. You were at the hotel at the time.'

'The hotel?'

'The Astoria. Do you remember?'

'There was a rose petal on my shoe,' I said. Lychev and Petrov exchanged a look.

'Anna was desperate to find you and warn you not to go to the apartment,' Lychev went on. 'Catherine went to Saburov's to look for you but you'd already gone and no one knew where.'

'Where is she now?'

'In a safe house not far from here,' Lychev said.

'Where is here?' From what I could see of the room it was bare and none too clean.

'We're in the Vyborg,' Petrov said with a grin. 'You're back where you started, with the workers.' He helped me sit up. 'You and Anna are going to Paris.'

'What are you talking about?'

Petrov laughed and turned to Lychev. 'He doesn't seem very grateful, does he, after all our hard work?' Turning back to me, he said, 'We've arranged everything – the tickets, the false papers.' He produced a small packet. 'They're in the name of Mr and Mrs Spirodovich,' he said, placing them by the bed.

'What is this about Paris? I'm not going to Paris. I'm not going anywhere.'

'I'm sorry to have to be the one to tell you this, Spethmann,' Petrov said, obviously enjoying himself, 'but until four days ago, in spite of a little trouble with an over-zealous policeman' – he turned to grin at Lychev – 'you were a respected psychoanalyst and upstanding member of the St Petersburg bourgeoisie. Sadly, since the explosion at the Bolshoy apartment, you are now a wanted murderer. Your picture is all over the newspapers.'

Even when he put a copy of *The Orator* in my hands and I saw my own face staring back at me I could not believe it. The story was not long – three or four paragraphs only – but I experienced the same difficulty I had with Zinnurov's note: the words were clear enough but meaning and consequence were too tortuous to take in.

'You're in this too,' I said, looking up at Lychev.

'Lychev has also gone from hero of the St Petersburg bureau of detectives to wanted fugitive,' Petrov said. 'It's an unhappy blow for the Party, but we'll get over it.'

'I always knew the day would come,' Lychev said evenly. 'In many ways it's a relief.'

Petrov's tone became suddenly sombre. 'If Gan catches you, he will show you no mercy.'

'I am aware of that.'

My eyes were very tired, my head heavy.

'He's fallen asleep,' I heard Lychev say.

'Let him rest,' Petrov said. 'He's got a long journey tomorrow.'

'Any news of Berek Medem?' Petrov asked.

'Nothing,' Lychev replied. 'After the Astoria, he disappeared.'

'He'll still be in St Petersburg. What about the fiddle player?'

'Kopelzon? He's back at his apartment,' Lychev said. 'I suppose he has nothing to worry about.'

'Nothing,' Petrov said. 'Gan won't allow anything to happen to him. At least not until they have carried out the assassination. After that, Gan will throw him to the wolves.'

'Do you think Kopelzon knows?'

'Of course not. He's so egotistical he probably thinks the new regime will make him a duke or a prince.'

There was a brief pause. I heard Lychev say, 'May I speak frankly?'

'Go on,' Petrov answered with a hint of suspicion.

'Once they kill the tsar Gan will use the public hysteria to attack us. I am not convinced we will survive.'

'I think you underestimate the organisation's resilience,' Petrov said curtly.

'We can stop them if we want,' Lychev went on. 'They still need Rozental's double and we know where he is.'

'Where?'

'At the house on Kirochny Street – Kavi's watching it now. Eliminate the double and the plot falls apart.'

Petrov's voice was stern. 'The Central Committee has made its decision. We are to do nothing to hinder the assassination.'

There was a silence.

'Have I made myself clear?' Petrov repeated.

I heard them argue. I heard Lychev's voice rise insistently. Petrov was shouting. At least the bed was not tipping up.

Twenty-Six

I f you are knocked down in the street, my father used to say, check your wallet and your balls. I didn't care about my wallet. My head ached and there was a low humming in my ears. But I could see. I could feel my toes. I could wiggle my fingers. No broken limbs. I brought my hand up to my face. I needed to shave. I touched the hair on my head. It was brittle, not uniformly but in patches; I could crush individual strands and rub them between my fingers until they crumbled to dust. My hair had been scorched.

I was lying in a bed that was not mine, in a room I did not know. Smoke from the coal fire combined with the paraffin lamps and the building's general dampness produced a sharp odour that stung my nostrils. I had a hacking cough. Wherever I was, it was a poorer quarter – back where I started, where my father the baker started.

I decided to get up and immediately fell asleep again.

A cool hand was stroking my brow. I opened my eyes. Catherine. Her huge blue eyes were troubled and concerned. I had forgotten how long her eyelashes were.

'Your mother always envied you your eyelashes,' I said. She smiled and kissed me.

'How do you feel today?'

'My head hurts,' I said.

'You said that yesterday.'

'Were you here yesterday?'

'I've been here every day. They couldn't risk taking you to a hospital so they arranged for your friend Dr Sokolov to treat you. Your injuries were superficial, some minor burns and cuts and bruises, but you suffered a concussion.'

'What day is it?'

'It's the 26th – Thursday. Mintimer brought you here after the explosion five days ago. You're looking a lot better than you did then,' she said, narrowing her eyes to scrutinise me. She helped me sit up and started to re-arrange the pillows.

'The police are looking for me,' I said.

She took my hand and squeezed it. 'I know. Because of the murder in the apartment.'

'That wasn't me,' I protested, my voice catching on the acrid air.

'I know – Mintimer told me everything. The police are looking for him as well. They know he's a Bolshevik. Don't worry, as long as we get you on the train, you'll be safe.'

'I'm not going, Catherine. I'm not leaving you.'

'You have to,' she said matter-of-factly.

'Then you must come too,' I said.

'No, I'm staying,' she said with equal bluntness.

'Why?' I protested.

'I've joined the Party,' she said.

I filled up with fear and rage and outrage. I swung my feet to the floor. 'I will kill Petrov!' I said. 'I will kill him!'

'I haven't joined because of Petrov.'

'Who then? Who persuaded you? Was it Lychev?'

She laughed at my anger. 'You're behaving like a bourgeois paterfamilias.'

'I am a bourgeois paterfamilias. I am your father and you are my daughter. You are not even nineteen years old. You are still at university. What about your studies?'

231

'They had nothing more to teach me,' she said.

'I will not allow you to throw your life away like this.'

'Papa, I don't think you understand. My old life is over. After what happened at the Astoria and the Bolshoy apartment, Colonel Gan raided our house. I'm in hiding now, the same as you.'

'Then you have to come with me. I will tell Petrov and he will make you come.'

I saw the familiar look of determination and will come into her eyes. It cost her a great deal, it went against her fierce spirit and all her instincts, but she fought down the temptation to fly into a rage with me.

'If you want,' she began in an ominous tone, 'I will give you my reasons for joining. I will spell them out, one by one, starting with the condition of the people who live in these streets –'

'There is nothing you can tell me about these streets. I was born here, don't forget!'

'Peter Zinnurov was born the son of a peasant. He may remember something of that life but even if he does it makes no difference. He doesn't experience it any more than you experience life in the Vyborg.'

'I don't want to have this conversation,' I said.

'Fine,' she said. 'I'm not interested in it either.'

Her mind was made up. It was another battle I would not win.

'I think,' I said after a time, 'I would be less hurt by what you're doing if you would only show some sadness at the fact we are parting.'

'I am sad,' she said.

'You don't seem it.'

'Children can never look as sad as their parents want.'

'I don't know,' I said. 'The children of other parents seem to manage.'

'Then they're pretending,' she said. 'Would you like me to pretend for you? Would that make you feel better?'

'Yes,' I said.

She laughed and put her hand in mine. 'I don't believe you. You have always looked for the truth. Your work is all about the truth, isn't it?'

Catherine had always been a realist. Even as a child she understood that some decisions, however painful, were inevitable and there was no use in crying; her mother – and I, to some extent – preferred to make and see some sign of distress or sadness before the acceptance.

She said, making her voice softer now, 'The life we knew is over, it's past. All we can do is start again, a new life – a better one. I will start here.'

'Then I will too.'

She said, 'You want to make what you had before, and you can't do that in St Petersburg.' She smiled. 'Don't look so worried.'

'I am worried.'

'There's no need. I'm not alone any more. I'm part of something now, an organism in which each protects the other and together we are strong.'

'You should really talk to Petrov about the reality of this precious organism before you start rhapsodising to me,' I said sharply. 'The organism he described to me is full of jealousy, bitterness and betrayal.'

She smiled tolerantly. We looked at each other. I felt low and empty but it was Catherine who, to my surprise, started to cry. I held her head to my chest and kissed the top of it and stroked her fine, white-blonde hair. She gave herself fully to my embrace, for once, sinking into me as her mother used to do. I whispered her name over and over. This was what I wanted. If not sadness, then at least authentic feeling. Eventually, I released her.

'Are you hungry?'

233

I said I was. She left the room. A few minutes later she returned with tea and bread and cabbage soup.

'What time is it?' I asked.

'It's just gone midday. Here, eat,' she said, raising a spoon to my lips. 'You've got a long journey ahead of you. The train leaves from the Finland Station at ten o'clock tonight. Anna will be on it.'

'Are you angry?' I said. 'I promised you I wouldn't see her.'

She pushed the spoon around in the bowl and without looking at me said, 'I made you promise you wouldn't – there's a difference.'

Coming from Catherine, this was a fulsome apology for past errors.

'What do you think of her?' I asked lightly. 'Do you like her?'

She threw me a sharp look. I should not have pushed my luck. Her mouth started to form the word 'No', but then she forced a smile to her lips, trying to make it as sincere as possible. 'Yes,' she said. 'I do, and she loves you very much.'

Most of us take for granted that people lie to spare another's feelings. I never had, not with Catherine.

We were interrupted by the sound of raised voices next door.

'Petrov's here,' she said. 'He wants to say goodbye to you. I'll leave you to get dressed.' She indicated under the bed. 'Lidiya packed a bag with your clothes and some books and things. I'll be outside.'

'Catherine,' I called to her as she went to the door. 'How is Rozental doing? In the tournament?'

'He's second from bottom,' she replied. 'All the chess people say he has no chance of winning now.'

So it had all been for nothing. Gan's plot to manipulate the most wanted terrorist in Russia into doing his bidding and killing the tsar had stumbled on the one element he could not

234

control yet should have had every right to expect to calculate accurately. He bought Kopelzon and fooled Berek Medem, but he could not orchestrate the outcome of a series of games whose very logic should have made them the most predictable element in the whole complex. Gan had overlooked the human factor. He had overlooked Rozental. His plot had claimed the lives of Gulko and the unfortunate Leon Pikser. It had claimed the lives of Tolya and Medem's two companions in the corridor of the fourth floor of the Astoria. And of how many others? All for nothing. The plot had collapsed of its own accord.

My joints were stiff and my shoulders and lower back ached. I moved like an old man. I almost fainted as I pulled the valise from under the bed, and again as I struggled into my shirt.

As I dressed, I realised I would never see Kopelzon again. I would never hear his music, with all its passion, grace and waywardness; and its unique promise – that escape from human thraldom was almost within reach. Now I knew otherwise, for the discrepancy between the man and his playing had been brutally exposed; the promise was worthless. Kopelzon's playing claimed for its author the best of human instincts, but the actions of the man were in no way commensurate with these. The illusion was gone. I began to cry.

As I pushed the valise back under the bed, I noticed a box and pulled it out. It contained the clothes I had been wearing on the night of the explosion. They were blasted and torn. The right leg of my trousers was entirely shredded. My coat was scorched and spotted with blood. I felt in the pockets. There was something hard and heavy – the gun the man hiding in the bedroom had let fall. I had not handled a weapon of any kind in many years – I had not hunted since before Catherine was born – but I had never been afraid of guns. I inspected it

235

carefully; it was a German Mauser. I released and emptied the magazine and, after clearing the breach, carefully counted the bullets before reinserting the magazine into the housing. I pushed the gun into the waistband of my trousers, knotted my tie, took a deep breath and went to the door.

The room was small and low-ceilinged and the floorboards dusty and bare. It was empty but for a number of rude wooden chairs set around a simple table on which, among several newspapers, stood an empty bottle of Georgian wine and two dirty glasses. There were plates of unfinished *bitky*, pickled mushrooms and boiled potatoes.

Gregory Petrov leaned back in his chair, looking grey and strained. Lychev was on his feet. I had interrupted them in the middle of an angry disagreement. Lychev turned away, not wanting me to see his discomposure. Petrov assembled a smile.

'So you finally decided to get up, Spethmann,' he said jovially. 'Not before time. Your train leaves tonight.'

Though obviously exhausted, he was beautifully turned out in a cream-coloured linen suit, dark-blue cotton shirt and handmade shoes; not the dress typically associated with a tribune of the people and particularly incongruous in these surroundings. But Petrov was never less than his own man. He opened a silver case and offered me a Turkish cigarette. I shook my head. He lit one for himself and one for Catherine.

'You have your tickets, Mr Spirodovich?' he asked.

I took the papers from my pocket and examined them.

'You are a resident of St Petersburg, Mr Spirodovich,' he said. 'You are an engineer and you are travelling to Paris to consult with the firm of Lajannière & Philibot about the proposed construction of a new bridge across the Neva.'

'They're forgeries,' Lychev said, 'but of the best quality. You will have no problems at the border.'

'And to make your long journey as agreeable as possible,' Petrov said with a grin, 'we've also arranged for your lovely wife Zinaida to travel with you.'

Anna's photograph in the travel document was not flattering. An older woman, strained and tired.

'Where is Anna?'

Petrov stood up. 'Patience, Spethmann. The police are looking for you and, with equal zeal, Zinnurov is looking for Anna. The Mountain's affection for his daughter is truly astonishing. The arrangements have been made with great care. Don't mess them up.'

He collected his hat and coat and glanced towards Catherine. 'The metal workers have called a strike,' he said by way of explanation. Catherine gathered her things.

'You're going?' I asked.

'Catherine is now my secretary,' Petrov answered for her. Turning to address Lychev, he said sternly, 'Your orders are very specific, Lychev. See that you carry them out.'

The two men glared at each other. Struggling to contain his annoyance, Petrov turned to me and held out his hand. 'I don't know if we will see each other again, Spethmann, so I'll just say good luck.'

'Why are you helping me?' I said. 'I'm not one of your organisation. I don't approve of what you do or stand for, or the fact that you've recruited my daughter.'

'I don't approve of you either,' he replied with a grin. 'But you helped me and I know how to repay my debts.'

'I'm not sure I ever did help,' I said. 'I tried, but you would never allow me.'

'As for Catherine,' he went on. 'I have the impression she makes her own decisions.'

He smiled again and squeezed my hand. Catherine came up to kiss me.

'I'll see you at the station tonight,' she said.

Twenty-Seven

W hen we were alone, Lychev said, 'You should rest.' He looked utterly miserable as he dropped into one of the chairs at the table. I had never seen him like this. He studied one of the newspapers, tossed it aside in disgust and picked up another.

'Did you find out why Gan had Gulko killed? Why did he order the murder of a newspaper editor who had nothing to do with the plot?'

'Catherine got Yastrebov a job at a restaurant –'

'Leinner's – yes, I know.'

'By chance one night a newspaperman was among the diners – Gulko. Yastrebov probably didn't know who he was so it's likely another of the waiters or diners pointed Gulko out. In any case Yastrebov, who had started to have second thoughts, approached Gulko and told him the fascinating story of how he'd become involved in a plot to kill the tsar. Perhaps Gulko believed him, perhaps not – it's entirely possible he thought Yastrebov a fantasist. Unfortunately for him, Gan, who was keeping an eye on the plotters to make sure they were doing what they were supposed to do, couldn't take the chance. He had Yastrebov killed that night and the following morning Gulko was assassinated as he crossed Politseisky Bridge on his way to work. The rest you know.'

Lychev's tone made it clear he wanted me to leave him.

'May I take this paper?' I said, picking up the *Petersburgskiye Vedomosti*.

'Help yourself,' he said morosely.

I would have gone back to my room had I not noticed the headline: 'The King is Dead!' I glanced at the other papers. *Vecha* and *The Orator* had identical headlines: 'Checkmate'.

My first thought was that something had happened to Rozental but, taking up *The Orator*, I saw that the story had nothing to do with chess. The previous afternoon the body of Oleg Ivanovich Delyanov had been pulled from the Neva. The veteran Bolshevik had been shot in the back of the head and his body bore the marks of torture. A chess piece had been found on a string around his neck – a king.

'You found your traitor, I see.'

Lychev made a facetious grunt. 'So the newspapers say.'

His tone put me on alert. 'Are you saying they've got it wrong?'

'Why do people turn traitor?' Lychev asked rhetorically. 'There is always a motive, there is always something they get in return, tangible or otherwise. If you have a taste for luxury, the Okhrana can give you money. If you have an embarrassing past, it can keep your secrets secret. If you are a nobody, it can give you a sense of importance. If you have enemies, it can wreak revenge on your behalf. But Delyanov was a modest man, not highly intelligent but well enough liked. He always seemed to me indifferent to possessions and money. His clothes were old and patched. He had a wife, a fat old woman on whom he doted. He never had mistresses, he didn't go to prostitutes. Most of all, he believed in the workers' struggle. He lived for the revolution.'

'You don't believe Delyanov was King?'

'Where is his motive?' Lychev said. 'I don't see it.'

'Why didn't you prevent Delyanov's murder, if you thought he was innocent?'

'The Party made its decision.'

'You say "the Party" as though it's an entity.'

'It is.'

'But it's made up of individuals. Individuals made the decision, not the entity.'

He looked at me with contempt. 'This is Party business. It has nothing to do with you, Spethmann.'

'My daughter is now part of your organisation,' I said, 'an organisation so rife with treachery that its members torture and kill each other. That makes it something to do with me.'

Lychev picked up the bottle, emptied the last remaining drops into a glass and knocked it back.

'If Delyanov isn't King, who is?' I said.

He shook his head. 'It could be any one of fifty people – an underground worker, a trade union leader, a member of the Central Committee.'

Lychev grabbed the bottle again and, turning it upside down over his glass, started to shake it as if it were wilfully withholding its contents. He tossed the empty bottle across the room. It hit the floorboards but did not break. Neither of us spoke for some long moments.

'Why were you and Petrov arguing?' I said.

Lychev got up and went to the window.

'What orders did he give you?'

He hesitated a moment, then, with his back still to me, said, 'He was reminding me of the Central Committee's decision to allow the assassination to go ahead.'

'But the plot has already fallen apart,' I said. 'They needed Rozental to win, and he isn't going to.'

'Gan has been planning this for months. He and Zinnurov have been preparing the ground for years. They are on the verge of seizing power. Do you really think they would have staked so much on the outcome of a chess tournament? Don't be ridiculous.'

'Then how do they propose to do it?'

'Last night we found out that a certain chess player has had the honour of being invited to a very special occasion.'

'Rozental?'

'Precisely. He was the only player to receive the invitation. Not even Lasker was invited.'

'What is the occasion?'

'A recital to be given by your friend Kopelzon at the Mariinsky Theatre tonight. The tsar and tsarina will be present. The double will take Rozental's place and do the deed, and by morning Bolsheviks will be hanging from the lampposts the length of the Nevsky. But don't worry, Spethmann. You'll be in Paris with your lover.'

I looked at my watch. It was coming up to two o'clock. I went to the door.

'What do you think you're doing?' I heard Lychev call after me.

I ignored him and started down the mouldy wooden staircase. Lychev hurried after me and grabbed me by the arm.

'Petrov left strict instructions you are not to leave this house until it is time to go to the station,' he said.

I shook him off and continued down the stairs. I emerged into a squalid, narrow street. Drying clothes hung on lines strung from the windows above. There was a horrible, fetid stink from the open drains. I had no idea where I was. I started walking.

'Spethmann, wait!'

I turned back to see Lychev at the entrance to the building. He strode towards me.

'What are you doing?' he said.

'I'm going to stop Medem.'

'And how do you propose to do that?'

'I'll go to the police and tell them everything.'

Lychev began to shake with laughter. 'Obviously I haven't

made the situation clear. You are wanted for murder, Speth-mann. You'll be arrested the minute you go to the police – that's if they don't shoot you. And let's say for some reason they don't, that they've run out of ammunition or been overtaken by conscience, to whom do you think the police will report? To Colonel Gan.'

'I have to try. I have to do something. It won't just be Bolsheviks hanging from the lamp-posts. There must be a way,' I said angrily and turned to go.

Lychev grabbed my arm.

'There is,' he said.

Lychev drove past St Petersburg Metals. Workers were pour-ing from the factory gates. It was too early to be the end of their shift. I saw some men unfurl a huge banner with the legend: 'Freedom and Bread!' Further along we passed men, women and children forming up with more banners and placards, proclaiming the Metal Workers' Union to be on strike.

'Petrov's called a strike,' Lychev explained. 'This is his own union, this is where he started. He joined when he was fourteen. By the time he was sixteen he was one of the local leaders. Have you ever heard him speak in public?'

'I tend to avoid political meetings,' I said.

'You don't know what you've missed. Gregory Petrov is electrifying. When you listen to him, the hairs on the back of your neck stand up. You shiver and you think: I will go to the ends of the earth for this man.'

Lychev had to make a detour to avoid getting caught up in the procession. It was after three by the time we got to Alexandrovski Bridge; scattered advance parties of strikers and their families were already crossing it. They were chanting '*Bread and Freedom!*' and the name of their hero, Gregory Petrov.

242

'Are you still interested in what happened in Kazan?' Lychev said out of the blue as we were crawling across the bridge. 'Before I had to disappear, I received a full report from my former colleagues there.'

'Go on,' I said.

'You remember there was an unexplained killing?'

'Of the intruder?'

'It turns out the intruder was not bent on robbery, but on revenge.'

'Revenge on whom?'

'There were two men in the house, though neither lived there. It belonged to the mother of one of them. His name was Oleg Yuratev. The file, or rather files, on Yuratev are large.'

We weaved in and out of the traffic. We passed a captain of gendarmes trying to turn back the marchers.

'Yuratev's grandfather was a serf. His son, Yuratev's father, was conscripted into the army, though not before impregnating a young woman – Irina – in his village. The rumour-mongers and gossips claimed there had been no legal marriage. The child did not see his father until the soldier returned home at the conclusion of the Crimean War, by which time he was almost ten. By all accounts, he was precociously intelligent and already beyond his mother's control. His father soon disappeared again and his mother turned to drink and probably also to occasional prostitution. Apparently, a local priest took an interest in young Oleg and saw that he got an education. But he had a hard time at university – he was a peasant, after all, and illegitimate.'

Lychev turned and gave me the kind of look that usually presages surprising information.

'It was at university that young Oleg became involved in a terrorist group, the People's Will. According to them the only hope of saving the Russian soul was by action, by the deed, the bomb and the gun. In 1876 the district governor was assassinated by a young man with a pistol – none other than Oleg Yuratev. His deed propelled him up the hierarchy of the organisation and he became a member of its executive committee. More assassinations followed. Police officials, government officers, local governors, tsarist ministers. Yuratev's efficiency and dedication solidified his reputation among his comrades. There was just one problem: the man they so admired for his commitment to the revolutionary cause was a traitor.'

We were almost across the bridge.

'It's not clear whether Yuratev was a double agent from the beginning of his terrorist career or whether he had become disillusioned and offered his services to the secret police. But he was instrumental in destroying the People's Will and for his achievements he received a new name, amnesty and the seed money with which he later made his fortune.'

'Zinnurov?' I said.

'The files do not give Yuratev's new name, but there can be little doubt. Peter Zinnurov and Oleg Yuratev are one and the same man.'

Lychev let the information settle.

After a time I said, 'What does this have to do with the killing of the intruder in Kazan?'

'Yuratev had travelled to Kazan to meet the officer from the Okhrana with whom he had worked while he was a member of the People's Will. Somehow one of Yuratev's former comrades found out they were in the house of Yuratev's mother. He broke in and tried to kill them both – and he nearly succeeded. Both men were very seriously injured. They would have died had not a young girl been found wandering the streets covered in blood and crying that there had been a murder.'

'Who was the Okhrana officer in the house with Zinnurov?'

'I'm sure you've probably already guessed.'

'Colonel Gan.'

'He was a captain then.'

We were on Liteiny Prospect. The turning for Kirochny Street was coming up.

'Wait a minute,' I said. 'I have to see Rozental.'

'There's no time,' Lychev shot back.

'Saburov's house is just up here. We'll be ten minutes.'

'No,' Lychev shouted.

'I've let Rozental down badly. I have to see him.'

Lychev let out a curse as we passed Kirochny Street and continued towards Saburov's house.

The ballroom accommodated three of the five tables and smaller adjoining rooms the other two. By the time we arrived the games were well under way. Groups of spectators milled about, shifting from one table to another as battles flowed and ebbed. Rozental was nowhere in sight.

'Excuse me,' I whispered to a spectator, 'who is Rozental playing?'

The spectator pointed to the middle table in the ballroom at which Lasker sat, his legs crossed high up, his right arm dangling languorously over the back of his chair, a cigar between his fingers.

'Whose move is it?' I asked.

'Lasker's. Rozental captured with the knight on d2.'

I searched the room but still couldn't find him. 'Where is he?' I whispered.

'Have a close look over there,' Lychev put in, directing my attention to a large potted palm to my right, behind which, after a moment or two, I discerned the lurking figure of Rozental.

'It's bizarre,' the spectator put in, only then registering my singed hair; his gaze passed discreetly over it before he went on. 'He makes his move then goes off and hides behind the palm. He only comes back when Lasker makes his move and presses his clock. He's losing a lot of thinking time. He's second from bottom – can you believe it? Who would have thought the great Avrom Chilowicz would perform so badly?'

I told Lychev to wait. 'Don't be long,' he said as I approached the potted palm.

'Avrom Chilowicz,' I ventured. 'What are you doing there?'

There was no reply.

'Shouldn't you be at the board, studying the position?'

'I have no need to study it,' Rozental answered, his voice barely audible.

'But why are you hiding like this?'

'I'm not hiding.' His face was partially obscured by the palm's sharp fronds but I could see his nervous, sad brown eyes.

'Then what are you doing?'

'I don't want to be any trouble to anyone.'

'Who would you be trouble to?'

'Dr Lasker,' he said after a moment. 'I don't want to cause my opponent any offence.'

'But you're not offending him.'

'My presence offends him. I am offensive to everyone.'

'That's not true,' I said. 'Please, Avrom, come back to the table.'

He shook his head – no.

I felt angry with myself. I had not succeeded in helping him in the least. And I felt desperately sad: Rozental's talents were no less considerable than those of the greatest players present, but I saw all too clearly now that the man from the shtetl would never achieve anything like the success even of his inferiors. It was not that his chance for greatness had passed – the chance itself had never been anything other than an illusion.

'Goodbye, Avrom,' I said.

'Goodbye,' he said. The word had as much meaning for him as it did for a child responding to an adult he did not know.

I turned to go back to Lychev. To my horror, only a few paces away, Saburov stood in good-natured clubby conversation with two other members of the St Petersburg Chess Union. He was nodding in vigorous agreement with something one of his companions had just said. For a moment I thought he might not see me, but then he suddenly looked up, instinctively alerted by the scrutiny of another, and his eyes met mine. His jaw dropped and his face went white.

I went up to the table, where Lasker was still sunk in thought, and whispered to Lychev, 'I've been recognised. Let's go.'

As we started away, the spectators sent up a sudden murmur of speculation. Looking back, I saw Lasker taking the knight on d2 with his queen. He pressed his clock to start Rozental's ticking. As one body, the spectators turned their gaze to the potted palm, from which Rozental duly emerged, eyes cast down, arms rigidly at his side, hands clenched. He took his seat and, after the briefest glance at the new position, moved his f-pawn one square forward. He suddenly cocked his head and started to swipe at the flies tormenting him. He pressed his clock, whispered 'Excuse me' and went back to the palm. One or two of the spectators sniggered.

Saburov and his two companions were staring after us.

We descended the stairs and walked briskly to the door. As we got to the street, someone shouted, 'Stop those men!'

We ran for the car, which Lychev had parked outside the Marie Hospital pointing towards the Nevsky. He jumped into the driver's seat while I cranked the engine. Looking past the car to Saburov's house, I saw half a dozen or so men emerge onto the steps. They shouted and pointed in our direction. Then two braver souls started sprinting towards us.

247

The engine spluttered into life and I leaped in beside Lychev.

'We'll have to double back later,' he said, making for the junction with the Nevsky, 250 *sazheni* away.

At this time of day the Nevsky is always crowded with people, buses, taxis, droshkies, lorries, carts, cars and private carriages, and I was worried that we would be overtaken by the men coming after us. But today the great avenue was almost deserted; what little traffic there was on the road was heading in the opposite direction, the drivers peculiarly grim-faced.

'We're in luck!' Lychev said as he pressed the accelerator.

We left our pursuers behind at the corner with Liteiny Prospect. Lychev continued over the Fontanka, a smile of satisfaction playing on his lips.

Something was wrong.

'What's going on?' I said.

A woman hurried past us, following the carriages and droshkies going in the opposite direction. Then came four or five men. They stopped and stared back the way they had come with what seemed like puzzlement and apprehension before running on. People were stampeding, spilling out onto the road, colliding with one another in their desperation to flee.

But from what?

At the Armenian Church sheer numbers forced us to a halt. Lychev shouted and blew the horn but there was no question of going forward. He threw the car into reverse and tried to back up, but the crowds flowing around us made any movement impossible.

I looked at my watch. It was almost 4 p.m.

'We'll have to go on foot,' Lychev said, springing out of the car. 'Come on!'

I climbed out after him.

A child stumbled and fell in front of us. A youth running behind cleared the prostrate form with a leap but those who followed could not avoid him. A dozen or more people were caught up in the collision. Men started screaming.

That was when the first shots were fired.

One of the men who had been crawling away from the pile-up pitched violently forward, as though someone had kicked him in the behind. I saw another man stagger, his legs uncertain, his arms reaching desperately for support. He got to a lamp-post and clung to it like a sailor cleaving to a mast in a storm. There was a large bloody wound at the small of his back. The ground beneath his feet was treacherous, his legs could not be trusted, yet still he would not give up. I watched horrified as he gathered his forces for one last effort. He let go of the lamp-post, tottered a step or two and collapsed face down in front of me.

I bent down to him. He was still breathing. The bullet had torn through the seat of his trousers, fractionally to the right. I turned him over. He breathed out heavily and gasped 'Mother'.

'Spethmann, come on!' Lychev shouted.

I glimpsed a soldier outside the Duma, his bayonet fixed. We stared at each other for a moment before he seemed to lose interest in me and ran on, perhaps to some other quarry.

Lychev pulled me up. 'We have to go!' he shouted.

'Help me get this man off the street,' I shouted back.

There were more shots, three or four, though it was impossible to tell where they were coming from or what the intended targets were.

'Leave him!' Lychev screamed. 'We have to get to Kirochny Street. Now!'

'We can't leave him,' I shouted.

Lychev threw me a disgusted look, then started off by himself. I struggled to lift the man but he was a dead weight.

Someone came up, a worker by his dress, and said, panting, 'Is he hurt?'

'He's been shot.'

'Quickly,' the man said, 'before the soldiers get him.'

With some difficulty the two of us hauled him up.

'Get him into the church,' I said as we staggered forward. 'What's going on down there?'

'We were coming up the Nevsky,' the man said breathlessly, grunting under the strain. 'Everything peaceful, and all of a sudden the soldiers started shooting. God knows how many they've killed. It's Bloody Sunday all over again.'

We were less than twenty *sazheni* from the church when two Cossacks bore down on us.

'Save yourself!' the man shouted, suddenly dropping the wounded man. 'They'll kill us!'

He took off but did not get more than ten paces before he was overtaken.

The second Cossack was bearing down on me. I was mesmerised by the extraordinarily beautiful, flowing movements with which he controlled his mount. His long moustache was grey and we were so close I could see that his skin was pitted and flecked with red. He adjusted his weight in readiness for the strike, leaning smoothly to the right.

He stretched his sabre, then jolted sharply back in the saddle before flopping forward and galloping harmlessly past. The sabre that clattered to the ground next to me was already stained with blood; I would not have been the Cossack's first kill of the day.

Lychev was holding a pistol in his hand. I looked down at the man I had tried to help.

'Leave him – he's dead.'

Lychev pulled me into a narrow passage that ran alongside the church. Within minutes we were on the Fontanka Embankment. We crossed the canal and quickly found ourselves, once again, on Liteiny Prospect, somewhat north of Saburov's house. I had to pause to recover my breath. I felt light-headed and weak. At the Cathedral of the Transfiguration, where Kirochny joins Liteiny, a tram had been set on fire.

Twenty-Eight

Number 19 Kirochny Street was the address Berek Medem had given to Yastrebov in Moscow when he had recruited the ardent young idealist. As far as the conspirators were aware, they were still safe there. They did not know that Yastrebov had told Catherine about it and that through me it had come to the attention of Lychev.

Kavi was in the building opposite, in a second-floor apartment Lychev had rented. He was bored and frustrated, the more so for having heard something of the commotion in the city. A man of the street, a fighter, he bridled at the inactivity his role as monitor forced on him. He was further disconcerted when Lychev told him why we were there.

'I won't cry if the tsar is killed.'

'It won't just be the tsar who dies,' Lychev said tersely. 'Gan and the Baltic Barons will use the assassination as an excuse to crack down on us. We'll be annihilated.'

Kavi scratched his chin. 'I don't know, Mintimer,' he said. 'If the Central Committee has decided to let it go ahead –'

'They only decided because Petrov persuaded them. The double will be leaving for the theatre soon. If we're going to do this, it has to be now.'

'There has to be discipline, Mintimer. Once an order is given it has to be carried out.'

'You know in your heart, Kavi, that I'm right. You know that this will be a disaster for us.'

252

'Not just for you,' I put in. 'For everyone.'

Kavi scowled and Lychev examined the floor. I had nothing to say here.

'I don't like to go against the Central Committee's orders,' Kavi said.

'If we don't, there won't be a Central Committee. There won't be a Party. The Baltic Barons will be in control.'

Kavi paced the floor, grunting and gesturing. 'We'll be in big trouble,' he said.

'Bigger than hanging from a lamp-post?'

Kavi stopped, looked up at the ceiling and exhaled. 'All right,' he said at last. 'But you can do the explaining.'

'I'll tell them I lied to you,' Lychev said, clapping him on the back. 'I'll say I told you that the Central Committee changed its mind.'

Kavi took out his knife and tested its sharpness.

'There's no need to kill him,' I said. 'All you have to do is keep him from the recital.'

Kavi shot me a pitying look.

'Wait for me here,' Lychev said to me. 'When I come back we'll make our way to the Finland Station. It's not yet 5 p.m. Even if we have to walk all the way, we have plenty of time.'

Kavi broke open a large revolver in front of us and carefully loaded each chamber before snapping it together again.

'Make yourself some tea,' Lychev said. 'I'll be back soon.'

'Wait a minute,' I said. 'Was Yuratev's mother also in the house in Kazan the night the intruder broke in?'

'No,' Lychev said. 'According to the police reports she had died two years earlier.'

So Zinnurov had been telling the truth, about this at least. Anna must have conflated her passing with the brutal assault she witnessed as a thirteen-year-old girl.

'How did she die?'

'After a fall. The death was recorded as accidental.'

'Was there some doubt?'

'As a policeman reading between the lines, yes, a lot of doubt.'

Had Anna been right, after all? 'Do you think Zinnurov killed her?'

'Not according to the detective who investigated the case. He thought Zinnurov was protecting the real killer.'

'Who was the real killer?'

'Are you sure you want to know?'

I said nothing.

Lychev said, 'Irina Yuratev was not some child's beloved babushka. She was a drunken, foul-mouthed, coarse old woman.'

It may or may not have been true. Who was I to know? But even had she been this and worse, it hardly excused murder.

Lychev and Kavi checked their weapons one last time. Lychev pulled back the slide of his automatic, slamming a bullet into the firing chamber.

'Oh, Spethmann, I meant to ask,' Kavi said. 'How did your game with Kopelzon go?'

It took me a moment to realise what he was talking about. 'We never got to finish it,' I said.

'You mean the move I gave you was all for nothing?'

'I'm afraid so.'

He laughed as he pulled the door closed after him.

All for nothing.

I went to the window at the front of the apartment. A minute or two later, I saw Kavi and Lychev, hands stuffed in the pockets of their overcoats, start across the street for the house at number 19.

In a few hours all this would be over. The guests would arrive at the Mariinsky and make their way to the White Hall. Kopelzon would be more nervous than usual. He would scan the faces, expecting at any moment to see Rozental's double turn up. And then everyone would rise and bow as the tsar and tsarina came to take their seats. Where was the double? Kopelzon would be sweating now. Where was the double?

I would be on a train to Paris with Anna.

Lychev and Kavi were approaching the door of number 19. They took a quick look around. Lychev nodded and took out his pistol. The huge Cossack kicked at the door, once, twice. The sound of the shattering frame carried all the way across the street. The top hinge broke and the door swung open.

Lychev and Kavi dashed inside.

I knew they would kill him but even so I flinched at the first shot. I was about to turn away when I saw someone stumble backwards through the broken door.

Kavi still had his gun in his hand but there was nothing he could do with it. He collapsed heavily on the pavement.

A moment later, Lychev emerged, hands above his head, surrounded by half a dozen men armed with pistols and carbines. They were followed by Colonel Gan, impeccable in his Household Cavalry uniform. With him was the man I had once briefly mistaken for Rozental. A motor carriage pulled up and the double got inside. As it drove away, Gan turned to Lychev and offered him a cigarette. Lychev shook his head.

It was only then that I noticed two of Gan's men hurrying across the street. They were coming to get me.

I was on the landing before I realised that if I tried to escape from the front of the house I would run into Gan's men. I ran back into the apartment, slamming the door behind me. There was a gun in my pocket but I knew I would never use it.

I raced into a bedroom at the back and went to the window.

255

It would not open. I went to the bathroom where the window was already open. I looked out. Below was a garden. It was a long way down.

They were at the door.

I looked out again. There was a tree but I would never be able to reach its branches.

They were kicking in the door, just as Kavi had.

I climbed onto the ledge. There was a pergola with a thin, insubstantial plant growing over it. I heard the door shatter. I leaped into the air, pushing out as far as I could.

Two faces looked down at me. For a moment I was not sure where I was or why they were interested in me. One of the faces ducked inside, the other shouted at me to stay where I was.

I got to my feet, struggling out of the trailing branches of the plant and the broken wood of the pergola. A bewildered child in a sailor's suit was staring open-mouthed from a window on the ground floor. I turned and ran the length of the garden. My right hip hurt and by the time I reached the gate in the far wall I was already hobbling. Glancing back, I saw the man in the window take aim with his pistol. He fired three or four shots.

I ducked through the side streets. I ran through pain. I ran from fear. After ten minutes or so I could go no further. Had I turned then to find my pursuer, gun in hand, but a pace away, there would have been nothing I could have done. My breath had given out. My heart was pounding. I put my hands on my knees, bent over and retched. I wiped my mouth, gulped for air and went on.

Even with the most detailed map I would not now be able to reproduce the course of my flight. I don't remember crossing the Nevsky, I don't know how I got to Minsky Street. I don't remember that at any point in my flight I took a decision to go there, but of course I must have. It could not have been by chance. I do remember seeing in the streets the pitiful detritus of the strikers' procession – the abandoned placards, umbrellas, boaters and shoes. From time to time I heard the dry crack of a rifle shot but for the most part there was silence. Shop windows had been smashed, but not many. Near the Yusupov Palace I passed what looked at first like a collection of rags lying on the pavement. It turned out to be a dead body, around which a small group of bored policemen had gathered.

Minsky Street.

I had arrived. I looked at my watch. It was 6.18 p.m. The recital was for 7.30 p.m. Kopelzon might well have left for the theatre already.

Twenty-Nine

M y appearance at his door took him by surprise. He tried
to push it shut but I barged through to the small, over-
furnished room. There were turkey-work cloths and cushions
scattered over the furniture, photographs of himself in Paris
and Moscow, posters for his concerts, a phonograph, sheet
music, books and, on a little table in the centre of the room, a
chessboard.

He was already in his dress suit. He looked lined, haggard
and oppressed. He smelt musky and sour.

'You look as though you didn't expect to see me,' I said,
going to the chessboard.

'I'm warning you, Otto,' he said, 'I have a gun. I will use it if
I have to.'

'You won't have to,' I said. 'I just want to finish our game.'

'I don't have time for this,' he said, glancing anxiously in the
direction of the bedroom.

'Do you have company?' I said.

'That's none of your business.'

'Is it your friend Berek Medem?'

'It's a woman, actually.'

'I'm sure she won't mind. It'll only take a minute,' I said,
setting up the position from our game. In spite of himself he
was watching with interest. 'I have the win. I have it all
worked out.'

'Nonsense,' he said dismissively. 'It's a dead draw.'

'No, Reuven,' I said. 'It's a forced win.'

'You're deluding yourself,' he said. 'You're attacking my f-pawn with queen and king, I'm defending with equal forces. You can't win.'

Spethmann–Kopelzon
After 46 . . . Qc7. Spethmann claims to have found
a forced win. Is he right?

I put my hand out to the queen. This much Kopelzon expected. He also expected me to play it to g7. Instead I moved it to h6. He squinted at the board. I do not think he yet realised that the position was fatal, but I could see he was beginning to have doubts.

'Who's in the bedroom?' I asked. 'Anyone I know?'

'Someone I happen to be deeply in love with,' he said, looking up from the board, 'if you must know.'

'Really?' I said. 'That's new for you, isn't it?'

'We're going to get married, actually,' he said sharply.

'Congratulations. Is she coming to hear you tonight?'

He looked at me with suspicion. 'You won't stop us, Otto,' he said. He opened the drawer of the table and brought out a revolver.

259

'We're playing chess, Reuven,' I said. 'There's no need for that.'

'Are you alone?' he asked.

'Yes.'

'Where's Lychev?'

'He was arrested an hour ago,' I said, 'by Colonel Gan.'

He searched my face and, satisfied I was telling the truth, he placed the gun on the table beside the taken pieces, though still within reach. I was no threat to him.

He played his queen to e7. 'I'm still guarding the pawn with queen and king,' he said with a thin smile of satisfaction. 'You won't get it.'

I played my queen to g7. Kopelzon narrowed his eyes. Now he apprehended something of the danger.

'How did you ever come to meet Berek Medem?' I said.

'You've heard of the recital I gave at the Paris Opera? Two years ago this August? Do you know, Otto, people boast of having been present. When they talk about it, it's with awe. They don't talk about me as a musician – no! That night they heard a messiah who touched their souls.'

He looked down at the chessboard.

'You're running out of moves, Reuven,' I said.

He played his pawn to a6. I played mine to a3.

'Berek was there that night. He heard me. He came backstage. There were the usual women, old and young, all of them begging to have the opportunity to entertain me privately. I would have obliged, the prettiest at least.' He smiled; his carnality had always been plain. 'But I saw this man and for the first time in my life I sensed a power greater than my own.'

He moved his a-pawn another square forward. I did the same. He sat back, regarding the pieces almost as enemies.

'You're in zugzwang, Reuven,' I said.

260

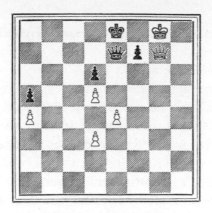

Spethmann–Kopelzon

After 50 a4. Zugzwang. Black is running out of moves.

He stared at the board, not wanting to believe what he was seeing. He had no choice but to move the king away from the defence of the f-pawn. His hand trembled as he moved the king to d8. I played at once, moving my queen to f8.

'Check,' I said quietly.

He played his queen to e8, a forlorn blocking of the check; it would change nothing. I played my king to g7. The f-pawn would fall after the exchange on f8. The game was mine.

Spethmann–Kopelzon

After 52 Kg7. Black is in zugzwang. Whatever Kopelzon does, he will lose the f7-pawn, and with it the game.

261

It was not in Kopelzon's nature to be a good loser. He did not formally resign. He did not turn his king over. He did not offer to shake hands. He got to his feet.

'You look very pleased with yourself,' he said.

'You can have no idea how unhappy I am,' I said.

I got up. I said, 'Don't go to the recital, Reuven. You've already ruined Rozental. Don't destroy still more lives.'

'Are you pleading for the tsar?' he said with a sneer. 'After all he has done?' He picked up the gun from the table. 'Just this afternoon he set the Cossacks on a demonstration of workers. They're saying more than thirty people were killed – and that's just today, here in St Petersburg!'

'I beg you, Reuven, for pity's sake.'

'Pity? Pity?' he spat back. 'And where is your pity, Otto? Where are your tears? You are Dr Otto Spethmann' – he made the name sound utterly distasteful – 'you have made your own way in the world. Good for you. You have left the shtetl and the Pale behind. Why not? It's nicer to live in a big house on Furshtatskaya Street than in a stinking wooden shack next to a cattle market. But, Otto, the men and women and children you left behind cannot follow you to a better life. In Dvinsk, your father's brothers are still alive. You have cousins and aunts and nieces and nephews. They have lice in their hair and holes in their teeth, and they live entirely without hope that tomorrow will be better than today. If you're so overflowing with pity, go to your uncles. Go to your nephews. Lavish your pity on them. And then, when you've looked in the faces of the children who will never know anything but squalor and violence, ask yourself this question: now that I have seen what I have seen, am I going to turn my eyes away?'

He stared at me with contempt. He had always held me in contempt. This was the truth of it. It was not incompatible with his love for me, which I believed even at that moment was genuine.

'Get out, Otto! Go and bury your head in the sand,' he said, marching to the door. 'That way you won't have to see the suffering all around you.'

'By killing the tsar you will end the suffering?' I asked.

He transferred the gun to his left hand so as to unlock the door. 'I know that if we do nothing, nothing will change.'

I started to laugh.

'What's so funny?' he said suspiciously.

'You play the part so convincingly.'

'What part?'

'Spare me the lines you used on the poor souls you duped when you were in Paris and London. Spare me the tears, Reuven.'

He did not move as I withdrew the Mauser. He had not expected this.

'How long have you been in the pay of Colonel Gan?' I said.

He blanched. I did not wait for an answer. I am not sure that he had one. Even as the bullet struck him he did not believe it.

'Oh,' he gasped, staring into my eyes.

I heard movement coming from the bedroom and swivelled round, ready to shoot again.

A woman, flushed and still sweaty, ran into the room and let out a cry. Her silk robe came open. She was naked underneath, her body as shiny as an egg yolk.

Minna did not even glance at me. She went forward to Kopelzon. Blood was blooming over his white dress shirt. His face had drained of colour. She helped him into a chair.

I picked up the telephone and asked to be put through to the artistic director of the Mariinsky Theatre. I told him that Reuven Moiseyevich Kopelzon was sadly indisposed and would not be able to play that night.

I put the phone down.

263

'I'm sorry, Minna,' I said.

Minna buried her head in Kopelzon's lap and started to weep. I waited with her until Kopelzon took his final breath. She did not believe me. But I was sorry.

I crossed Krukov's Canal and made my way to the Mariinsky Theatre. I saw a troop of Cossack guards with long hair and in scarlet tunics trot out of the square, their sabres flashing and their horses glistening with health and sweat. They were escorting a four-horse calèche away from the theatre. In it I glimpsed the tsar in an admiral's uniform and the tsarina in a brocade dress and diamond tiara. Other carriages were following the tsar's. Forty or fifty curious onlookers, held back by white-coated gendarmes on either side of the main entrance, watched as the guests departed from the recital that would never take place.

It was 9.10 p.m. I had less than an hour to get to the Finland Station. Gendarmes, soldiers and Cossacks were still roaming the near-empty streets, swinging their clubs and rifle butts at anyone who ventured out. None of the taxi drivers in the square was prepared to take me across the Neva, saying it was still too dangerous after the riot in the afternoon. Eventually I found a droshky. The driver agreed to take me as far as the Alexandrovski Bridge. From there I walked to the station. Catherine and Anna were standing together at the ticket barrier, looking anxiously about. Catherine was the first to see me and she ran into my arms.

Thirty

I t was the first time we had spent the night together and not made love. This is the real world. This is what love in the real world is like. I tried to recall the last time Elena and I had made love but could not. What a thing to forget. The real world.

The attendant had insisted on lighting the stove in the sleeping car even though the night was mild. I had a terrible headache. I slipped out of the bunk and dressed as quietly as I could. My right hip had all but seized up.

'What's the matter?' Anna said sleepily.

'Nothing,' I said, stroking her hair and kissing her. 'Go back to sleep.'

'I don't want to stay in Paris.'

'Let's see how we feel when we get there,' I said. 'We can rest for a day or two and then decide where to go.'

'I would like to see London.'

'Sleep,' I whispered, 'sleep.'

'My mother had a half-sister – Ivana,' she said. 'She was quite a bit older. She married a lovely man when she was twenty-six. She and her husband never spent a single night apart in all the time they were married. They died within three months of each other.' She smiled sadly. 'I don't know why I told you that.'

I kissed her. 'Don't worry,' I said. 'I won't be long.'

I walked the length of the corridor, limping as I went, and passed through the door at the end of the carriage. An

265

attendant in a black blouse and belt, with wide trousers tucked into his polished boots and a round fur cap, asked if he could be of assistance.

'Is the restaurant car still open?' I asked.

'If his honour continues for two more carriages he will find it.'

The car was empty. I took a seat and ordered a brandy.

'Where are we?' I asked the attendant.

'We'll soon be in Wirballen,' he said. 'His honour has his passport ready? The guards will check his papers and baggage there. Is there anything else his honour needs?'

'Do you think you could find me a pen and some writing paper?'

He returned a minute or two later with pen and paper. I wrote the date, 27 April 1914, 'near Wirballen' and 'My darling daughter . . .' Everything at the station had been so fraught. I had a thousand things to say to her yet I could not find a way to say any of them.

I squinted through the window out into the darkness. I turned back to my letter but I wrote no words.

The train's brakes ground and squealed and we started to slow. We were coming into Wirballen. I finished my brandy and made to go back to Anna. The attendant stooped to look out of the window.

'Strange,' he said as the train came to a halt. 'We're not due in Wirballen for another twenty minutes.'

The engine huffed. Steam billowed back, clouding the view.

'Very strange,' the attendant said, going off in search of someone who would tell him what was going on.

I settled back into my seat. Ten minutes later the attendant returned. He had no explanation for the delay. I ordered another brandy.

After an hour the train started up again. The lights of the town came into view. Was it possible Gan had discovered my escape route? Would Lychev have confessed? I debated with myself whether I should rouse Anna. Should we get off the train and try to find another way out of the country?

'This is getting very odd,' the attendant said.

'What's going on?'

'We're not pulling into the station.' He scratched his head. 'They're putting us in a siding.'

I looked out the window. Instead of the station platform I saw the silhouettes of sheds and cranes and industrial buildings.

A passenger entered and asked why he couldn't get off the train. Others behind him started to mutter and complain. After some moments the chief attendant came and explained the delay would be a short one and they would soon be at the station.

'Why can't we just get out here and walk the rest of the way?' one of the aggrieved passengers said.

'No one is allowed on or off the train,' the chief attendant said firmly. 'Those are our orders.'

'What do you mean your orders?' a passenger shouted back.

I got up and went quickly to the sleeping car. Policemen were patrolling the track outside.

Anna was profoundly asleep. I shook her once. She moaned but did not wake. Why bother her with this? I thought. There was nothing to be done, except to wait. I returned to the restaurant car, by now filled with bored and frustrated passengers.

At 3.15 in the morning the train suddenly lurched backwards. Dozing passengers with the clammy sheen of sweat on their brows looked up hopefully. At once the attendant became the recipient of a score of shouted enquiries.

'I don't know,' he kept protesting, 'I don't know anything.'

We were being shunted back onto the main line. A cheer went up when we pulled forward again and the station came into view in the thin, early-morning light. I hurried for the sleeping car.

267

Anna lay in exactly the same position as I had left her, as deeply asleep as the child the parent carries from carriage to bed after a long journey late at night. I ran through the possibilities: Had Lychev confessed? Had he revealed the details of our escape? Or was our delay simply a matter of the track's integrity, the engine's health, the timetable's soundness? Trains in Russia were frequently late. I did not want to worry her. I returned again to the restaurant car.

The train pulled into the station. Within a couple of minutes the car had emptied as passengers went to gather their luggage. I was again alone with the attendant.

A man entered at the far end. He wore no hat but I did not recognise him at first because he was the last person I was expecting to see.

Gregory Petrov slid into the seat opposite and offered me a cigarette.

'What are you doing here, Gregory?' I asked.

'I'm here to offer you a deal on behalf of a third party.'

'That's interesting,' I said. 'Who is this third party?'

He licked his lips. 'Peter Zinnurov.'

'I didn't know you were friends.'

Petrov's eyes were tired and sad. 'I loathe everything about Zinnurov. Everything.'

'But you have come on his behalf,' I said. 'At his bidding.'

'Let me tell you about my brother,' he said, putting a cigarette between his lips and lighting it. He inhaled deeply. 'The one who was arrested with me when I was a kid.'

'You told me you made that story up.'

He blew out a jet of smoke and sniffed. 'Sadly, no – it's a true story.' The facile grin he had fixed to his face gave way to a truer, melancholy expression. 'The officer in charge of our case was as good as his word. Ivan and I were both sent to prison as subversives. We were children. I was sixteen – Ivan a

268

year younger – but I knew, in my bones I knew, I would survive. Ivan was made differently. He was frightened. The guards were vicious, the cell was dark and cold. Sometimes when he cried I got angry and told him to pull himself together. He would just go silent. He was so skinny. Tiny, thin little arms, hollow cheeks and big eyes. He was so small.'

The attendant brought us brandy. Petrov threw his down in one gulp and ordered another. On the platform the first bell sounded: fifteen minutes to departure.

'In the end I couldn't stand being in the same cell, just couldn't bear it any longer. Guilt, I suppose.' His eyes were moist. He chewed his lower lip. 'I bribed a guard with a few cigarettes to move me to another cell. It was a Saturday, in the afternoon. The next morning the guard came into my new cell. "Your brother's dead," he said. "He hanged himself during the night." He was fifteen. Another month and he would have been sixteen.'

Petrov stared at me. 'There's a lesson for you there, Otto. Never confess. If your brother hangs himself, that's his business – not yours.'

'You don't really believe that, do you?'

'I have to,' he said. 'How else does a man live in the real world?'

He stubbed out his cigarette and put his elbows on the table, interlacing his fingers.

'I often think to myself: What would have happened had Ivan not killed himself like that? My life would have been very different. At the time I despised myself for still being alive. I wanted to kill myself like Ivan. I wanted to hang myself. Someone came to me. He was omnipotent. Maybe everyone seems omnipotent to the prisoner, but I tell you, Otto, the minute I laid eyes on him I sensed his power, his absolute power. He was still, he hardly moved a muscle, and he looked at me with calm eyes. Sometimes you come across someone and they know everything about you, they know the secrets in

269

your soul. He was like that. I couldn't beat him in an argument. In everything I said he got the better of me. And he twisted what had happened with Ivan until he had me believing it was not me who was responsible for the fact he ended up dangling from the bars of a prison cell with a rope he made from his own shirt, but the Party. The Party killed Ivan. That's what he persuaded me to believe. I never thought it would be possible to hate myself even more than I hated myself after Ivan died.'

'You too, Gregory?' I said.

He nodded slowly. 'Colonel Gan always finds your weakness, and once he has it, he never lets go.'

I had only ever seen Petrov as a man with an unbreakable addiction to the crude and vigorous life, a troubled and, to a very large degree, self-loathing patient, fatigued in body and spirit by the very irascibility and high-spiritedness that, notoriously, made him who he was. I had sensed in him a desperate need to unburden himself but he never let me get close. He had once offered an analogy: a married man who loved his wife and was devoted to his children who nevertheless conceived a passion for another woman. That man was torn and confused. How could I have overlooked what he had been saying? He had been telling me all along: Petrov was in thrall not to a wife and mistress, but to two masters – Gan and Lenin; the Okhrana and the Party.

The second bell rang: five minutes to departure. The train would leave immediately after the third bell.

'Gan and Zinnurov are very angry, Otto,' he said, a smile playing on his lips. 'Have you any idea how difficult it is to kill a tsar? Have you any idea of what Gan was having to do to make the assassination look like it was carried out by Jewish terrorists? It's a conjuring trick, a juggling act. And just when he's got all the balls in the air, you go and shoot the most important one out of his hand. They underestimated you, Otto. I warned them not to

270

but they didn't listen. When they found Kopelzon, they couldn't believe you'd killed him. You were his best friend!'

He shook his head with amusement, and then sighed heavily.

'Sadly, neither Gan nor Zinnurov shares my sense of humour. Gan gave an order for you to be assassinated.'

He enjoyed the reaction the news provoked in me.

'It's all right, Otto. I intervened. I persuaded them to let you live.'

'How?'

'I said that if anything happened to you I would go to the Bolshevik delegation in the Duma, confess that I have been spying for the Okhrana all along, and resign. Gan is a rational man. He saw at once that I am worth much more than your death, which, after all, would be a pure act of spite.'

'Why would you bargain for my life?'

He said nothing for some moments, then he looked at me with something like mild annoyance for my lack of understanding. 'You helped me, Otto,' he said quietly. 'I would have killed myself had it not been for you.'

I heard my name called. Anna was approaching the table.

'Go back to the sleeping car,' I said.

Petrov got to his feet and bowed courteously.

'What is he doing here?' she said, looking at Petrov with a mixture of anxiety and distaste. 'Did you know he was on the train?'

'Actually I wasn't on the train,' Petrov said. 'I came by a later one.'

'Go back to the sleeping car, Anna,' I said. 'I'll be there in a minute.'

Petrov said, 'It's better if she stays.' He looked apologetically at me. 'If it were up to me, Otto, I'd be happy to let the two of you go.'

My hand moved to the gun in my coat pocket.

'Have you seen the police and soldiers out there?' Petrov

271

said. 'Are you going to shoot them all? Please, sit down and listen to what I have to say.'

Neither Anna nor I moved.

'Please,' Petrov said.

Slowly we took our places, side by side. Anna put her hand in mine.

'The Mountain wants his daughter,' Petrov said, looking to Anna.

I clutched Anna's hand. 'No,' I said. 'Never.'

Petrov peered through the window as though looking for someone. We saw the head guard in his silver and red braid checking his pocket watch.

'Take a look out there,' Petrov said.

Anna and I looked out to the platform. Among the passengers, policemen and porters were two tall, elderly men, one dressed in topcoat and hat, the other in the uniform of the Household Cavalry.

'Oh my God,' Anna cried, 'they've got Catherine.'

I jumped to my feet. Petrov held me by the wrist. He said quickly, 'It's all right, Otto. Trust me. Catherine will be fine as long as you do as they say.'

Zinnurov pushed Catherine forward. She looked tiny compared to the men. Her head was bare and her jaw set.

I wrenched free from Petrov and put my hands to the window. 'Catherine!' I shouted.

I made for the aisle but Petrov got up to block my way. 'You can have her, Otto,' he said. 'It's all right, you can have her. I've arranged everything.'

I looked at him, not understanding what I was hearing. Then comprehension came, and with it an awful, shuddering jolt.

'No,' I said.

I ran the length of the restaurant car, barging past passengers struggling with their baggage, and got to the door.

'Father!' Catherine shouted. She started forward, only to be pulled back by Gan.

'Let her go!' I shouted.

'My daughter for yours, Spethmann,' Zinnurov said calmly.

Petrov was behind me. 'They were going to kill Catherine and snatch Anna back by force,' he whispered urgently. 'I negotiated this deal for you. Don't let me down, Otto. It's the best you can get in the circumstances.'

The head guard was looking along the length of the train, checking that everyone was aboard.

I reached into my pocket and wrapped my fingers around the Mauser's butt.

'Don't be a fool,' Petrov said, his voice hardening. 'You and Catherine will both be killed.'

The guards began slamming the doors shut as the last of the embarking passengers climbed aboard. I glanced back inside the restaurant car. Anna was gone. I rushed inside. She wasn't there.

The head guard rang the final bell. Anna was on the platform.

'Anna!'

I ran back to the door where Petrov was waiting. Anna was slowly walking towards her father.

A guard came to close the door but Petrov held it open.

'Catherine, come! Now!' Petrov shouted and held out his hand, as the train started to crawl forward. Zinnurov released her and she ran towards us. I swung her aboard. She clutched me ferociously to her and would not let go.

'Goodbye, Otto,' Petrov said, leaping out onto the platform.

The train picked up speed. I looked back over Catherine's shoulder. Anna's eyes met mine and her lips moved. Her hand rose slowly, a forlorn leave-taking. Then Zinnurov put his arm around his daughter and led her away.

The attendant reached past us and pulled the door to. The

train accelerated and the lights of the station started to fall behind. I led Catherine into the restaurant car. On the table was a single chess piece. It was the white king from my Jaques set, the final confession from the patient I failed most.

'They say they'll kill Mintimer if we say anything about what happened,' Catherine said when I got her settled.

'And if we don't?' I said.

The question had not been intended seriously. Whatever we did, whatever we said, Gan and Zinnurov would go unpunished. They would destroy as many people as they had to, guilty and innocent, in pursuit of their ambitions.

I put my arms around Catherine and kissed her. She rested her head on my shoulder. We did not speak.

By mid-morning we were passing across the great plain of Poland. Desolate villages rolled past one after another. The poverty here had made Kopelzon cry. Kopelzon was a hypocrite, but he was probably telling the truth about his tears. Kopelzon was a hypocrite but his questions remained: What do you do if you are born into misery and deprivation? How do you look at your firstborn and not curse yourself for having brought flesh of your flesh into this place? And for those of us not born as they are, who do not know the fields of weeping, is the question any less urgent? What do we do? What do we do when we know that the time will come when fathers and mothers will no longer accept that their children have to have the lives they have lived? Rage and numbers will force the issue. It cannot be avoided. Nothing Colonel Gan or Zinnurov or Maklakov or the tsar or any of his ministers or generals could do would prevent a settling of accounts. They could tighten the chains: they could arrest, imprison, persecute and denounce. Or they could loosen the chains: they could mollify, apologise and promise. It would make no difference. They were in zugzwang. When things reach this pitch we are all in zugzwang. Past wrongs will not be forgiven. Rage and numbers will tell.

Spethmann–Kopelzon

St Petersburg, 1913–14

1.e4 c5 2.Nc3 Nc6 3.g3 g6 4.Bg2 Bg7 5.d3 d6 6.Nge2 e5 7.h4 h5 8.Nd5 Nce7 9.Nec3 Nxd5 10.Nxd5 Be6 11.c4 Bxd5 12.cxd5 Bh6 13.b4 Bxc1 14.Rxc1 b6 15.Bh3 Nh6 16.Qd2 Kf8 17.0–0 Kg7 18.f4 exf4 19.Rxf4 Re8 20.Qb2+ Re5 21.bxc5 bxc5 22.Rxc5 g5 23.hxg5 Qxg5 24.Rc2 Kh7 25.Rg2 Rg8 26.Qf2 Qe7 27.Rf6 Kg7 28.Rf4 Kh7 29.Bf5+ Nxf5 30.Rxf5 Rxf5 31.Qxf5+ Kh6 32.Qf4+ Rg5 33.g4 hxg4 34.Rxg4 Kh5 35.Rg2 Rxg2+ 36. Kxg2 Qc7 37.Qf5+ Kh6 38.Qf6+ Kh7 39.Kg3 Kg8 40.Kh4 Qb6 41.Kh5 Kf8 42.Kh6 Ke8 43.Kh7 Qc5 44.Qg7 Ke7 45.Qg5+ Ke8 46.Kg8 Qc7 47.Qh6 Qe7 48.Qg7 a6 49.a3 a5 50.a4 Kd8 51.Qf8+ Qe8 52.Kg7 1–0

Those with an eye for these things may notice that the game bears a remarkable similarity to King–Sokolov, Swiss Team Championship, 2000.

Acknowledgements

I have said before that when conflicts arise between histor-
ical fact and the demands of the novel, the novelist settles
them in favour of the latter. There was a great chess tournament held in St Petersburg in April–May 1914 (the games
were annotated by Siegbert Tarrasch in the tournament book
(reprinted by Caissa in 1993)), but there was no participant
called Avrom Chilowicz Rozental; chess enthusiasts will have
their opinion on the identity of the man on whom they think
he is based. I owe the interpretation of 'master of the fly' to an
article by Grandmaster Nigel Davies in the *Jerusalem Post*.

Similarities may also be observed between *Zugzwang*'s
Gregory Petrov and the real-life Bolshevik militant Roman
Malinowski, aspects of whose strange career are described
in David Shub, *Lenin* (Pelican, 1976), Stephen F. Cohen,
Bukharin and the Bolshevik Revolution (OUP, 1980), and most
recently in Simon Sebag Montefiore, *Young Stalin* (Weidenfeld & Nicolson, 2007).

For the general social and political background of late-
Tsarist Russia, the most important works on which I drew
included: Richard Pipes, *Russia Under the Old Regime* (Pen-
guin, 1979); Sidney Harcave, *First Blood: the Russian Revolution of 1905* (Bodley Head, 1964); W. Bruce Lincoln, *In War's
Dark Shadow: the Russians before the Great War* (Dial Press,
1983); Christopher Read, *Religion, Revolution & the Russian
Intelligentsia, 1900–1912* (Macmillan, 1979); S. Stepniak, *Life*

Under the Tzars (Downey, n/d); Vera Broido, *Apostles into Terrorists* (Maurice Temple, 1977); Norman M. Naimark, *Terrorists and Social Democrats* (Harvard, 1983); Derek Offord, *The Russian Revolutionary Movement of the 1880s* (CUP, 1986); Maurice Baring, *A Year in Russia* (Methuen, 1907); Maurice Paléologue, *An Ambassador's Memoirs* (3 vols, Octagon edn, 1970); and Laura Engelstein, *The Keys to Happiness: sex and the search for modernity in fin-de-siècle Russia* (Cornell, 1992).

For St Petersburg: Boris Ometev & John Stuart, *St Petersburg: Portrait of an Imperial City* (Cassell, 1990); I.A. Egorov, *The Architectural Planning of St Petersburg* (Ohio, 1969); Nigel Gosling, *Leningrad: history, art, architecture* (Studio Vista, 1965); Julie A. Buckler, *Mapping St Petersburg* (Princeton, 2005); W. Bruce Lincoln, *Sunlight at Midnight* (Basic Books, 2000); Robert B. McKean, *St Petersburg Between the Revolutions* (Yale, 1990).

For the Okhrana: Ronald Hingley, *The Russian Secret Police* (Hutchinson, 1970); Dimitry Pospielovsky, *Russian Police Trade Unionism* (Weidenfeld & Nicolson, 1971); Charles A. Ruud & Sergei A. Stepanov, *Fontanka 16* (Sutton, 1999); A.T. Vassilyev, *The Okhrana: the Russian Secret Police* (Harrap, 1930); Nurit Schleifman, *Undercover Agents in the Russian Revolutionary Movement* (Macmillan, 1988).

For the Jewish/Polish dimension: Joshua D. Zimmerman, *Poles, Jews and the Politics of Nationality* (Wisconsin, 2004); S.M. Dubnow, *History of the Jews in Russia and Poland* (3 vols, Jewish Publication Society of America edn, 1946); Hersh Mendel, *Memoirs of a Jewish Revolutionary* (Pluto, 1989); Mikhail Beizer, *The Jews of St Petersburg* (Jewish Publication Society, 1989); Paul Kriwaczek, *Yiddish Civilization* (Weidenfeld & Nicolson, 2005); Hans Rogger, *Jewish Policies and Right-Wing Politics in Imperial Russia* (University of California, 1986); Gennady Estraikh & Mikhail Krutikov (eds), *The*

Shtetl: Image and Reality (Legenda, 2000); Gérard Silvain & Henri Minczelles, *Yiddishland* (Gingko Press, 1999); Leo Trepp, *The Complete Book of Jewish Observance* (Simon & Schuster, 1980).

For Spethmann the psychoanalyst: *The Complete Psychological Works of Sigmund Freud*, ed. James Strachey (Vintage edn, 2001), especially vols IV (*The Interpretation of Dreams I*), V (*The Interpretation of Dreams II*), VII (*A Case of Hysteria*), X (*Two Case Histories: 'Little Hans' and the 'Rat Man'*), XXII (*New Introductory Lectures on Psycho-Analysis and Other Works*); Henri F. Ellenberger, *The Discovery of the Unconscious* (Basic Books, 1970); Reuben Fine, *The Psychology of the Chess Player* (Dover, 1967); Peter Gay, *Freud: a life for our times* (Dent, 1988); Janet Malcolm, *Psychoanalysis: the impossible profession* (Knopf, 1981).

For miscellaneous chess matters: Hans Kmoch, *Rubinstein's Chess Masterpieces: 100 selected games* (Dover edn, 1960); Frank Marshall, *Best Games of Chess* (Dover edn, 1960); J. Hannak, *Emanuel Lasker: the life of a chess master* (Dover edn, 1991); Aaron Nimzowitsch, *The Praxis of My System* (Dover edn, 1962).

The trend among novelists to compete with Oscar winners in pouring out heartfelt thanks to all and sundry has been criticised, justifiably. Some debts, however, are too important not to mention. So, briefly but sincerely, I would like to express my gratitude to: Alexandra Pringle, Karen Rinaldi, Roger Alton, Marc Quinn, Ruth Rogers, Paul Simon, John Mulholland, John Saunders, Tim and Hector Moss, Daniel King, Maeve Magee, Sharon Smithline, Jojo Tulloh and Vince Stevenson.

A NOTE ON THE TYPE

The text of this book is set in Berling roman. A modern face designed by K. E. Forsberg between 1951 and 1958. In spite of its youth it does carry the characteristics of an old face. The serifs are inclined and blunt, and the g has a straight ear.